NOT THE KILLING TYPE

Lorna Barrett

BERKLEY PRIME CRIME, NEW YORK

THE BERKLEY PUBLISHING GROUP
Published by the Penguin Group
Penguin Group (USA) Inc.
375 Hudson Street, New York, New York 10014, USA

USA | Canada | UK | Ireland | Australia | New Zealand | India | South Africa | China

Penguin Books Ltd., Registered Offices: 80 Strand, London WC2R 0RL, England
For more information about the Penguin Group, visit penguin.com.

This book is an original publication of The Berkley Publishing Group.

Berkley Prime Crime Books are published by The Berkley Publishing Group.
BERKLEY® PRIME CRIME and the PRIME CRIME logo are
trademarks of Penguin Group (USA) Inc.

Library of Congress Cataloging-in-Publication Data

Barrett, Lorna.
Not the killing type / Lorna Barrett.—First Edition.
p. cm.
ISBN 978-0-425-25222-2
1. Miles, Tricia (Fictitious character)—Fiction.   2. Women booksellers—Fiction.
3. Murder—Fiction.   4. New Hampshire—Fiction.   I. Title.
PS3602.A83955N68 2013
813'.6—dc23   2013009624

FIRST EDITION: July 2013

PRINTED IN THE UNITED STATES OF AMERICA

10   9   8   7   6   5   4   3   2   1

Cover illustration by Teresa Fasolino.
Cover design by Diana Kolsky.
Interior text design by Laura K. Corless.

For Deb Baker,
who made all this possible

ACKNOWLEDGMENTS

A writer's life can be quite lonely, but not when your friends are just an e-mail away. I couldn't get through the day without my staunchest supporters Jennifer Stanley and Leann Sweeney, who keep me on an even keel, even as we race to see who will finish her manuscript first. Those daily word count tallies keep us all honest.

Another form of camaraderie comes from my pals at the Cozy Chicks blog: Ellery Adams, Deb Baker, Heather Blake, Julie Hyzy, Kate Collins, Maggie Sefton, and Leann Sweeney. (Look for us online: CozyChicksblog.com)

Pat Remick is always cheerfully ready to help me when I need to verify my New Hampshire facts. Thanks for all the local color, Pat.

Always in the background, but ready to help when called upon, are my editor, Tom Colgan; his assistant, Amanda Ng; and my agent, Jessica Faust. Thanks for being there.

I love receiving notes from readers, and try to answer every one. If you haven't already checked out my website, I hope you will. It contains all kinds of interesting facts and other information on the Booktown Mysteries, as well as some of Angelica's most-requested recipes: www.LornaBarrett.com. You can find me on Facebook, Twitter, and Pinterest, too!

Happy reading!

NOT THE KILLING TYPE

ONE

"Can I freshen up your coffee?" Darlene Boyle, one of the Brookview Inn's waitresses, eagerly asked, brandishing the polished chrome pot over the linen-clad table.

Tricia Miles looked up from her crumb-scattered place setting. "No, thank you," she said and put a hand over her cup, just in case Darlene decided to pour anyway. The truth was she'd had more than enough coffee, but she didn't think she could make a discreet exit for the ladies' room—not with her eagle-eyed sister, Angelica, sitting next to her. But Angelica's attention was focused on the front of the dining room—as it had been during the entire Stoneham Chamber of Commerce breakfast.

Tricia had other company at the table for six—her former

assistant, Ginny Wilson; and Michele Fowler, the manager of Stoneham's newest enterprise, the Dog-Eared Page, a cozy pub on Stoneham's Main Street. Still, they'd all run out of polite chitchat, and boredom now reigned. Darlene represented a new conversational victim.

"How's that son of yours?" Tricia asked.

Darlene positively glowed. "Now that he's been nominated by our local congressman, he's just put in the paperwork for the Naval Academy. He refuses to even consider any other college. I don't know what he'll do if he's not accepted."

That seemed unlikely. Mark Boyle was Stoneham High's pride and joy. He'd won every scholastic prize he'd gone after, and scholarship opportunities abounded, much to his single mom's relief. But all seventeen-year-old Mark could ever talk about was the Naval Academy. The kid was motivated to earn what he could toward his schooling. Summers he was employed at the Brookview, lifting, carrying, hauling garbage—whatever needed doing—and Tricia had never seen such a hardworking young man.

"Anybody else want coffee?" Darlene asked, but the others shook their heads and fidgeted in their seats. Smiling, she moved on to the next table, was likewise rebuffed, and retreated to the coffee station at the side of the room to set down the pot and join her colleagues, who were also waiting for the meeting to begin. Or rather, they waited for the meeting to finish so they could ready the room for the inn's lunch crowd. Chubby and cheerful Henry Dawson—a fixture at the Brookview Inn, and nearly as old as Tricia's part-time employee, Mr. Everett—greeted her with a smile, as did Ginny's fiancé, Antonio Barbero, who managed the inn for Nigela Ricita Associates.

The noise level in the room was as high as Tricia had ever

heard. The November meeting was always well attended, and this one was no different. She didn't even recognize half the members, many of whom owned businesses that contributed nothing to Stoneham's reputation as a book town. Doctors, dentists, day care centers, a pizza parlor, and more.

Tricia turned back to her tablemates. Angelica sighed, both bored and agitated. "When is he going to make the announcement?" she grated under her breath. The who was Angelica's former beau, Bob Kelly, president of the Stoneham Chamber of Commerce. The what was the annual Chamber election.

"Who knows?" Tricia made to get up, but Angelica's arm swung out to grab her, holding her firmly in her seat.

"You can't miss this."

"You've been saying that for half an hour. Nature is calling, and I must listen," Tricia said, but Angelica didn't let go. Meanwhile, Bob was too busy gabbing, laughing, and generally enjoying himself to move the monthly breakfast meeting along.

"It looks like I'm going to have to make a real show of leadership and take matters into my own hands." Angelica grabbed her water glass and a spoon, stood, and tapped on the glass. It took more than a minute for the noisy room to quiet down, but soon enough every eye was fixed on her. She wasn't hard to look at. Dressed in a black blazer and slacks, white turtleneck, with a necklace of jet beads, she looked authoritative but approachable. Angelica took great care of her skin and applied only as much makeup as was necessary. She'd also recently gone back to a shorter hairstyle and, with freshened highlights, looked younger than her forty-seven years.

Bob Kelly also stood and moved to the lectern, sudden

annoyance creasing his brow. "Was there something you wanted to ask?" he inquired tersely. A year before he wouldn't have been so brusque. A year before his relationship with Angelica had been of a romantic nature. That was before he cheated on her. The phrase "hell hath no fury like a woman scorned" certainly applied to Angelica, who'd previously been cheated on by four husbands. And she was about to drop yet another bomb on Bob.

"This is November," Angelica reminded him. "Time for the annual election for Chamber of Commerce president."

All eyes turned toward Bob. He waved her comment aside. "Yes, and I'm very pleased to serve the Chamber for—what is it? The eleventh year now?" He laughed, but nobody in the audience joined him. "Now, did anyone else have a concern?"

"Excuse me, Mr. Kelly," Angelica said, and there was ire in her gaze. The members turned their heads toward her. "But you can't be elected for a twelfth term if we haven't had an opportunity to vote."

Bob laughed. "Yes, of course you're right. Now since I'm running unopposed—"

The heads turned back to Bob. Tricia began to feel like a spectator at a tennis match.

"How do you know you're running unopposed if you haven't opened the floor for nominations?" Angelica asked. Everyone looked back to Bob, who appeared positively shocked at the idea that someone would actually run against him for the job. He had a poor—or was it a selective?—memory. Angelica had told him she intended to do just that some three months before.

"Well, as a formality," he said, backpedaling. "I open the floor for nominations."

Tricia knew her cue when it came. "I nominate Angelica

Miles," she said. There was a gasp from those assembled, as all eyes turned to take in the sisters.

"But-but," Bob stammered.

Angelica's smile was positively evil. "Talk about gob-smacked," she muttered.

"I'll second that," Ginny called out. Good old Ginny. Of course, she'd been in on the plan, as well. She'd been Tricia's assistant at her mystery bookstore, Haven't Got a Clue, for over two years until several months before when Ginny had been offered the manager's job at the Happy Domestic, a charming little shop filled with home décor accessories and books pertaining to that same subject.

Out of the corner of her eye, Tricia saw another figure stand. "I'd like to nominate myself, if that's all right."

Tricia, Angelica, and Ginny turned in unison to take in the man. Stan Berry was known around the village as "the sign man." He had a shop in his garage over on Oak Street. He always wore flannel shirts and jeans, and as he rarely ever spoke at Chamber meetings, nominating himself for Chamber president took everyone by surprise.

"I'll second that," said John Marcella, owner of the convenience store up on the highway.

It was Angelica's turn to look gobsmacked. She had figured she could easily defeat Bob, who was not universally loved by the booksellers. He owned most of the real estate on Main Street and, during the past few years, had inflated the price of the leases to the point of forcing some of the merchants out of business.

"Well-well," Bob stammered. If he'd been shocked by one person challenging his iron-fisted control of the Chamber, two absolutely blew him away. He stood there, mouth open—speechless.

"What's the protocol in situations like this?" asked Nikki Brimfield, owner of Stoneham's bakery, the Patisserie.

Everyone looked back at Bob. "Uh . . . we've never had a situation like this," he admitted. "I'll have to consult the Chamber's charter and get back to . . ."

"According to the charter," Angelica said, and all eyes turned back to look at her once again, "the nominees must be given time to state their qualifications for the job before the voting commences."

Tricia clenched her teeth and rubbed her aching neck, hoping the speechmaking wasn't going to turn into long-winded harangues. When he got going, Bob was difficult to silence, and Angelica was just as fond of singing her own praises. Stan was the wild card. Tricia crossed her legs and raised her hand. "Perhaps we could take a short recess before that happens."

"No, let's get it over with," said Alexa Koslov, one half of the married couple who owned the Coffee Bean, the only place in town to get piping-hot espresso and other gourmet coffees. "I've *got* to get back to my shop."

"I'll second that," said Glenn Baker, owner of Baker Funeral Home. "I've got two showings this afternoon."

Bob seemed seized by indecision. Apparently he'd never even given a moment's thought to the idea that he could be replaced as Chamber president before the meeting's end. "Well . . . I guess so. Let's hear from you, Stan."

"Whatever happened to ladies first?" Angelica groused.

Again the audience turned as one as Stan stood once more, this time looking a lot more formidable. "The current leadership of the Chamber of Commerce has been serving our community for more than a decade. In that time it has vastly favored the booksellers, a minority of its members, over the rest of the organization. It's about time that changed. If you vote for me, I'll see that each and every business member has equal representation."

Enthusiastic applause followed. Angelica gave Tricia a worried look. "He still hasn't told us his qualifications," she muttered, channeling some great ventriloquist. She never even moved her lips.

Once the noise had died down, Nikki Brimfield raised her hand. Berry called on her. "That's a great platform, Stan. But have you ever held any kind of leadership role before?"

Stan nodded. "I own my own business. Isn't that leadership enough?"

Nikki frowned, but others in the audience again applauded. Tricia wasn't sure if she could count on Nikki to vote for Angelica. Since she became engaged to Tricia's former lover, Russ Smith, Nikki seemed threatened by Tricia's presence. And although Tricia had been seeing someone else off and on for more than a year, Nikki's jealousy hadn't abated.

Stan hadn't answered Nikki's question. His was a one-man business. Had he ever managed a workforce—or even one employee?

Michele Fowler, manager of Stoneham's newly opened pub, the Dog-Eared Page, raised her hand, but Stan ignored her and instead acknowledged John Marcella.

"What can we hope to see once you're our Chamber president?"

Stan seemed to stand a little taller. "The first thing I'll do is reduce the membership dues—and the mandatory participation in stupid ideas like planting flowers and hanging banners around town."

Tricia's mouth dropped. The tourists—the very people who came to Stoneham, spent money, and had not only revived the near-dying town's economy, but made it possible for businesses like Berry's to flourish—were not only attracted to the pretty village because of the booksellers, but thanks to the very things Berry wanted to eliminate.

His suggestions received a lukewarm response as a number of those in attendance—especially those whose businesses flanked Main Street—looked dubiously at each other. Both Berry's and Marcella's businesses were located off the beaten tourist track, and admittedly, they weren't on the receiving end of such attention-getting devices.

"Do you have anything else to add?" Bob asked gravely.

Again the members' heads swiveled to look at Stan. "Yeah. We'd also stop promoting moronic events like Founders Day. I'm sure everyone can agree that it was a major fiasco!"

Several people gasped at the reference. Back in August, a small plane had crashed into the village's picturesque gazebo, killing the pilot and one of the Chamber members. Naturally, the rest of the planned festivities had immediately been canceled—at great expense to those who'd been participating in the event.

Michele was now frantically waving her hand, trying to gain Berry's attention, but he refused to look in her direction.

"I believe Ms. Fowler has something to say," said Antonio Barbero at the back of the room. Not only was the handsome young man with the lilting Italian accent the manager of the Brookview Inn, but he was a Chamber member *and* Ginny's fiancé.

Stan sat down, but Bob gave Michele the nod to speak. She stood.

"Mr. Berry, what other plans do you have for the Chamber, especially with a slashed budget to work from?" Her pleasant English accent always seemed to encourage people to listen to what she had to say.

Berry didn't bother to stand. "I'll cut the newsletter down to once or twice a year, and make these breakfast meetings quarterly instead of monthly—and in a much cheaper venue," he added with a sidelong glare at Antonio, whose expression darkened. Darlene and Henry turned their gazes to their boss and looked worried.

"But how can we make progress with so little communication?" Michele asked, perturbed.

"You can always call me at my shop. And that's another thing. We can get rid of the Chamber office, which would save us thousands of dollars in rent every year."

"Excuse me, Stan," a testy Bob interrupted. "But I *own* the building the Chamber office is housed in and the yearly rent is exactly twelve dollars. That's one dollar a month."

"Well, then we'll get rid of the utility costs *and* that secretary you hired. She won't have much to do after we downscale the newsletter and cut these meetings by seventy-five percent."

No one commented on these last suggestions, and Michele sat down, looking absolutely horrified.

A slashed budget. Quarterly meetings? A curtailed newsletter? No secretary to take care of the day-to-day operations of the Chamber? Tricia felt as shaken as Michele looked.

"But most of all, it would be clear that there'd be no conflict of interest with some members getting preferential treatment as there is today." At this, Stan turned to stare at Bob.

"I beg your pardon?" Bob demanded.

"Mr. Kelly, you own most of the storefronts on Main

Street. Most of the Chamber's resources have been funneled into bolstering the businesses located there. You collect the rents and, I might add, raise them on a frequent basis, which makes it harder for the rest of us to compete."

As far as Tricia knew, Berry wasn't competing for business with anyone else in Stoneham. To whom did he refer?

Before she could ask, Angelica stood and cleared her throat. "If I may speak now, Mr. Kelly," she said, and the look she gave Bob was enough to sear the hair off the top of his head with laser-like precision.

Bob seemed shaken by Berry's accusation and muttered, "Go ahead, Ms. Miles," and he sat down once again.

Angelica stood to her full five-foot-six-inch height—plus two inches for heels—poised and confident. "Ladies and gentlemen of the Stoneham Chamber of Commerce, it's my heartfelt ambition to serve you as your next president. Not only would I build on the work by my erstwhile predecessor, but I'd expand upon it." She leveled her gaze at Berry. "Not only would I increase the floral offerings during the spring, summer, and fall seasons, but I would encourage those businesses not directly on Main Street to do the same."

She took in the group at large. "As I'm sure some of you might remember, Stoneham was in the running for the prettiest village in New England and made the list of finalists. The publicity brought in quite a lot of people to our fair village."

"That was my idea," Bob said, raising a hand to claim ownership.

Angelica ignored the outburst. "Thanks to the opening of several new businesses—the Paige Dialysis Center, the Sheer Comfort Inn, and the Dog-Eared Page, and investment here at the Brookview Inn—we've also seen quite a jump in visitors."

"All done on my watch!" Bob called out.

Angelica frowned and leveled an annoyed glare at Bob. "I believe it's *my* turn to speak, Mr. Kelly."

"Hear, hear," Michele said, and Tricia and Ginny dutifully applauded.

Bob glowered.

Angelica continued. "Not only would I promote our Chamber and its members, but I would seek out and encourage new development to take place here in Stoneham."

"And just how would you do that?" Marcella asked with a sneer.

"Networking. Both online and in person."

He turned away with a snort of derisive laughter.

Russ Smith, the editor of the *Stoneham Weekly News*, stood. "It doesn't sound like you'd be offering the Chamber any more than its current president is already doing."

Bob beamed with approval at this comment, while Angelica somehow managed to keep her face impassive. Russ had never much cared for Angelica, even during the year or so Tricia had dated him. The feeling was mutual.

"In closing, I want it known that, as Mr. Berry has pointed out, with me in charge, there'd be no conflict of interest. I don't own any real estate on Main Street." With that, she sat down. Polite applause followed.

Russ turned back to face the front of the room, his steno pad and ballpoint pen at the ready. "And what have you got to say for yourself, Bob?"

Bob returned to the lectern, his chest puffed out so that it was straining against his Kelly Realty sports coat. "This

conflict of interest accusation is totally baseless. I have no
financial interest in any of the businesses on Main Street."

"I beg your pardon, but isn't your real estate office located
on Main Street?" Marcella accused.

"Yes, but that has no bearing on the improvements the
Chamber has made for the businesses located there."

A rumble of mumbling circled the room. Russ waited
until it subsided to speak again. "Do you have anything else
to add?"

"I believe my record speaks for itself," Bob asserted, his
head held high. "I brought the booksellers to Stoneham. I
made this village a destination spot. I deserve the continued
respect of my colleagues, and I deserve to remain the head
of the Stoneham Chamber of Commerce."

Modesty was not one of Bob's strengths.

Everyone looked at each other in the hushed silence that
followed.

An uncomfortable Tricia grabbed the edge of the table
and stood. Her bladder was about to burst. "May I make a
suggestion? Why don't we recess for ten minutes to allow us
all to think over all the candidates' platforms, and then we
can vote."

"Splendid idea," Michele agreed.

"Ten minutes it is," Bob agreed and banged his gavel
against the top of the lectern.

It seemed that quite a few of the Chamber members were
in the same predicament as Tricia. Half of those present got
up from their seats and made a beeline for the inn's wash-
rooms, which were located just outside the dining room.
Tricia moved to join the crowd, but a tap on her shoulder
made her turn. It was Ginny.

They moved out of the line of stampeding Chamber

members. Ginny leaned in closer to speak. "Stan Berry jumping into the race was sure unexpected."

"You're telling me," Tricia agreed.

"Still, I think Angelica's got a good shot. Bob's long overdue to retire from the job. I know I'm not the only member who'd like to see a breath of fresh air when it comes to leadership. I'm just surprised that the only other viable candidate seems more intent on dismantling rather than enhancing the Chamber's activities."

Tricia tried not to squirm and nodded. "I'm in complete agreement, although I do think Ange could be taking on far too much work. She's already got her café, her bookstore, and her cookbook-writing career. That's already more than I could handle."

Ginny nodded. "Me, too, and I don't even own the store I manage."

Tricia smiled. "You have more important things to worry about right now. Like your wedding next Saturday."

Ginny frowned. "Yeah."

"What's the matter?" Tricia asked, concerned.

Ginny waved a hand in dismissal. "I'll have to tell you later. This isn't the right time."

"You're still planning on marrying Antonio, aren't you?" Tricia asked, a bit panicked. She'd already bought her bridesmaid dress, shoes, and a matching bag, plus a lovely gift for the lucky couple.

"Of course. But things just aren't going the way I'd like. It's Joelle," she said and frowned. The wedding planner hired to take care of the upcoming nuptials. "I saw her outside in the lobby a little while ago. I swear, that woman harasses us more than she helps us. If she's not calling or arriving unannounced to bug me, she's doing the same to Antonio." She glanced at her watch and sighed. "I sure hope we get out of here soon. Brittney's never opened the store by herself before." Brittney Sanders had been working at the Happy Domestic for a little over two months. Ginny had once complained that Tricia hadn't given her enough responsibility—or the keys to Haven't Got a Clue—but now she seemed to feel the same way about her own store. To make matters worse, Brittney would be on her own for the entire weekend of wedding festivities. Ginny and Antonio had decided to delay their honeymoon until after the holidays and had planned a Caribbean cruise for early January.

Ginny peered around Tricia. She turned to see Antonio by the table with the coffee urns, beckoning his bride-to-be to join him. "Talk to you later," Ginny said and scooted away.

Tricia resumed her course for the ladies' room. There was sure to be a line. Would Bob hold the election before she could return? It might be one way for him to cheat Angelica out of at least one vote.

By the time Tricia made it to the lobby, the line for the restroom was indeed long. She wandered over to the inn's check-in desk where Eleanor McCorvey, the inn's sixty-something receptionist, seemed to be shuffling all the papers around her workstation.

"Lose something?" Tricia asked.

Eleanor didn't look up. "My letter opener. It was here last time I looked."

"When was that?"

"Ten–fifteen minutes ago," Eleanor said and sniffed as she shuffled through a pile of file folders. "I can't have lost it. I've had it for years. It's an antique—brass with a lovely heart on the top. My sister gave it to me for my birthday when I got my first part-time office job at sixteen. She's gone now, so it's kind of precious to me."

Tricia eyed the line to the ladies' room, which was definitely not moving, although no one else had joined the queue.

Eleanor grabbed a tissue from the box on her workspace and blew her nose.

"Are you okay?" Tricia asked, noting Eleanor's red eyes.

"Allergies; someone wearing a lot of perfume walked by earlier."

Could that have been Angelica? She was known to splash on a little too much of the stuff.

Tricia glanced at the line to the restroom, which still wasn't moving. "How're things going with you and Chauncey?"

Eleanor's romance with the owner of the Armchair Tourist had been the big story around Stoneham during the summer months. Chauncey Porter had undergone quite a transformation since he'd lost more than fifty pounds through a new diet and exercise regimen. Since they started dating, Eleanor, too, had lost weight. Tricia often saw the couple walking hand in hand through the village at night.

Eleanor set the files aside and finally turned her full attention to Tricia, smiling shyly, although her eyes looked puffy and her nose was rather red. Was she coming down with a cold? Tricia took a step back, just in case.

"Things are *wonderful*. I'm having the time of my life. We've even talked about going on a cruise next spring, that is if Chauncey can find someone to look after the store for a few days or a week."

"Sounds lovely," Tricia said, biting her lip. Her own situation was getting dire.

"Are you okay, Tricia? You look rather panicked."

"I really, really need to use the ladies' room, but as you can see, there's a line out the door. Is there another bathroom nearby I could use?"

Eleanor looked beyond her to the line of impatient women and then nodded toward the hall in the opposite direction from the restaurant. "There's a unisex handicapped washroom at the end of the corridor."

"Bless you," Tricia said and hurried off. She passed a small meeting room, complete with a table, computer, and a fax machine, set up for business guests to use. Next to it was a door with the universal sign of a wheelchair-bound figure. To be safe, Tricia knocked on the door. "Anyone in there?" She waited several seconds before she tried the door's lever handle. It obligingly moved. "Yes!"

She yanked the door open and, to her horror, found Stan Berry sitting on the toilet. It looked like he'd found Eleanor's letter opener.

It was sticking out of his bloodied chest.

TWO

"**Will this** *ever* stop happening?" Tricia groused and slammed the restroom door. She'd found a body sitting on a toilet once before—in her own store. That time it had been a visiting author, Zoë Carter, who'd been known for a series of historical mysteries. She'd been strangled. Tricia seriously doubted Stan Berry had written anything other than invoices and checks.

She took a couple of deep breaths to calm her suddenly jagged nerves. Since there was a minimum of blood staining Stan's clothing, he must have died almost instantly. His expression of slack-jawed surprise was sure to stay with her when she closed her eyes for any length of time during the coming days.

Torn, she glanced down the hallway. On the one hand,

the odds of Angelica winning the election for Chamber president had risen considerably, but on the other, Tricia still
needed to find an unoccupied bathroom.

Instead, she fished her cell phone out of her purse and
punched in Antonio's phone number. He answered almost
immediately. "What can I do for you, Tricia?"

"You're about to have a terrible PR problem. Meet me
down the hall in front of the inn's first floor handicapped
bathroom." She snapped her phone shut. She should have
punched in 911. But then, the dispatcher would probably
tell her to stay on the line and guard the body until law
enforcement arrived. To do that, Tricia would need to be
wearing Depends.

Tricia was practically dancing in agony when Antonio
jogged down the hall to meet her.

"What is wrong?"

Tricia threw open the washroom door. "This!"

Antonio's olive-toned skin immediately went a shade
lighter, and he, too, slammed the door shut.

"I've *got* to go to the ladies' room. You call 911 to report
it, and I'll explain everything to Chief Baker when he gets
here."

"But—"

Tricia didn't wait for the rest of his reply and hurried
down the corridor. She made it back to the lobby, relieved
to see the line to the restroom had dwindled.

Once her immediate situation was taken care of, shock
began to set in, upsetting her stomach, and Tricia wished
she hadn't splurged on a Danish for breakfast. She returned
to the restaurant as Bob was calling the meeting back to
order.

"Since we don't have prepared ballots, we're going to vote

by a show of hands," Bob was telling those assembled, but Tricia hurried up to the lectern. Her stomach churning, she tugged at Bob's jacket, pulling him away from the microphone.

"We can't hold the election today," she said softly.

"Oh, yes, we can," Bob grated, his eyes blazing. "And the sooner the better."

"No, we *can't*." She leaned in closer to whisper in Bob's ear. "I just found Stan Berry dead in the handicapped bathroom. It looks like he's been murdered."

Bob's eyes bulged. He turned to look at her, outraged, and put his hand over the lectern's microphone. "What kind of a sick joke is this, Tricia?" he demanded.

"No joke. And you'd better close the doors to this room and make sure nobody leaves. Chief Baker will be here any moment, and—"

To prove her right, the sound of sirens cut through the din of those conversing at the freshly cleared tables.

"Uh, folks, before we begin," Bob said, nervously, "let's shut those doors so we aren't disturbed."

Angelica stood. "We can't start without Stan. Just where is he?"

Bob turned to Tricia and lifted his hand as an invitation for her to speak.

Tricia swallowed but stepped up to the microphone. "He's-he's . . . down the hall. Mr. Barbero is with him."

"Well, someone should go get him. We need to vote. Our members need to get back to their businesses," Angelica stated.

"Yeah," several members called out in unison.

"Um . . ." Tricia looked to Bob for help, but he'd taken a step back, his arms crossed over his green blazer, his expression glib.

"He's-he's . . . dead."

"Very funny, Tricia," Nikki said, annoyed.

"No, really. I've found other bodies before and I can assure you . . . Stan is no longer with us."

Except for the sound of the furnace rumbling away somewhere in the bowels of the building, the room went absolutely silent. Everyone glared at Tricia until the French doors at the back of the room burst open and Chief Baker of the Stoneham Police Department, who was also Tricia's sometime boyfriend, significant other—lover—stepped into the dining room.

"Folks, there's been an accident. I want everyone to stay in your seats." He looked directly at Tricia, his expression distinctly annoyed, and raised his right hand. He motioned with his index finger for her to join him. "Ms. Miles, you and I need to have a little talk."

"You never should have left the body until the police arrived," Baker scolded Tricia. He paced the lobby, which teemed with the entire Stoneham police force. "And why on earth didn't you call it in yourself?"

Tricia leaned against the wall outside the dining room, watching as one of the officers cordoned off the building. "I've already told you, I didn't want to be standing in a puddle of my own—"

"Yes, yes," he said, but he was clearly unhappy about it. The fact that he'd called her out of the dining room, and then made her wait almost twenty minutes before speaking with her hadn't improved her mood.

From her vantage point, Tricia could see Eleanor was still at her post, quietly sobbing into a damp tissue.

"Did you talk to her yet?" Tricia asked, nodding in Eleanor's direction.

"No. She's still pretty upset. I'll speak to her when she gets herself under control. Meanwhile, the murder weapon belonged to her. Do you think she's capable of killing someone?"

"Not a chance. In fact, before I found Berry in the washroom, I stopped to talk to Eleanor. She was about to open the morning mail and was looking for her letter opener. She said she'd had it only minutes before. The lobby was pretty crowded with people heading for the johns and milling around; anyone could have picked it up."

Baker nodded.

Tricia glanced at her watch. It was already ten thirty. Thank goodness her assistant, Pixie Poe, and her part-time employee, Mr. Everett, both had keys to Haven't Got a Clue and would open the store without her. In the past she hadn't been so generous when it came to giving that kind of access to her employees. The booksellers who didn't have employees were probably furious to still be detained. Every minute away from their shops meant lost income. And there was a tour bus scheduled to arrive before noon.

"What can we do to expedite the police interviews?" Tricia asked Baker. "Some of us need to get back to our stores. It's well past opening."

"Sorry for the inconvenience, but I'm sure Mr. Berry was looking forward to opening his shop as well—that is before one of you killed him."

Tricia bristled. "How do you know it was one of the Chamber members? It could easily have been a guest here at the inn. Or someone who walked in off the street."

"That's what we need to ascertain. And we can't do that

without interviewing everyone who was in the building at the time of the murder."

"At least I have someone minding my store. You'd better interview the others before Angelica, Ginny, and me."

"I asked my men to do just that." He threw a look in Eleanor's direction. Her sobs were winding down to hiccupping sniffles. "I'm going to talk to the receptionist now," he said and glanced in Eleanor's direction. She grabbed a fresh tissue from the box on her desk and wiped at her swollen eyes. One of the uniformed officers stood by, guarding her. Had they already decided on her as their chief suspect?

Baker turned back to Tricia. "By the way, isn't this the second time you've found a body on a toilet?"

"Yes, it is, and I'm sure I'm going to hear that same question thirty or forty times in the next couple of hours—complete with leering looks and snickers."

Baker shrugged and moved away.

With nothing better to do until it was her turn to be questioned, Tricia reentered the dining room. Every eye turned to look at her. To say they were unhappy was putting it mildly. If their expressions were to be believed, they blamed *her* for Berry's death. As she walked toward the table where she, Angelica, Ginny, and Michele had been sitting, she heard more than one person mutter, "jinx." Head held high, she ignored them.

She sat down. Ginny looked anxious, but Michele immediately leaned forward, placing a hand on Tricia's. "You poor thing. Are you all right?"

Tricia nodded, grateful for the kind words. So many of the others were staring daggers at her. "Where's Angelica?"

Michele nodded toward the front of the room. A somber

Angelica stood speaking to one of the patrolmen, with Bob nodding in agreement, and Antonio standing nearby. Had the former lovers called a truce?

"Was it too terrible?" Michele probed.

Before Tricia could answer, another uniformed patrolman, who stood by the lectern, leaned over the microphone, his gaze centered on their table. "No talking, please."

Tricia sighed and Michele sat back, looking chagrined. Tricia knew the drill. The cops didn't want the potential witness pool to contaminate each other's version of their whereabouts or what they may or may not have seen before the body was found. Still, she knew she wasn't the only one who felt like she was being held hostage.

It was going to be a very long morning.

Tricia watched as Angelica turned and walked back to their table, while the officer pulled out a cell phone.

"What's going on?" Tricia asked, as Angelica took her seat. But Angelica shook her head and then pressed her index finger against her lips to shush her sister.

The officer flipped the phone shut, consulted with Bob for a moment, and then Bob stepped up to the lectern once again.

"We have a *big* problem. The election was supposed to take place today, but obviously that can't happen now."

A man was dead in the washroom and he was worried about the election!

"However," Bob continued, "our charter says it must happen in the month of November. Our next meeting is scheduled in late December. If we wait more than a week, we'll be into the high holiday season, and none of the retail merchants can afford to abandon their business to come to a Chamber meeting. I've already cleared it with Mr. Barbero, and therefore, I propose we hold a short meeting right here next Wednesday morning."

John Marcella raised his hand. "You realize that's the day before Thanksgiving, don't you?"

Bob nodded. "I sure do. But many of you will be opening your doors early on Black Friday. It's the biggest sales day of the year, and I doubt I could get any of you to gather back here for a meeting."

"You got that right," Marcella said.

"Then let's have a show of hands," Bob suggested. "Those who agree?" Just about everybody's hand shot up. "Those opposed?"

Tricia could only see Marcella's hand raised. Why would he care about the timing of the meeting? His was a 24/7 business with plenty of employees to keep it running during his absence.

"Motion carried," Bob said and banged his gavel on the lectern.

It wasn't a good solution to the election problem, but it would have to do. Tricia looked at Angelica, who seemed resigned to the situation.

"The officer says we'll have to remain here until everyone is questioned," Bob continued, "but they've called in the Sheriff's Department to come and help take our statements. Hopefully we'll all be out of here by one or two o'clock."

The room erupted into a cacophony of groans and complaints. Bob banged his gavel five or six times until order was once again restored. "Now, now—let's show a little restraint. After all, one of our members has been killed."

At least he finally seemed to have taken note of that fact.

Henry entered the room, pushing a cart with a couple of tables and chairs on it. He set them up at the front of the room, and then stood to one side. Most likely he was going to be interrogated, too. It was then a couple of uniformed deputies entered the dining room, no doubt there to help with the interviews. With only two of them, it was going to take a long, long time.

Tricia sighed, disappointed in herself for not tucking a book into her purse that morning. Just in case . . .

THREE

Lunchtime came and went. If circumstances had been different, Tricia would have ordered the inn's luncheon special, which the menu board out in the lobby had said would be honeycrisp apple salad. It sounded delicious. Of course, thanks to Stan Berry's murder, they weren't serving that day, Tricia would just have to make do.

When Baker had finally allowed her to leave, she'd tried sneaking out the inn's back entrance, but a TV crew from Manchester's Channel 9 News had been lying in wait, hoping to get a quote from the notorious Stoneham Jinx of Death. She managed to get in her car without making a comment and went straight back to Haven't Got a Clue and hoped she could scrounge a container of yogurt from her refrigerator.

Tricia parked her car in the municipal parking lot and

walked to Haven't Got a Clue. She peeked in through the big display window to see that things were quiet at the store. Her cat, Miss Marple, dozed among the books in the front display before her. Since the store was bereft of customers, Mr. Everett walked between the shelves with his lamb's-wool duster, making sure everything was spotless, and Pixie was stationed behind the register, her nose buried in a book.

When the bell over the door rang, Pixie looked up and smiled. "I see the screws finally sprung you."

Pixie's nomenclature was always colorful, no doubt because she'd not only spent a great deal of her life reading vintage mysteries, but also because of what she'd picked up when she'd been a guest of the state in the New Hampshire Prison for Women. Before she'd turned her life around, Pixie had been what Mr. Everett would call "a lady of the evening." Not that Mr. Everett would even utter such a phrase in reference to his fellow employee. At least not to Pixie's face. He was a gentleman, after all.

"Are they close to an arrest?" Pixie asked, her eyes wide with interest.

Tricia shrugged out of her jacket. "I doubt it. There's no motive for the murder. At least, not that anyone I know could tell. But I'm sure the police will be looking at Angelica and Bob Kelly as their chief suspects. They were running against Stan for Chamber president—if that's what you could call it. They must've known for all of ten minutes that he was in the running before the poor man was killed."

"And did you find the body, Ms. Miles?" Mr. Everett asked, although from the tone of his voice he already seemed to know the answer.

Somehow Tricia managed a nod, feeling ashamed and not meeting his gaze.

Pixie shook her head, her dyed black pompadour bobbing. While her hairstyle remained the same from month to month, Tricia never knew what color Pixie's hair might be on any given day. She'd gone from carrot orange to blonde to red to brown, and now to black. She'd been humming Elvis tunes of late, so Tricia suspected that's why she'd gone to a shade to match that of the King of Rock and Roll.

Pixie should have been born in another age. She dressed exclusively in vintage clothes that were popular from Glenn Miller's heyday up to the golden age of rock, and wore her hair to match. She gazed at Tricia and shook her head sadly. "Lady, you got the worst luck in the whole friggin' world."

"Tell me about it," Tricia said and sighed, and unbuttoned her coat.

"Who would want to kill Mr. Berry?" Mr. Everett asked, aghast.

"No one I know," Tricia admitted, "but then I barely knew him."

"Ya think his death really had anything to do with the Chamber election?" Pixie asked. "I mean, honestly, what would the other candidates gain?"

Miss Marple seemed to levitate onto the cash desk; her head suddenly appeared in Tricia's hand, desperate to be petted. Of course, Tricia complied. "Bob's ego is all tied up in wanting to control how the commercial side of the village runs. And there's no doubt about it, Angelica wants the job, but she honestly has the merchants' best interests at heart, and she certainly doesn't want it enough to kill someone."

"*Yow,*" Miss Marple said, as though in confirmation.

Again, Pixie shook her head. "Yeah, well, the cops will probably think otherwise. No offense to your boyfriend or nothin', but I ain't met a flatfoot yet who wasn't crooked at least once or twice in his career and willing to look away from hard evidence in order to make a collar."

"Let's hope that only happens in vintage mysteries," Tricia said. She wanted nothing more than to change the subject. "Have you had many sales today?"

Pixie shook her head. "It's been slow going. Mr. E tells me that things will pick up the closer we get to the holidays. I can't wait. I've got me some really cute Christmas sweaters that I found at a thrift store in Nashua. I can't wear them the rest of the year, so I plan to give 'em a good workout between now and New Year's."

Oh, dear. At least Pixie's Haven't Got a Clue green work apron would cover the worst of them.

"When are we going to decorate the store for the holidays?" Pixie asked, suddenly sounding as excited as a child on December 24.

"We haven't done too much in the past," Tricia admitted, as Miss Marple settled down on the counter, resting her head on her front paws and purring contentedly. "Just some artificial greenery and a small tree in the window. We decorate it with paper stars. People buy them for a dollar or more donation and we contribute the money to a literacy organization."

"Oh. That's nice . . . I guess," Pixie said, sounding less than enthused.

"The children who benefit from our customers' generosity seem to enjoy the books," Mr. Everett said. "Last year Ms. Miles allowed me to deliver them to a party for underprivileged youth. We sent along cookies from the Patisserie, too."

"Cookies are good," Pixie agreed unenthusiastically, "but don't you think if we did a super job of decorating that we might sell a lot more books? You know, get people in the holiday spirit and in the mood to spend, spend, spend."

"What did you have in mind?" Tricia asked, dreading the answer.

Pixie's eyes widened. "Let me give it some thought and get back to you in a couple of days."

"Okay," Tricia said and smiled, all the while dreading whatever Pixie might come up with. Pixie had a tendency to throw herself wholeheartedly into things.

The shop door opened and thankfully it was Angelica who swooped in. "Sorry I didn't wait for you at the inn, Trish, but I just had to get away from those vultures," she said dramatically.

"You mean the cops?" Pixie asked with glee. She loved to disparage any branch of law enforcement.

"Yes." Angelica hung her head and let out a loud theatrical sigh. "I'm afraid poor Sarge"—Angelica's bichon frise—"couldn't wait. It looks like I need to buy a steam cleaner for my rugs. And now I've got to suffer until the next meeting before I know if I'll be the next Chamber president or just a fashionable sore loser."

"Perhaps you could use the interval to campaign," Mr. Everett suggested.

Angelica's eyes widened as her frown turned upside down. "Why, that's a wonderful idea, Mr. Everett. I'm surprised I didn't think of it myself."

Mr. Everett smiled, apparently not taking in the last part of Angelica's statement. Tricia could envision Angelica's mental gears churning away. "Did you have any *other* reason for dropping by?"

"Of course. I need your opinion." Angelica grabbed Tricia's arm and hauled her off toward the readers' nook. Miss Marple raised her head from her front paws and took this as an invitation to join them. She jumped down from the counter and trotted over to the big square coffee table just as the sisters sat down.

Angelica's eyes were wide. "What if I *do* become the next Chamber president? I was wondering what to do about Frannie."

Frannie Mae Armstrong managed the Cookery, Angelica's cookbook store, located right next door to Haven't Got a Clue. Frannie had taken the job, and a fat pay increase, after ten years as the secretary/receptionist at the Stoneham Chamber of Commerce. Bob hadn't treated her with the respect she deserved, and with her new responsibilities at the Cookery, she'd positively blossomed.

"You weren't thinking of offering Frannie her old job back, were you?" Tricia asked.

"Let's face it, Betsy Dittmeyer"—the current Chamber receptionist—"is about as welcoming as a mistreated pit bull. Frannie has a way with people. She can charm all kinds of information out of them."

"Yes, but won't she think you're offering to demote her?"

"Why?" Angelica asked, petting Miss Marple, who seemed to enjoy it.

"Her job title, for one. You've got to admit, store manager is much more appealing than receptionist. That's about the lowest of the low when it comes to pink-collar jobs."

"She could be the Chamber's office manager," Angelica countered.

"And will the Chamber pay her the same wage she was making before she came to work for you?"

Angelica's face fell. "Oh. That is a sticky subject."

"And she's got affordable health care now, too, thanks to you. She didn't have that when she worked for the Chamber."

Angelica seemed to sag. "Oh, dear, I hate it when you're right. But what a terrific asset she'd be back in her old Chamber position. If I do win, I'll be stuck working with Betsy. That is *if* I kept her."

"Unless you've got a plausible reason to fire her, you'd be looking at a possible lawsuit for unjustified termination."

Angelica stopped petting the cat, shaking off the accumulation of loose hair from her hand. "Oh, dear. Trust you to have a logical mind."

"I'm just looking out for your best interests, dear sister." Tricia frowned, watching the cat hair gently land on the carpet, knowing she'd be getting out the carpet sweeper as soon as this visit was over. "Ange, are you really sure you want to take on the job of Chamber president in addition to everything else you've already got going?"

"We've talked about this over a hundred times during the last few months. Bob has done a credible job, but it's time for a change. I could take Stoneham to the next level. If we had the right marketing plan, we could be welcoming customers year-round instead of just six months of the year." She sighed. "I should've gone into more detail about my plans at the meeting, but as Mr. Everett says, I can be out there campaigning for the next five days. Of course, now that Bob knows he's got competition, he's going to be out there beating the bushes with a plank. Lucky for me, and thanks to his materialistic nature, he's persona non grata with a number of the Main Street business owners."

Tricia laughed. "Especially you."

Angelica fought a smile. "Yes." She quickly sobered. "You've *got* to help me plan my campaign strategy."

"What strategy? You've made your pitch. You'll either win or lose. And I'm afraid that those who agreed with Stan will probably vote for Bob over you. You didn't say you'd raise membership dues, but if your agenda is as ambitious as you outlined at the meeting, you'll probably have to do just that. And not everyone who runs a business here in Stoneham is in the black like the two of us."

"I know that. But I was hoping . . ." She let the sentence trail off and looked away as though distracted.

"Hoping what?" Tricia asked.

"Well, that maybe we could convince Ms. Nigela Ricita to make a generous contribution to the flower fund. I mean, she's got two businesses on Main Street, plus the Sheer Comfort and Brookview Inns. She's now vying with Bob as the biggest stakeholder in the village."

"She doesn't *own* the Brookview. She's just a partner. And she doesn't own the building that houses the Happy Domestic, either," Tricia reminded her.

Angelica waved a dismissive hand. "She's got a vested interest in the village."

"How are you going to convince her to open her wallet?" Tricia asked. "Do you know how to contact her?"

"I've tried e-mailing," Angelica admitted, defeat coloring her tone. "Antonio answered it. What's this woman afraid of, anyway? That we'll bite her if she actually shows up?"

"Maybe she just values her privacy. Or maybe a lot of people bug her for money and it's easier not to talk to them than continue to hear the constant whine of *gimme, gimme, gimme*."

Angelica sighed and shrugged. "You're probably right. But I sure could cinch this election if I had her support."

"You've got Antonio's support. Surely that carries some Nigela Ricita weight."

"That's true."

"It still beats me why you want to do this anyway. I thought you wanted to be the next Paula Deen. Why don't you concentrate on that?"

"I've been rethinking my goals," Angelica said, looking wistful. "Now I want to be the next Martha Stewart. I like the idea of having a plethora of companies and products to offer the public at large."

"A finger in every pie?" Tricia asked.

Angelica's smile was wry. "Exactly. And I figure I can learn a lot by networking with other people within the state-wide Chamber of Commerce network."

"How long would you want to hold the job?" Tricia asked.

"Oh, only a year or two. That's all I'd need. I'm a quick study."

That she was.

Angelica stood. "Look, I'd better be going. The lunch crowd will be thinning over at Booked for Lunch and I'd better go help with the cleanup." She looked down at Tricia. "Are you coming over for your usual tuna plate?"

Tricia shook her head. "Not today. It's time for Pixie and Mr. Everett to go to lunch."

As if in agreement, Pixie, who'd been unabashedly eaves-dropping, headed toward the back of the store to grab her coat.

"I'll call you later," Angelica promised and steered for the exit.

"Good afternoon, Ms. Miles," Mr. Everett said.

"Ta-ta!" Angelica called and exited the store.

Pixie came back just as the door closed behind Angelica. She carried Mr. Everett's jacket, too. "We're going to the Bookshelf Diner. They've got liver and onions on the special board today. Want us to bring something back for you?"

Tricia shook her head. She'd lost her appetite for the day—and maybe tomorrow, too—when she'd found Stan Berry dead on the toilet.

"We'll be back in an hour," Pixie promised, and she and Mr. Everett headed out the door. The phone rang, and Tricia moved to stand behind the cash desk before she picked up the heavy black receiver of her circa-1935 telephone. "Haven't Got a Clue, this is Tricia. How can I help you?"

"Tricia, my love. It's so good to hear your beautiful voice."

Oh, dear. It was Christopher, Tricia's ex-husband. The one who had dumped her four years before. Christopher, who'd abandoned his lucrative career as a stockbroker, run away to the Colorado mountains to find himself, and then had reappeared on her doorstep some three months before.

"All settled in?" she asked hopefully. Christopher had decided Colorado was too far away from his past life, had recently relocated to the East Coast, and was renting a cabin in the White Mountains just a few hours north of Stoneham—at least a few hours as the crow flies. By road, it took a bit longer.

"Pretty much," he said. "This morning I went into town for a newspaper. The convenience store had a TV on. There was a story developing about a murder today in Stoneham. I saw you on a piece of news footage leaving the—"

"You don't have to remind me. I was there."

Christopher laughed, and something inside Tricia ached. Oh, how she had missed that laugh. "Angelica tells me you have a penchant for finding bodies," he said.

"When did you speak to Angelica?" Tricia asked suspiciously.

"A few months back. She said some of your neighbors call you the village jinx."

Her sour mood intensified. If Tricia ever heard that word again . . . "Why did you call?" she asked, perturbed.

"I'll be heading your way soon and hoped that maybe we could have lunch or dinner together."

"You're coming to Stoneham?" Tricia asked. She really didn't want to see Christopher. Memories of his rejection, their separation and eventual divorce, were still all too painful.

"Portsmouth, actually. I've got a job interview."

"I thought your new, frugal lifestyle gave you the latitude so that you never needed to work again."

"It has, but let's face it, I was good," he said, sounding smug. "I still have a few clients and now there's no stress, no quotas to meet. I feel like a human being once again. And, to be honest, I'm a little bored."

"I'm glad to hear you've returned to some semblance of your old self," Tricia said, and she meant it. She would always love Christopher and, indeed, he almost sounded like the man she had fallen in love with. Almost. And almost was no longer good enough. She thought about her relationship with Chief Baker. How come she was settling for what he was able or willing to give? She shook the thought away, concentrating on her ex once more, hoping he would just find somebody else to share his life with and stop popping back into hers.

"As it turns out," he continued, "I have a strong desire to feel useful. Everyone needs to feel useful. And all I need to conduct business is an Internet connection to consult via long distance."

Did they have broadband in the mountains? Tricia shrugged. It really wasn't her problem. "When are you arriving?" she asked, resigned.

"The day after tomorrow. I'm not sure about the timing. Will you meet with me?"

Tricia looked out the front display window. Up the street, and very much out of sight, was the Stoneham police station. Was Grant Baker there right now? He hadn't been pleased when Christopher had shown up out of the blue back in August. Tricia had been careful not to mention that he called periodically, and usually for silly reasons—like to wish Miss Marple a happy birthday or to ask a question about someone they'd known back in Manhattan.

"I don't know. Maybe you'd better call me after you've conducted your business," she said.

"Does Chief Baker have a problem with us seeing each other?" Christopher asked with reproach.

"I don't see why he would," she said, thinking about the year or more she'd hung around waiting for Baker when his ex-wife was ill and he felt the need to be with her during her recovery. Tricia wasn't about to tell Christopher that.

"Then let's tentatively plan it. I'll book a room at the Brookview Inn and let you know when I get into town."

Tricia sighed. She really shouldn't encourage him. And yet . . . "Very well." There, that sounded like she was just putting up with him—which she was. She had no illusions about them ever getting back together, and if he was smart, he wouldn't, either. "I'll talk to you then."

"Okay. Give Miss Marple a pat on the head for me," he said.

"I will."

"Bye."

"Bye."

Tricia replaced the receiver in its cradle and let out a sigh.

Miss Marple jumped up on the counter with a cheerful "*Brrrrpt!*"

"Yes, that was Christopher. He's coming to town." She petted the cat. "That's from him."

Miss Marple nuzzled her head against Tricia's arm, and her purring went into overdrive. The sound brought back a vivid memory from earlier that day. The fan in the inn's handicapped restroom had been running when she'd found Stan Berry. The low hum should have been rather soothing, like a cat's purr. The sight of Berry dead had been anything but a balm to the nerves.

Suddenly the quiet became incredibly unnerving. Tricia pivoted and strode over to the shop's stereo system, then shuffled through the stack of CDs until she came to a favorite full of cheerful Celtic tunes. She decided to make a fresh pot of coffee, too, just in case the store was flooded with afternoon customers.

As she filled the pot from the restroom's tap, she wondered if she could keep busy enough to stop thinking about real death and concentrate on selling the fictional kind to her customers.

FOUR

The preholiday shopping season seemed to have skipped that particular Friday in November, at least for Haven't Got a Clue. It was exactly one week until Black Friday. Things would be different on that day. Tricia—and every other proprietor of a retail establishment in Stoneham—hoped.

When closing time finally arrived, Tricia was more than ready to pull down the shade on the main display window and turn the OPEN sign to CLOSED. Mr. Everett had already left for the day by the time Pixie finished vacuuming the carpet and grabbed her coat from a hook in the back of the store.

After the morning she'd had, Tricia wasn't looking forward to spending the evening alone. She loved Miss Marple with all her heart, but the little gray cat preferred to nap in the evenings rather than chat, and Tricia felt the need for company.

Tricia turned to Pixie. "We've had a long, boring day. How would you like to join me at the Dog-Eared Page for a glass of wine?" she asked, and realized it was the first time she'd ever invited her newest employee to join her in an after-work excursion.

Pixie's eyes widened with a hunger like that of a starving puppy. "Oh, I would love to—thank you," she said, sounding wistful, but then her mouth drooped. "But I can't. It's a condition of my parole that I not frequent businesses that serve alcohol. Just in case I'm tempted to . . . you know," she said and rolled her eyes.

Take up her old life as a prostitute? Yes, Tricia could see the danger that frequenting a bar might pose. She forced a smile. "Maybe we'll do breakfast before the holidays, then. We can invite Mr. Everett to join us, too."

"That would be great," Pixie agreed and shrugged into her moth-eaten fur coat. "But as long as you're going to the bar anyway, have one for me."

"I'll do that," Tricia said.

"Good night," Pixie called and headed out the door, which seemed to close with a terrible finality.

Tricia found herself standing in the middle of her too-quiet shop, a feeling of panic building within her. She had to get out of there! She had to be around people—laughter—*life*!

Somehow, she managed to finish her end-of-day tasks before she gave Miss Marple a few kitty snacks to hold her over until her dinner, grabbed her coat and purse, and flew out the door.

The lights were on and Tricia could hear the sound of music as she crossed the street and approached the Dog-Eared Page. Since they'd opened several months before, she found she liked to occasionally visit in the evening after working hours and before dinner. Too often Chief Baker was working late, and she found she couldn't resist the urge for companionship—but it was usually fellow Chamber members, or even her own sister, who were apt to show up.

On that night, she entered the warm and inviting tavern filled with boisterous customers and music, looked around, and saw Ginny and Antonio sitting at the bar, conversing with its manager. Angelica was nowhere in sight. Tricia took off her coat, hung it on one of the pegs in the corner, and headed for the bar and the empty seat next to Antonio.

"Can I join you?" she asked.

Antonio turned at the sound of her voice and stood. "Ah, Tricia. We would love it. Please sit."

Tricia took the offered seat, soaking in the ambience.

"What brings you out on a cold night like this?" Ginny asked, toying with the plastic stir stick that protruded from her short glass. A gin and tonic, Tricia surmised, by the lime that rested on top of the ice in her glass.

"There's nothing good on TV," Tricia fibbed. She hadn't even consulted the schedule for that evening.

"Don't tell that to the group over there watching the hockey game on TV," Michele advised. "What'll you have?"

"Chardonnay," Tricia said.

Moments later, Michele put a cocktail napkin and a stemmed glass of wine down in front of her.

"So what's the big topic of conversation tonight?" Tricia asked.

"Stan's murder," Ginny answered.

Suddenly, coming to the bar didn't seem like such a good idea. "Oh, no—let's talk about anything *but* the murder," Tricia begged.

"How about the Chamber of Commerce election?" Michele asked.

Tricia shook her head and took a sip of her wine. "Too close to the same subject. And anyway, I think I know how the three of you are going to vote."

They all nodded, not bothering to suppress smiles.

Michele looked at Antonio. "I've been meaning to ask you, dear boy, what does our boss think about someone getting killed in her inn?"

Antonio glowered. "She was not at all pleased. This could make for much bad publicity."

"I thought we weren't going to talk about the murder," Tricia protested.

"Oops, sorry," Michele apologized, but she didn't look at all guilty.

"And do we have to talk about our employer, as well? Everybody badgers me about the dear lady. It gets annoying," Antonio grumbled.

"Surely you don't think *we're* annoying?" Michele forcefully demanded, straightening up in umbrage.

Antonio held out his hands in submission. "Ah, never you, dear ladies."

"Then will you tell us about her?" Michele asked hungrily. She leaned forward, resting her elbows on the bar and her head in her hands.

Antonio sighed and sipped what looked like Campari on ice. "She is a very private woman."

"We get that," Ginny said. "But you can't blame us for being curious."

"You mean Antonio hasn't even spilled the Nigela beans with you?" Tricia asked.

Ginny's smile was coy. "We try to leave our work lives behind when we're at home."

"Go on," Tricia urged, grinning.

Antonio shrugged. "There's not much to tell." He looked thoughtful for a few moments. "You see . . . my father did not marry my mother. It is still a sore point with me."

"Oh," Tricia said, and suddenly wished she hadn't prodded so hard.

"But he did marry Nigela. I met her when I was eight. I came to stay with them for a summer. My father . . . he was not so interested in having a bastard son, but Nigela was very kind to me. Always."

"Did you see her much after that summer?"

"Only when she would come to Firenze. Even after they divorced, Nigela would send me money for school clothes and books. When I was seventeen, my mother died. Nigela brought me to America to go to university."

"So she's an American?" Tricia asked, surprised.

Antonio nodded. "*Sì.*"

Tricia had thought Ricita was an Italian name. Could it be the woman's current married name?

"Did you ever live with her?" Michele asked.

Antonio shook his head. "She had remarried. Her new husband did not want the bastard child of her ex-husband in their home. I'm sure you can imagine the difficulties. But she paid for my schooling and we saw each other often. When I graduated, my heart told me I should go home to Italia."

"You were homesick," Michele said with understanding, her English accent sounding just a wee bit stronger. "I've been that way a time or two myself over the years."

Antonio nodded. "But I found Italia was no longer my home. You see, there was no one there for me."

"Ohhhh," the three women chorused in sympathy.

"So, I asked Nigela if I could return to America. She was overjoyed. Not only did she pay my way, but she asked me to work for her, which I have been very happy to do. She is my second mother. She has given me opportunities I never would have had in Italia. I would do *anything* for her."

"Like keeping her private life completely private?" Tricia asked.

He nodded. *"Sì."*

"Then how about answering a question that doesn't pertain to her private life," Michele said. "Why is she investing so much money in Stoneham?"

Antonio laughed. "She likes it here."

"She's been to Stoneham?" Tricia asked, surprised.

"Oh, many times," Antonio said.

"Why doesn't she let people know when she comes?" Ginny asked.

"She believes if people knew she was here, she would be treated differently," Antonio explained.

"How?" Tricia asked.

"That people would . . . how do you say it? . . . fall all over themselves."

"I'm your fiancée. She could have met with *me*," Ginny grumbled. "I'm not about to fall all over her."

"So she's been to the Brookview?" Tricia asked, hoping to deflect her friend's ire.

Antonio nodded. *"Sì.* Under an assumed name."

"Does anyone at the inn know her secret identity?" Tricia asked. Good grief. It sounded like they were talking about a superhero!

Antonio shook his head.

"So that's how she knew what colors to paint the lobby, and what rug to choose," Ginny said thoughtfully.

"It certainly looks nice," Tricia agreed.

"Nigela is gifted with many talents," Antonio admitted.

"Is she or isn't she going to be at our wedding?" Ginny asked with a slight edge to her voice.

He shrugged. "I would hope so. But I cannot blame her if she does not come. As I said, she does not want people to be sicko . . . sicko—" He struggled with the English word.

"Sycophants?" Michele suggested.

Antonio nodded. "Sì."

"I'll be very hurt if she doesn't come," Ginny said, sounding just a little childish. "After all, you said she was like a second mother to you. What loving mother would skip her son's—even a stepson's—wedding day?"

"If she does, she has her reasons, and I would respect that," Antonio said solemnly.

"You can always send her pictures—and the wedding video," Tricia suggested.

Antonio smiled. "That is true."

Ginny's gaze returned to the oak bar top and what remained of her drink. It wasn't hard to fathom what she was thinking. It was time to change the subject.

"Has everybody finished decorating for the holidays?" Tricia asked.

Michele waved a hand around the bar. "As you can see, I haven't even started. I've got a big box of lights, garlands, and faux greenery in the back room. I thought I'd wait a few more days before I transform the place."

"The Happy Domestic is all decked out," Ginny volunteered. "How about Haven't Got a Clue?"

Tricia sighed. "Pixie is eager to start. She wants floor-to-ceiling decorations. I think I'll have a fight on my hands to keep things simple and dignified."

Ginny laughed. "Oh, go ahead and indulge her. You might see an uptick in sales this year."

Tricia thought about what Ginny wasn't saying. "Do you think I've been too restrained in the past?"

Ginny turned her attention back to what was left of her drink. "A little."

Tricia felt her mouth tighten. Had Ginny been too intimidated to say so when she'd worked for Tricia—or hadn't she cared? "What would you suggest?"

Ginny's eyes widened. "Ribbon. Lots of it. Put some bows on the books that don't have dustcovers. The portraits on the walls have glass over them. Get some colored dry-erase markers and draw on Santa beards and hats. Liven the place up a little bit."

Liven the place up? Tricia found the very idea of belittling the famous—and long-dead—authors absolutely abhorrent.

"Miss Marple might like to help you, too," Michele suggested. "I used to put a bell on my cat's collar at Christmastime. It was very cheerful."

"Miss Marple doesn't wear a collar," Tricia said, knowing her cat would not like one, either.

"You could dress her up as Santa, too," Ginny suggested. "She'd look really cute in a little red coat and hat. They're made with elastic so that you can tuck them under her chin and around her belly."

"I don't think she'd like that, either," Tricia said. Defacing portraits—dressing up her cat? What were they thinking?

Antonio eyed her, his mouth set. "Tricia is like me. She

likes dignified decorations. Nothing over the top. The inn will be decorated this weekend. I invite you to arrive on Sunday, before the wedding rehearsal, to see how lovely it all looks."

"I'd almost forgotten about the rehearsal," Tricia admitted. "I'll look forward to seeing everything all spruced up for the holiday."

"Did Nigela choose the decorations?" Michele asked.

Antonio nodded. "Our guests will feel as though they have come home for the holidays. And since we are fully booked through the rest of the month, as well as December, there will be plenty of people to enjoy them."

Tricia didn't want to jump back on the Nigela Ricita bandwagon once again, and decided she'd had enough companionship for one night. She took one last sip from her glass, set it on the bar, and stood. "I've got a hungry cat waiting for me at home. I'd best be going." She paid for her drink, leaving the change on the bar for the tip jar.

"Good night," her friends chorused. Tricia gave them a smile and a wave and headed for the door where she'd left her coat. She put it on and exited the pub.

The cold air hit her with the force of a sucker punch. She looked left and right for traffic, but there was none. She also noted that most of the storefronts on Main Street had already been decorated for the holiday season. The white fairy lights on By Hook or By Book were utterly charming. Tricia wouldn't mind adding a string of lights to her front display window, and maybe around the front door. They were attractive yet dignified, just like Haven't Got a Clue.

Pixie might want to deck the halls with far too many decorations, and Tricia decided she must stand firm. That settled, she crossed the empty street. Less than a minute later she was inside the store and heading for her loft apartment, with Miss Marple trotting up the stairs after her.

Despite the fact she'd spent the better part of the last hour with friends, Tricia realized she still felt unsettled. There were things she needed to talk about, but not with Ginny, Antonio, or Michele. As she fed Miss Marple and set out a bowl of fresh water, she made a decision and picked up the kitchen extension. It rang twice before it was answered.

"Hello," Angelica said.

"What are you doing tonight?" Tricia asked.

"Not a damn thing. I was thinking about making myself a vegetable stir-fry. Why?"

"Do you want to go somewhere for dinner?"

"What have you got in mind?"

Tricia hadn't had anything in mind, but stir-fry sure sounded good. "How about we go out for Chinese? But you have to drive. I've just come from the Dog-Eared Page."

"Oh, and you didn't invite me?"

"Sorry. How about that dinner?"

"I've already got my keys in my hand. Let's go."

FIVE

The drive to Merrimack, where a fine selection of Chinese restaurants could be found, would have been pretty quiet if Angelica hadn't blathered on and on about her campaign strategy. Tricia wasn't sure what it was she wanted to tell her sister, only that she had to get something off her chest.

The white linen tablecloths were protected by table-sized plate glass, and the napkins were linen instead of paper for the nighttime crowd. The restaurant was filled with people, conversation, and cheerful ethnic music played in the background. A large saltwater fish tank divided the dining room, where a variety of colorful fish swam lazily back and forth, probably wondering why they were held prisoner in such a tiny space when they—or their forebearers—had once had an ocean in which to roam free.

Angelica perused Madam Lu's menu with the same level of concentration she gave her literary contracts.

"It's only food," Tricia reminded her.

Angelica looked over the top of her reading glasses and glowered. "I suppose you're going to choose the steamed vegetables—sans rice, soup, or egg roll."

Tricia shrugged. "I splurged on a Danish for breakfast, so I really should rein in my dinner choice."

"You're not overweight. You don't have high cholesterol or blood pressure. Can't you ever just let go and enjoy yourself?"

Tricia looked down at her menu and fought sudden tears.

The waiter returned with a sweating pitcher of water and filled the glasses that sat before them, his expression eager to please. "You like something else to drink?"

"I'll have a Beefeater martini, up, with two queen olives," Angelica said without hesitation. She looked at her sister expectantly. "Tricia?"

"I'll have the same," Tricia blurted.

Angelica blinked, startled.

"You order now?" the waistcoated waiter asked.

Angelica shook her head and set her menu aside. "Not yet. Please bring our drinks. We might need some time to think this over."

The waiter nodded enthusiastically and hurried away.

All kinds of emotions seemed to be bubbling up inside Tricia, and she fought the urge to burst into tears. Angelica reached across the table and rested her hand on Tricia's. "Trish, honey, something is terribly wrong. I think it's time you told me what's going on."

Tricia bit her lip and shook her head. She wasn't sure she could articulate what was on her mind—not without crying, anyway. That she felt picked on by Ginny? That wasn't it. That Christopher's imminent arrival had triggered both anger and nostalgia, while Stan's murder was sure to drive Grant Baker away? And why had she wanted to go to a public place when she could have unburdened herself quite nicely in Angelica's—private—kitchen?

Angelica's fingers curled around Tricia's and the touch brought a flood of memories from the past. How many times had their beloved grandmother done the same thing when her childhood problems had seemed so overwhelming? Tricia's vision blurred as she looked up at her sister and noticed how much Angelica resembled their father's mother.

"Please tell me what's wrong," Angelica whispered. "Maybe I can help."

It was then Tricia burst into tears.

Suddenly Angelica was beside her in the booth, her arms encircling Tricia's shoulders, their heads resting against each other. "Tricia, Tricia," Angelica soothed. "Come on, tell your big sister all about it," Angelica implored and pressed a paper napkin into Tricia's hand.

"My life is such a mess," Tricia blubbered and blew her nose.

Angelica squeezed her tighter. "Tell me all about it."

Tricia shook her head and Angelica pressed a kiss against her cheek. "Come on. We can't solve this unless you bare all."

Tricia knew she was right, but the vast ocean of emotion she'd been denying for such a long time engulfed her like a tsunami. She cried and cried and cried.

The drinks arrived, and she was sure that the other restaurant patrons around them were staring at them in discomfort, but for the very first time in her life, she didn't care. Crying in a public place was embarrassing, and yet somehow very liberating. Angelica held on to her, kissing her head, rocking her, and cooing comforting words into her ear. When at last the tears started to subside, Tricia found herself wiping her eyes with the other cocktail napkin. She looked up into her sister's worried face to find compassion, not derision.

"You're going to be okay," Angelica assured her. "We're going to figure out what's wrong and make it right. I promise."

Tricia blinked back the last of her tears and returned her sister's hug. Angelica planted one last kiss on Tricia's head—not unlike the ones she gave her dog—before she moved back to the other side of the booth.

The waiter was suddenly there, offering Tricia a fistful of clean paper napkins, his expression wary.

"We're going to need a few minutes," Angelica said. "Maybe ten or fifteen," she elaborated.

The little man bowed and scurried away.

Angelica lifted her martini glass. "Now, tell me what's wrong. But first, I think we should toast."

"To what?" Tricia asked miserably.

"The future, of course. And may it be fabulous for both of us."

Fabulous? Both of them were probably considered murder suspects by the chief of the Stoneham Police Department—and not for the first time, either.

Tricia studied her sister's face. Except for the time she'd witnessed Angelica's ordeal dealing with her fear of closed-in spaces, Tricia had never seen Angelica crumble—and especially not in public. Panic, maybe. Crumble? Not a chance.

Angelica never even blinked in the face of adversity. For the first time, Tricia envied her sister for that quality.

Tricia took a tiny sip of her drink. It was watered down, as most restaurant drinks seemed to be. She set her glass back down on the paper napkin.

"Something set you off," Angelica said quietly, setting her own glass on the table. "Now what was it? And let me remind you that everything in your life *isn't* in ruins."

"Oh, but it is. And the worst is my situation with Grant."

"Oh, it's always a man," Angelica commiserated.

"I can predict what's going to happen," Tricia began. "Tomorrow morning he's going to come into the shop—or worse, call me—and say, *You found the body. I have to consider you a suspect,* and will treat me like—"

"Like shit," Angelica supplied.

Tricia nodded. "Until the truth comes to light, and then he'll want to pick up where we left off as though nothing happened."

"The skunk," Angelica cried and took another sip of her drink.

Tricia swiped one of the rough napkins against her nose once again. "I don't think I can do that anymore."

"Of course you can't," Angelica agreed. "So what *will* you do?"

Tricia thought about it for a moment. Baker was a sweet, tender man—when he was emotionally available, but that was far too infrequently. How many times had he canceled a date? Date? What were they? More often than not the times they got together he'd come to her loft with a pizza or a sub sandwich, stay the night, and then disappear for a week or two.

Tricia had been reluctant to admit it, but the fact was

that being with Grant Baker was not much better than being alone. It had been eons since she'd spent a night at his place. They'd had a few hurried lunch dates during the past few months, but not much more.

"Are you ready to call it quits?" Angelica asked.

Tricia eyed her drink, picked it up, and took a fortifying sip. She nodded. "I should have known where we stood when he chose to stand by his sick ex-wife."

"I don't think you can fault the man for that," Angelica admonished.

"No, I don't. But it's now obvious to me that he'd choose anything—job, ex-wife, maybe even his car—over me."

Angelica sighed. "I'm sorry you have to go through this."

Tricia shrugged. "That's not the half of it. Christopher has resurfaced again."

Angelica frowned. "What does *he* want?"

Tricia shook her head. "He's got a job interview—but it's on the weekend. Who holds interviews on a weekend?"

"Not a corporate client. Maybe someone with big bucks who needs an honest financial advisor. You did once speculate that was the reason Christopher gave up his career. That he couldn't stand misleading clients into making risky investments that his superiors were pushing."

Tricia sighed and nodded. "If nothing else, Christopher never lied to me, and I do believe if he'd had to stay in that gonzo Wall Street environment much longer he would have gone crazy. But instead of just giving up his job, he gave up his whole life!"

Angelica took another sip of her drink. "The thing is, you don't *have* to see him. You don't even have to talk to him."

"I know. But bottom line, I'll always care for him. I like the idea that we can still be friends, if not life partners."

"Maybe Grant Baker feels the same way about his ex-wife," Angelica suggested.

It was Tricia's turn to nod. She, too, took another sip of her drink. She didn't really enjoy a martini, and wished she'd ordered something a bit more tame, since that apparently was her style. These days, she wasn't quite sure what her style was.

"Anything else bothering you?" Angelica asked sincerely.

Tricia shrugged. "Ginny intimated that my decorating style—well, that *I'm*—stuffy."

"Tricia, dear, you *are* stuffy," Angelica confirmed. "That said, you command a lot of respect in Stoneham—that village jinx label not withstanding. You have dedicated employees, wonderful friends, Miss Marple, and of course Sarge and me."

Tricia ran her index finger around the bottom of her glass and nodded. She felt beaten, exhausted from exorcising her demons. But she also felt a lot calmer after giving in to the tears that had been hanging around the periphery of her soul for far too long.

Tricia became aware of the hopeful waiter standing nearby. As she glanced directly at him, Angelica said, "Not yet," in the same voice she used to admonish Sarge.

The waiter went away.

She turned back to her sister. "Trish, answer my next question from your gut—and not the part of your brain that wants to censor all you say or do."

Tricia looked up. "That sounds ominous."

"Not at all." Angelica removed the little pink sword that skewered the olives in her martini. She bit down on the first olive, pulled it free, and chewed, then put the sword and remaining olive back in her glass. She swallowed. "What would make you happy?"

World peace.

A cure for cancer.

No cruelty—ever—to animals, children, or the elderly.

"Time," she answered simply. "Time for myself. Time to do as I please. Time enough to read all day. Time to repair all the old books I've collected that need some TLC. Time to do what I damn well please."

Angelica nodded, took another sip of her drink, and set down her glass. "Did you notice that nothing in your want-to-do list was spending time with a man?"

Tricia blinked, taken aback. Angelica was right. Her off-the-cuff answer had not included Grant Baker or Christopher Benson.

"Maybe what you need to do is take a day off once in a while," Angelica said reasonably. "Have you had one day off since you opened the shop?"

Tricia thought about it. Yes, she had. Well, almost. When she'd taken care of Angelica after she'd broken her foot three years before, she'd opened and closed the store, leaving Ginny in charge during the intervening hours. And of course, she'd had the last two Christmas days off. But other than that . . .

"Do you think I'm burned out?" she asked Angelica. The thought had never occurred to her.

Angelica shrugged. "You tell me."

Tricia considered the idea. Hell yes, she was burned out! She loved her store, but she hadn't really built a life that included it, but didn't revolve around it. She ran four miles on her treadmill every day. Ate the same yogurt breakfast, tuna plate lunch, and a makeshift dinner—unless, of course,

Angelica invited her over . . . or she invited herself. Most nights she read herself to sleep.

Of course, she didn't want her old life back, either. In those days, she and Christopher would go out to eat or bring home take-out food—every night! Either that or they dined with people she thought had been friends. People who seemed too busy to talk or spend time with her after the divorce.

What she did miss was fun—or at least enjoying simple pleasures. Shopping with girlfriends. Taking in a museum or a movie. Having an occasional manicure.

"Yes," Tricia said at last, "I *am* burned out. I love my store. I love every aspect of running it, but it has become my life. Since I opened it, I don't even have time to read all the mysteries I love, in addition to keeping up with what's new in the marketplace." She looked up at her sister. "What do you think I should do?"

Angelica leaned back against the tufted Naugahyde banquette, waved her hands in denial, and shook her head. "Oh, no. It's not up to me to tell you what to do with your life. If you sit quietly for an hour or so and listen to what your heart is telling you—and not rely on anybody else's expectations or suggestions—you'll find your own key to happiness."

"That was pretty profound," Tricia commented with the ghost of a smile. "Are you speaking from experience?"

Angelica shrugged. "It can't hurt." She seemed to shake herself and grabbed her menu once again. "We really should decide what we want to order."

Tricia picked up her menu and stared at the photo of steamed vegetables. She was sick to death of eating healthy all the time. She'd had a fruit Danish for breakfast and had spent the rest of the day feeling guilty about it. "I think I'll have shrimp with black mushrooms."

Angelica raised an eyebrow, but said nothing. "I'm going to have the yu hsiang beef."

They both closed their menus and placed them on the outside edge of the table so that the next time the waiter made his circuit he'd see they were ready to order.

Tricia looked at her sister—the person she'd always considered bossy and condescending, and realized that not once during their entire conversation had Angelica voiced her opinion or volunteered a suggestion on what Tricia should do to change her life for the better. For once, she'd actually treated Tricia as an equal.

Tricia managed a weak, pleased smile.

"Feeling better now?" Angelica asked.

Tricia nodded—let out a deep, cleansing breath—and allowed her smile to widen. She *did* feel better. Perhaps one needed a meltdown every now and then to clear the fog that settled around one's brain.

Angelica raised her glass.

"Another toast?" Tricia asked.

Angelica shook her head. "No, the same one. The future. May it be fabulous for both of us."

Tricia raised her glass and clinked it against Angelica's. She took a sip. The gin and vermouth tasted so much better than it had just minutes before. She savored it. She hadn't savored much in her life of late, and was determined she wouldn't miss the opportunity in the future.

SIX

After such a soul-wrenching evening, Tricia had climbed into bed, closed her eyes, slept deeply, and didn't awake until the alarm clock woke her the next morning. As she completed the daily four-mile brisk run on her treadmill, she considered what Angelica had asked the previous evening. What was it going to take to make her happy?

She'd made up her mind about several things, and with the decisions made, she knew she'd have to start implementing them. That said, she thought it best to deal with the tasks that had the lowest priority in her life. She had plenty of time to think more about, and tackle, the larger issues.

One thing, she knew: when it came to decorating for the holidays, she was *not* going to draw Santa hats and beards on the portraits of long-dead authors that lined the walls of her shop. What was wrong with dignified decorations? *They're boring,* Ginny had hinted. Tricia had seen the decorations at the Happy Domestic, but she hadn't really taken note of them. She had plenty of time before she needed to open Haven't Got a Clue and decided to pay Ginny a visit.

After showering, dressing, and feeding an eager Miss Marple, Tricia reached for the phone in her kitchen. It was too early to call the Happy Domestic's number. Ginny wasn't likely to answer it, so instead Tricia dialed her former assistant's cell phone number. She picked it up right away. "Tricia? This is early. What's up?"

"Need a coffee break? I'm buying. It'll only take five or ten minutes out of your day."

Ginny laughed. "I'm sure I can make the time."

"Great. I'll be there as fast as Alexa can pour."

"See you in a few," Ginny said and broke the connection.

After grabbing her coat, Tricia stopped at the Coffee Bean, bought two cups of their holiday blend, and headed to the Happy Domestic. The sign hanging on the door was still turned to CLOSED, but she tested the handle and it turned easily. Ginny was waiting for her, standing behind the cash desk, pen in hand, pricing Dolly Dolittle figurines, the extremely cute Victorian-esque angels that sparkled. "How did you know I didn't have time to make coffee this morning?"

"Maybe I'm psychic." *It's better than being considered a jinx,* Tricia thought, *or stuffy,* but wasn't willing to voice either opinion. She handed Ginny one of the paper cups. "We'll have to work extra hard to save the planet the rest of the day."

Ginny laughed, but then her expression sobered. "Have you heard anything more about Stan Berry's murder?"

Tricia shook her head. "Not since—we talked last night.

Speaking of which, you seemed a little upset." Nothing compared to what she'd gone through herself, but it made a good conversational opening.

"Did I?" Ginny asked.

"Yeah. At least when the conversation turned to Nigela Ricita."

"I'm more than a little tired of hearing about that paragon of virtue," she grated.

"But you hinted that—"

Ginny shook her head. "Antonio doesn't open up to me about her. But all I ever hear from everybody else are questions, like what is she like, who is she? I have no idea, and I can't help feeling annoyed by it all."

Tricia was sorry she'd even mentioned the woman's name.

"I'm really grateful she sent Joelle to work on our wedding, but I'm more than a little suspicious about Ms. Ricita's motives."

Joelle Morrison just happened to be the sister of Betsy Dittmeyer, the receptionist at the Stoneham Chamber of Commerce. She was also a wedding planner from Nashua who'd been working with Ginny on all aspects of the upcoming nuptials, from picking out the cake topper to the socks Antonio would wear on their big day. Yet everyone involved with the wedding thought of her as a dour, past-her-prime woman—although she was probably no older than Tricia—who loved to nag. She expected the wedding to come off without a hitch, and that everyone would step into line to make it happen. And that voice! It was often a squeal.

"How so?" Tricia asked.

"Well, with Joelle around we can keep our noses to the grindstone. She shows up with some product or other, lets me choose, and hightails it out of here. And she's awful pushy. I was looking forward to visiting shops and going through catalogs and having a good wallow while planning my wedding. Joelle's taken all that away from me."

"But you really don't have the time for all that—especially now," Tricia pointed out.

Ginny nodded. "No. But I feel like I'm missing out on a lot of the fun stuff that happens when you plan a wedding."

Tricia could relate to that. She'd made planning her wedding into a second job.

"As if that wasn't enough, Ms. Ricita keeps sending us tacky wedding gifts," Ginny continued.

"Oh?"

"Stupid stuff. What kind of wedding gift is an autographed photo of Lucille Ball in a bathing suit?"

"I hope you're kidding."

Ginny shook her head. "*That* was for Antonio. He's a big fan. If he can't sleep at night, I'll find him in the living room watching an episode of *I Love Lucy*. He has them all on DVD. He said he learned English watching them as a kid and still loves them."

"That makes sense," Tricia said, although not sure she believed it.

"The great and powerful Nigela sent *me* a tablecloth."

"Was it nice?" Tricia asked.

"Italian lace—handmade. I suppose it's very nice. I haven't actually taken it out of the packaging yet, but I did send her a thank-you note."

Trust Ginny to cover all bases. "Well, she doesn't really know you . . . yet," Tricia said, in what she hoped was an encouraging tone.

Ginny glowered.

"What else has she sent?" Tricia asked.

"Boxes of Italian chocolates—like I need that when I'm supposed to fit in my wedding dress in seven days. Oh, and a couple of cases of wine."

"Chianti?" Tricia asked.

"No. Dom Pérignon for us to use as we see fit, either at the wedding or at home, and Domaine Chandon for our guests."

"A case of each?" Tricia sputtered in disbelief. "That's a pretty pricey gift."

Ginny shrugged. "She probably got it wholesale. She's got connections."

"Nevertheless, it sounds like she wants only the best for you both."

Ginny's expression was positively sour. "Yeah, but for all the stuff she's done, she still won't give us an answer as to whether she's going to show up for our wedding."

"Have you considered that maybe she knows her presence could take the spotlight off of you and Antonio?"

Ginny frowned. "What do you mean?"

"It's *your* day to shine. Any loving mother—step or otherwise—wouldn't want to disrupt the happiest day of her child's life. Maybe her not showing up could be the greatest gift she could give the two of you."

"Maybe," Ginny said, but she didn't look convinced. She took a long sip of her quickly cooling coffee.

"Are you all set for the rehearsal tomorrow afternoon?"

Ginny shrugged. "I guess. It kind of burns me that we have to have it six days before the wedding."

"Logistics," Tricia said. It made sense. The inn couldn't shut down operations to accommodate the rehearsal on a day it would be booked solid with guests.

"Yeah, this is the biggest mishmash of a wedding I've ever seen."

"That may be, but with Angelica throwing you a party, you know whatever she serves is going to be delicious, and everyone will have a wonderful time—especially if you bring a couple of those bottles of champagne along."

"I was planning on doing that. And yes, it was very generous of Angelica to do this for us. I was a little surprised, to tell you the truth. We didn't exactly hit it off when we first met."

"All water under the bridge," Tricia said, grateful her sister and her good friend had managed to become more than acquaintances in the past year or so.

Tricia sipped her coffee and looked around the Happy Domestic. For all Ginny's teasing the night before, the decorations in her own shop were hardly over the top. They were feminine, dainty, and quite conservative. A pink tabletop feather tree was loaded with pastel ornaments on a myriad of subjects; pink flamingos, green and yellow fruit, and delicate white dogs and cats were just a few of the baubles on offer. White fairy lights were artfully draped across the display pieces, with a touch of artificial greenery here and there. Instead of the usual potpourri, the shop smelled of evergreen, although Tricia wasn't sure how Ginny had pulled that off, and truthfully, she wasn't interested enough to even ask.

She glanced at her watch. "Oh, my. The day is getting ahead of me. I'd better say good-bye and open my own store."

"Thanks for the coffee—and the chat. I really miss them every day. Brittney's a great kid, but . . . she's just a kid."

Tricia suppressed a smile. She'd thought the same thing about Ginny almost four years before. "If we don't talk before tomorrow, I'll see you at the Brookview for the wedding rehearsal."

"Don't remind me," Ginny grumbled and gulped the rest of her coffee before waving good-bye as Tricia headed out the door.

Tricia just had time to turn her CLOSED sign to OPEN and put the cash in the till before the shop door opened and Pixie backed into the store, looking like an enormous bear wrestling with a bulky cardboard box. The vintage fur coat had seen better days, but Pixie didn't seem to care, and since she hung it out of sight at the back of the store, it wouldn't offend Tricia's customers who were anti-fur.

"Good morning!" Pixie called as she staggered under the weight of the box on her four-inch heels. She dropped the carton on the sales counter with a loud thud. Miss Marple, who'd been sitting on her perch behind the register, jumped down and scampered away in fright.

"Sorry," Pixie called and shrugged.

"What have you got there?" Tricia asked, dreading the answer.

"Christmas decorations. Of course, this is just the first box."

The first box?

"How many more are there?" Tricia asked.

"Just three."

Tricia took in the size of the box, which could have housed a small oven. "The same size?"

"Just about," Pixie said with pride and unfastened the buttons on her coat.

"Just what's inside?" Tricia asked, fearing the answer.

"Oh, all kinds of neat stuff. Garland, ornaments, and I've

got a big artificial tree out in the car. It must be eight feet tall when it's put together."

"Where are we going to put it all?" Tricia asked, her stomach tightening with dread.

"I thought I'd put some nails up near the ceiling—"

"No!" Tricia said, rather emphatically.

"No?" Pixie asked, taken aback.

"I hate to be a killjoy, but I paid a lot of money to restore the walls and add the crown molding."

"Oh, yeah. I hadn't thought about that," Pixie said. "I guess I could tape them up."

Tricia shook her head. "I don't want the tape to take off any of the paint, either."

"Oh. Well." Pixie's joy had evaporated like water in the desert.

"Why don't we go through the box and see what would be appropriate for a mystery bookstore," Tricia said.

"Appropriate?" Pixie asked suspiciously.

"We are a shop that specializes in murder. And while we do want our customers to buy, buy, buy—we need to make sure the decorations are tasteful," Tricia explained.

Pixie frowned, turned away, and tossed her coat on one of the seats in the readers' nook. When she returned, she opened the carton's flaps. Inside was a tangled mess of ratty pink and blue garland, artificial greenery that was crushed and bent at odd angles, and colorful balls that had been wound with synthetic silk thread. Unfortunately, the threads were snagged and frayed.

Pixie's expression grew more and more dour. "You don't like any of this stuff, do you?"

Tricia tried not to squirm. "I'm very conservative when it

comes to decorating," she admitted. That sounded a lot better than being stuffy. "What other kinds of things do you have?"

"A bunch of figurines. Some carolers, Santas, reindeer. The usual Christmas stuff."

"Why don't you bring those in and we'll take a look," Tricia said.

"Don't you want *any* of this stuff?" Pixie asked, exasperated, and for a moment Tricia thought she might burst into tears.

Tricia bit her lip as she gazed at the junk that littered her sales counter. "Maybe we could use some of the greenery. In the back of the shop," she amended.

Pixie's lower lip trembled and her eyes filled with tears as she repacked the box.

"I really appreciate you going to all this trouble," Tricia started but decided she'd better not make the situation any worse by saying more. "Would you like some help bringing the other boxes in?"

Pixie shook her head. "Maybe I should just forget the whole thing."

"I'm sure there's *something* we can use," Tricia said, not that she believed it. Couldn't Pixie see the items in the box for what they were—someone else's cast-offs? But then, after spending so many years in the penal system, maybe she found anything of a holiday nature to be cheerful. A jail cell had to be the most miserable place on earth to spend the joyous season.

"Well, maybe we could go through another one of the boxes," Pixie said as she retrieved her coat. She gathered the carton in her arms and started for the door. "Could you give me a hand?"

Tricia hurried across the shop, opened the door, and held it as Pixie went out, letting in two customers. "Can I help you?" Tricia asked.

"Oh, nice store," the first woman said, looking around. The sixty-something woman was bundled in a buff-colored coat with a thin, pink handcrafted scarf, reminding Tricia of a toaster pastry. The woman's gaze landed on the string of portraits of long-dead authors. "Are those all famous chefs?"

"Chefs?" Tricia repeated. "Were you ladies looking for the Cookery cookbook store?" They nodded enthusiastically. "That's right next door. This is Haven't Got a Clue. We sell vintage and new mysteries."

The second woman, who wore a rather dramatic flowing scarlet cape, frowned. "I told you it was next door. But no— you never listen to a word I say."

"Louise!" the first woman admonished, embarrassed. "Please forgive my sister. She's been testy ever since the meno-pause hit."

"I am not!" said the other, who yanked open the door and stormed out.

Her sister's cheeks colored in embarrassment. "Sorry to have bothered you."

"No trouble," Tricia said and closed the door behind her. Had she and Angelica sounded like those two siblings? Un-fortunately, she had to admit they had. After the previous evening, she was still basking in their sisterly bonding, but no doubt she'd soon be annoyed with Angelica for some reason. Only the next time it happened, she might not get quite as irritated. The two of them would never see eye to eye on everything, but their relationship was the best it had ever been—and she wanted to keep it that way.

Pixie returned, carrying a smaller box that was still large enough for a dorm refrigerator. However, this time she didn't bother taking off her coat. Maybe she figured she'd be quickly dispatched to her car once again.

She opened the flaps on the box. Everything within it had been carefully wrapped in dry, yellowing newspaper. There must have been fifty or sixty of the little bundles. "See if you like any of these."

Tricia grabbed one of the bundles off the top of the pile and unwrapped it. To her delight, it was a small ceramic angel all in white, playing the violin. It was old—well, relatively speaking. It looked like the kitsch she'd seen in a home style magazine, and was probably fifty or sixty years old. The entire body was glazed white, but the eyes had been hand painted, as had the lips. The instrument was outlined in black and gold. "She's adorable."

"Do you really like her?" Pixie asked, sounding incredulous.

"I love her."

"There's lots more," Pixie said, her eyes going wide, and picked up another one. She unwrapped it. This was a solemn boy soprano dressed in a black choir robe. His mouth was a painted circle, and he held an open book in his tiny hands.

The women took turns opening each wrapped figurine. Each and every one of them was a joy to behold. Angels with puppies, angels with Christmas trees. Little figures that *were* Christmas trees, the top branches acting as hats, with a little gold star on top. Skaters. Santas. Mrs. Santa. Reindeer. Christmas planters. Elves. Girls in red and green who stood atop small music boxes. Angel candleholders and candle walkers. It didn't stop!

Finally Pixie shrugged out of her coat, letting it slip to

the floor, and the two of them finished unwrapping every one of the figurines. By the time they were through they had amassed an unsightly pile of crumpled old newspapers on the floor but had revealed an angel orchestra, an impressive choir, and enough other figurines to populate an entire Christmas village.

"I know they don't have anything to do with mystery books, but you have to admit they're pretty damn cute," Pixie said.

"That they are," Tricia agreed.

"And they *are* vintage—like the mysteries we sell. Can we show them off *somewhere*?" she asked, desperation straining her voice. "Maybe on one of the back shelves?"

"Back shelves, nothing. They're going in the front display window," Tricia said with a smile.

Pixie's eyes lit up, but then her face fell. "What about Miss Marple? She's liable to knock them over. You know how she likes to sleep there when the sun is shining."

Tricia thought about it for a moment. "Have you ever heard of earthquake putty?"

Pixie shook her head.

"It's kind of like clay. We could put down a sheet of Plexiglas, and then add a wad of the putty on the bottom of each figurine and make it look like they were holding up some of the books. I know we've got a stack of holiday paperbacks and anthologies stashed in the storeroom. We would nestle some angel hair around them; it would look like snowdrifts."

"That would look pretty keen," Pixie agreed.

"And maybe we could leave a spot free for Miss Marple to sleep, too. Otherwise, we'll just have to encourage her to nap somewhere else, and I'm not sure she'd like that."

"One of the other boxes has vintage cardboard buildings. They're covered in glitter and they are to *die* for," Pixie gushed.

"If they're as cute as these little guys—why not?" Tricia said.

"If it's a slow sales day, we could put the whole thing together this afternoon. I could go out on my lunch break and buy the other stuff we need," Pixie offered. "They've got everything at the big craft store up on Route 101. It's just a ten- or fifteen-minute drive."

"Oh, no, I couldn't ask you to use your lunch break to do it," Tricia said.

"I could grab a burger while I'm out. I'd *really* like to do this, Tricia."

There was no way Tricia could squelch that kind of enthusiasm. "Okay." There were still no customers in the store. "Why don't you go get the box with the little buildings and we can start planning our layout."

She didn't have to ask twice. Pixie snatched her coat from the floor, thrust her arms in the sleeves, and whooshed out the door.

Tricia picked up one of the figurines and smiled. Cute. Not at all stuffy.

SEVEN

Like children at play, Tricia and Pixie had a wonderful time planning their Christmas window display on paper. Eager to complete the project, they decided not to wait until the noon hour for Pixie to leave for her errands. When she arrived back at the store, Tricia was waiting with sandwiches to go from Booked for Lunch and the two worked around the customers who came and went. Several of the tourists took pictures of the display in progress and suggested that Tricia put photos of the completed village on the Haven't Got a Clue website.

Pixie was conversing with a couple of customers in the back of the store, waxing poetically about John D. MacDonald's Travis McGee novels, when Angelica came breezing through Haven't Got a Clue's entrance clutching a catalog in one hand, and a Booked for Lunch coffee to go in the other.

"Greetings and felicitations!" she called merrily and approached the sales desk, where Tricia was checking eBay listings for mystery box lots on her laptop computer.

"My, but you're in a good mood," Tricia said, smiling.

Angelica's answering grin was positively wicked. "That's because my heart is pure."

"Not with that smile."

Angelica laughed, set her purse down, and unzipped her jacket. "I've come for your opinion on a number of subjects. The first of which is the dessert for Ginny and Antonio's wedding rehearsal dinner tomorrow night. Should I bake a cake or make crème brûlée?"

Tricia thought it over. "Well, there'll be wedding cake at the reception. I vote for crème brûlée."

"Oh, good. That was my first choice, too. I just wanted a corroborating opinion. Do you think the bride and groom will approve?"

"I'm sure whatever you put on the menu will please them."

"How did you know I was going to print out tiny, absolutely adorable menus and put them on each place setting? Have you gained psychic powers?"

"I wish," Tricia said, but then thought better of it. Maybe she didn't want to know what everyone around her was thinking all the time. "Speaking of the bride, Ginny's all bent out of shape because Nigela Ricita isn't going to be at the wedding. It turns out she's Antonio's stepmother."

"Really?" Angelica asked, surprised. She shook her head with a sour quirk of her mouth. "You can tell that girl has never been married before. She should be thanking her lucky stars the woman's staying away."

"Did you have mother-in-law problems?" Tricia asked. She didn't think Angelica ever put up with someone else's bad behavior.

Angelica nodded. "With three of my four exes. Drew's mother had passed away years before we got hitched—thank goodness—or I'm sure she'd have been just as interfering."

"Christopher's mother was always nice to me. His dad was a treasure."

"Lucky you. But you're just as divorced as me, anyway."

"I only went to bat once," Tricia reminded her.

Angelica shrugged. "Your good luck." She turned her gaze to her right and squinted down at the display in Tricia's front window. "What's with Angelville?"

"Isn't it cute?" Tricia gushed. "It was Pixie's idea. We sell vintage mysteries, why not have vintage Christmas decorations?"

"They're not really in keeping with the décor in your store."

"I'll grant you that," Tricia said. "But Pixie's heart was in the right place, and I hated to disappoint her."

Angelica shrugged. "At least they're cute, not stuffy."

There was that word again. "Ange, do you really think my store comes across as stuffy?" Tricia asked.

"Well, it's tastefully stuffy. Dark walls, dark paint, tin ceiling. Pictures of long-dead authors lining the walls . . . kind of like a stodgy gentleman's-only club from another age. You have to admit, cheerful this place ain't."

Angelica was starting to sound just like Ginny and Pixie. "Well, they'll only be in the front display through the holidays. Any ideas on what I should do next?"

"Maybe you could hire a professional window dresser."

"Are my displays really that bad?"

Angelica shrugged. "They're . . . boring. A book here, a book there. Just the dust jackets seem to change. And you can't keep them there long because they'd fade in the sunlight," she said reasonably.

"That is a big problem," Tricia admitted. She crossed her arms. "What would you do differently?"

Angelica frowned. "Let me think about it for a couple of days. And if I can't come up with something, I'll find someone to come in and give you some ideas."

"Not if you have to import them from Boston or New York."

"Would I do that and stick you with the bill?" Angelica cried, offended.

"Of course not."

Angelica looked thoughtful. "Maybe that should be one of my campaign promises—to get help for Chamber members to upgrade their displays or store decoration. After all, if we want to win the Prettiest Village in New England contest, we *will* have to work at it."

"Do you *really* think there's much value in that?"

"You better believe it. And I can't say I'm sorry that I won't be running against Stan Berry with his horrible ideas to slash budgets and services to our members."

"Don't go around advertising that sentiment," Tricia warned. "Grant might think you had it in for Stan."

"I do wish the inn had surveillance cameras," Angelica said wistfully. "That would've solved the whole problem."

"I don't think Antonio or the owners could ever have envisioned a murder taking place just off the main lobby."

"No, but it would have proved everyone was where they said they were—and maybe given the killer something to think about. Maybe tomorrow night I'll talk to Antonio about adding cameras, at least to the lobby and the parking area. After all, aside from winning the Prettiest Village in New England, I'd like Stoneham to reclaim the title of safest village, too."

It had lost that distinction when Tricia found Doris Gleason dead in her shop some three years before. Tricia didn't like to revisit that memory.

"Oh, I almost forgot why I came in to visit," Angelica said and handed Tricia the catalog of tchotchkes she'd been holding.

"What is this for?"

"Possible campaign giveaways."

Tricia flipped through the catalog. "This looks like the kind of stuff authors use for promotion."

"Well, where do you think I got it? I *am* an author, and I *do* buy stuff from that catalog to promote myself and my books."

"I thought you just did bookmarks and postcards."

"I've given away pens, measuring spoons, spatulas. You can personalize just about anything. I was thinking of giving away rulers."

"Why? Because you want to rule the Chamber?"

Angelica nodded enthusiastically. "Great pun, huh?"

Tricia shook her head, resisting a smile.

"If I put in my order before three o'clock, I can have them delivered on Monday morning."

"You're going to pay for almost next-day delivery?" Tricia asked. This was Saturday, after all.

"You bet. I need to hand out as many as I can before the election on Wednesday morning."

"What are you going to have printed, *Vote for Angelica?*"

"Oh, nothing that blatant. I thought maybe *Angelica*

Miles. Entrepreneur. Author. Leader. How's that sound?" she asked eagerly.

"Not as bigheaded as I thought it would be," Tricia admitted, hoping that would be the end of the conversation.

"Bigheaded? Me?" Angelica asked, aghast.

"I'm only kidding. I can truthfully say that you would be a welcome breath of fresh air for the Chamber of Commerce."

"I'm glad you feel that way, because I'm going to depend on you to help me get the word out."

Get the word out? Just about every member of the Chamber had heard Angelica's pitch just the day before. Tricia sighed but managed a halfhearted smile. "Of course I'll help you. What do you need?"

"Just talk me up to our fellow Chamber members. But then, I would expect that even if I wasn't the best thing to happen to Stoneham since Hiram Stone opened his quarry back in 1822."

Oh, brother!

"I'll do whatever it takes to replace Bob," Tricia said. "Just answer me one question: Are you really—*really*—sure this is what you want to do?"

"As God is my witness," Angelica said and crossed her heart with her right index finger.

Tricia's smile widened. "Then let's make this happen."

Angelica waggled her eyebrows a la Groucho Marx. "All right." Then she sighed and sobered. "There's just one awful aspect to this whole campaign."

"Stan Berry's death," Tricia said.

Angelica nodded sadly. "Do you know if Bob left the dining room when he adjourned for the meeting for our bathroom breaks?"

Tricia shrugged. "I have no idea."

"Maybe you could worm that information out of Chief Baker. If not, then the Chamber members might actually think I *was* trying to eliminate my competition."

Now was not a good time to ask for favors. At any minute Tricia expected the phone to ring or the door to burst open for Baker to make his announcement that they couldn't see each other as long as the case was unsolved. The following discussion wasn't likely to be pretty.

"Where were you when the meeting recessed?" Tricia asked.

"Like everybody else, I was on my way to the bathroom."

Tricia did not remember seeing Angelica standing in the restroom line when she'd spoken to Eleanor. She'd probably already been inside the ladies' room at the time. There was no way she could even consider Angelica a suspect. And if Grant Baker did, she would somehow have to dissuade him of that notion.

The idea that she should have to do so disturbed her. And then there was the whole subject of their relationship—or lack thereof. She didn't want to think about that until she absolutely had to.

Tricia and Pixie had come to an understanding on the Christmas decorations, and Tricia and Angelica were on solid ground as well. It felt good. And she looked forward to witnessing Ginny's wedding to Antonio. Those two were soul mates, of that she was sure. And the wedding was guaranteed to be a wonderful time, whether Nigela Ricita attended or not.

Pixie staggered up to the cash desk, her arms full of books, with the customers in tow. As much as Tricia had loved having Ginny as an assistant, she'd sold almost 20 percent more books since Pixie had come on board.

"I'd better get going," Angelica said and grabbed her catalog and coffee. "See you later," she called over her shoulder as she left the store.

Tricia began to ring up the sale.

"Oops, looks like Angelica left her purse," Pixie said, picking up Angelica's enormous purse, which she'd left sitting on the floor in front of the cash desk. "Do you want me to run it over to the Cookery?"

Tricia shook her head and rang up the next item. "If she doesn't notice it's missing, I'll take it over there in a little while."

Pixie handed her the purse, which she set down on the floor behind the counter. As she finished ringing up the sale, Tricia remembered something about her conversation with Angelica. She'd asked if Tricia had seen Bob after he'd recessed the meeting for their break. That meant Angelica hadn't seen him, either. Did she suspect Bob of murder? She'd always defended him in the past, saying he was incapable of such a crime.

Had she now changed her mind?

When thirty minutes had passed and Angelica hadn't returned to Haven't Got a Clue to retrieve her purse, Tricia decided she had better return it herself. As she approached the Cookery, Tricia could see a Granite State Tour bus parked in the road near the municipal lot, revving its engine. Stepping inside the store, she found it full of customers and a somewhat frazzled Frannie trying to take care of all of them at once.

"Is Angelica around?" Tricia called over the heads of the people at the register.

"She hasn't come back from Booked for Lunch," Frannie called back and returned her attention to her customer. "That'll be twenty-seven dollars and fifty-three cents."

Tricia threaded her way through the crowd, yanking off her own jacket as she went, and moved behind the register to help. She stuffed Angelica's purse and her jacket under the cash desk and started putting books into bags, while Frannie rang up the sales.

Five minutes later, the last of the customers practically ran out the door—but made it to the bus before it took off, heading for the highway.

"Whew! That was an unexpected rush," Frannie said and slumped against the wall, effectively trapping Tricia. She gave Tricia a critical look. "I don't know what possessed you to come into the store when you did, but I'm grateful."

Tricia pulled Angelica's purse out from under the counter. "Ange left this in my store a little while ago. I thought she would've come straight here, but apparently she had another errand."

Frannie looked at her watch. "That little dog of hers is going to need to be walked pretty soon. I'm sure she won't be long."

"Maybe I'll wait a few minutes. If she doesn't show up, I can always take Sarge out for his constitutional."

"You are such a good person, Tricia."

"Or a sucker," she said with a laugh. She grabbed her coat and nudged her way past Frannie, circling around to the front of the cash desk. "So, what's the grapevine saying about Stan Berry's death today?"

Frannie's eyes widened, her mouth quirking into a sly

grin. "Perhaps Chief Baker ought to consider everyone in Mr. Berry's life as a potential suspect. Especially his recently dumped lady friend."

"Oh?" Tricia asked, right on cue.

Frannie nodded. "It seems Mr. Berry had a relationship with none other than Ginny's wedding planner."

"Joelle Morrison?" Tricia asked aghast. For some reason, she found it hard to believe that any man would want to be tied up with Joelle. And it looked like she'd been right.

Frannie nodded again, her eyes narrowing. She looked around, then straightened and leaned in closer, dropping her voice to almost a whisper. "It seems they were quite the item until just recently. Stan was forever plying her with Godiva chocolate and those gorgeous cupcakes that Nikki Brimfield makes and sells over at the Patisserie."

"Is that so?" Tricia asked. "You said until just recently."

"Uh-huh. I'm not sure why, but it seems the breakup was rather abrupt. One argument and they were kaput."

"How long ago was the split?"

"Sometime in the last two weeks." The way she kept nodding, Frannie seemed to be imitating a bobblehead. "Oh, yeah, she was a frequent visitor at Stan's house, not that she stayed the night, but it sure was late when she'd leave." Frannie lived on the same street as Stan and kept track of all her neighbors' comings and goings. "I'm pretty sure on those occasions when time got past her that Joelle would go to her sister's house and stay rather than drive all the way back to Nashua."

"How did they meet?" Tricia asked and hoped to God she would never be on the receiving end of Frannie's gossip mill.

"Her sister Betsy over at the Chamber of Commerce recommended him as a source when Joelle wanted a sign made for her business. You've seen that giant advertising magnet she hangs on the door of her car, right? She ordered it from Stan."

"I didn't realize he made such things."

"He orders them from one of the companies he deals with. I heard he gave her quite a discount if she promised to go out with him. That was the beginning."

"How long were they together?" Tricia asked, wondering if Baker knew about this liaison.

"Must have been close to a year."

"How come I never heard about any of this?"

Frannie laughed. "'Cuz you lead such a sheltered life. You've always got your nose in a book."

"Not *always*," Tricia said.

Frannie's smile faded. "I guess you're right. You do seem to spend an awful lot of time tripping over dead bodies."

"Stan was sitting on the toilet," Tricia reminded her.

"What a way to go," Frannie said and shook her head, trying to keep a smirk off her face.

Tricia didn't think it was funny. "I'd better get going," she said and turned for the door.

"Thanks again for helping me," Frannie called after her.

Tricia waved and left the store, immediately wishing she'd taken the time to button her coat. She huddled inside it, head down as the wind blew her hair in her face. She'd almost reached Haven't Got a Clue when—pow!—she crashed into someone. She looked up.

"I'm so sorry, I wasn't watching where I was going." Her coat flew open, and she struggled to get the hair out of her eyes.

"Going inside?" the man asked.

"Yes."

He opened the door and let her go ahead of him. Once inside, Tricia raked her fingers through her hair in a fruitless attempt to tame it. "Again, let me apologize."

The young man shook his head. He must have been in his mid-twenties and he looked awfully familiar. "Excuse me, but I was told I might find Angelica Miles here."

Tricia shook her head. "Not here, although she is my sister. She owns the Cookery next door, and the little café across the street, Booked for Lunch."

"That's where I just came from." He shoved his hand toward her. "Hi, I'm Stan Berry."

EIGHT

"Stan Berry," Tricia repeated, dumbfounded.

"My name is actually Stanley William Berry Junior. My friends call me Will."

"Do you always go around trying to shock people?"

He ducked his head and shrugged like a little boy. Tricia supposed he was trying to be cute, but she was not amused.

"Hi, Will," Tricia said and shook his hand. Though his touch was light, he held on just a little too long. Tricia pulled her hand away. "How can I help you?"

"I understand your sister was one of the last people to see my dad alive," he continued.

"Angelica and about twenty-five other people last saw your dad alive, including me."

"Then you must be Tricia Miles, the person who *found*

my dad." He said the words casually and didn't seem all that broken up about the death.

Tricia nodded. "Yes, I did. I'm so sorry for your loss."

Berry shrugged. "Not much of a loss, as far as I can see." At her confusion, he elaborated. "My dad left my mom and me when I was about three. I've heard from him now and then over the years, but I only came to Stoneham because a lawyer called me last night and said he'd made me the executor of his will."

"I take it that was a surprise."

He nodded. "To be perfectly honest, I'm shocked. It turns out he left me everything. He was never very good about paying child support. My mom didn't go after him, either. We might have had a better quality of life if she had. I guess he figured this might make up for it."

This attractive, well-dressed—and well-spoken—young man didn't look the worse for wear for being brought up by a single mother. And he didn't sound all that bitter about his experience, either.

"Why did you want to talk to my sister?" Tricia asked.

"I understand she might have had a motive for my dad's murder."

Tricia started. "I beg your pardon?"

"According to the Stoneham chief of police, she was running against him for president of the Chamber of Commerce."

"My sister is not a murderer," Tricia said rather louder than she'd meant.

"I figure it had to be either her or the other guy in the running." He pulled a piece of paper from his jacket pocket and looked at it. "A Robert Kelly."

"He's known around here as Bob Kelly," Tricia corrected. "And I seriously doubt he would kill your father, either."

"Who else would have wanted him dead?" Will asked. He was being awfully matter-of-fact about his father's murder.

Tricia didn't even have to think about it. "To be perfectly honest—you."

"Me?" he asked, and for the first time since he'd entered the store there was actually some inflection in his tone.

"You just admitted he abandoned you and your mother. That he didn't pay child support. That could be interpreted as a reason for murder."

"Revenge?" he asked, incredulous.

"People have been killed for a lot less." How many times had she uttered that phrase in the past couple of years?

Berry shook his head. "I've got too much at stake to lower myself to petty revenge."

"Such as?" Tricia asked.

"I've been interning for a pretty prestigious law firm in Boston. Weinberg, Metcalf, Henley, and Durgin."

"Ah, another lawyer," she said, knowingly.

"Well, maybe some day. And why do you say it like it's a dirty word?"

She shook her head. "Nothing of the kind. But it's true that lawyers are some of the worst offenders when it comes to upholding the letter of the law."

"Maybe in politics," he agreed, "but that's not what I aspire to."

"And what do you ultimately want to do with your life?" Tricia asked. Good grief. She'd only just met the man—did she really care what he aspired to, and why was she interrogating him anyway?

"Until last night, I intended to be a corporate lawyer. That's where the real money is."

It wasn't surprising he wanted to catch the attorney brass ring, if he'd been brought up in a home that had struggled to stay above the poverty line. "And what made you change your mind?"

"I told my boss I needed time off to take care of my dad's affairs. He told me it wasn't a convenient time. We were working on a big lawsuit," he added for clarification. "I told him murder was never convenient and that I needed to take time off."

"And he said . . . ?" Tricia asked.

"'Don't bother to come back.'"

Tricia stared at the young man in disbelief. "Isn't that grounds for a lawsuit?"

"It sure is. But I'd have to have some pretty deep pockets to defend myself against them."

Tricia had heard of that particular law firm. They were notorious for winning cases, even when the odds were stacked against them. "What are your plans?" she asked.

Again Will shrugged. "I thought I might hang around Stoneham for a while and decide my next move. I'd like to meet my dad's friends, try to figure out who he became."

"Did you know your father had ended a relationship a couple of weeks before his death?"

"We haven't talked in almost a year, but nothing my dad did surprised me. To tell you the truth, knowing his history, I'm astounded that he had a relationship that lasted more than a couple of weeks. According to my mother, he wasn't known to be monogamous for any length of time."

Was he expecting some kind of reaction to that news? It really wasn't any of Tricia's business. And bad-mouthing a dead man—and one's father—seemed to be the height of tastelessness. It was time to end this conversation.

"Is there anything else I can do to help you today?" Tricia asked.

Berry nodded. "Tell me where I can find Mr. Kelly."

"He owns Kelly Real Estate, a block north on the left. If he's not out showing a property to a client, you'll find him in his office or next door at the Chamber of Commerce."

"And what about your sister?"

Tricia happened to have a small stack of Angelica's business cards under the counter. She grabbed one and handed it to Berry. "You can call either number during business hours."

"Thank you," he said with a nod and pocketed the card. He started for the door but paused, turning back to face her once again. "Would you like to have dinner with me tonight?"

Tricia blinked, startled. This young man was at least eighteen years younger than her. And though flattered, she also wondered what his real motivation might be for issuing such an invitation. "I'm seeing someone," she answered succinctly, although that wasn't exactly true, especially under the current circumstances.

Will shrugged. "My loss, his gain. Still, I'm not leaving town for at least the next few days. I'm sure we'll see each other again. Until then." He nodded at her and left the store.

Tricia's gaze remained fixed on the door for long seconds after he'd departed.

Pixie wandered up to stand before her. Tricia hadn't noticed her presence during her entire conversation with Berry. "What was that all about?"

Tricia faced her employee. "I have no idea."

"He's pretty cute. You should've gone out with him."

Tricia frowned. "You know Chief Baker and I are"—she hesitated—"in a relationship."

"Who says you have to bed the guy? But a free meal is a free meal." Pixie shrugged. "Then again, who says you can trust that the guy's on the up and up? Everything he told you might be big fat lies."

That was true. Tricia did tend to take people at face value . . . until they gave her reason to do otherwise. And what if Pixie was right? She had nothing to lose by talking with Berry, and he might tell her something about his father that could be useful—something he wasn't likely to tell Baker. Maybe she had been too hasty in declining his invitation. But then . . . he more or less said he'd be back.

That thought gave her reason to smile.

NINE

"Oh, damn," Pixie swore from the vicinity of the coffee station and held a jar upside down, tapping the bottom. "We're out of creamer—and almost out of sugar, too."

Damn indeed. Tricia had been meaning to replace those staples the last time she'd gone shopping and had forgotten—again.

"If I'd known, I could've gotten them when I went out earlier," Pixie groused. She glanced at the clock on the wall. "Do you think we'll get many more customers before the end of the day?"

"That's debatable," Tricia said.

"We don't *have* to serve them coffee," Pixie offered.

"No, but coffee and cookies often help make people feel

comfortable. And a comfortable customer will feel like indulging him or herself. Why don't I just whip up to the convenience store and grab some replacements? It should only take me ten minutes."

Pixie shrugged. "Fine with me," she said and tossed the empty jar into the wastebasket, and wiped the counter while Tricia went to the back to grab her jacket.

In less than five minutes, Tricia pulled her Lexus into the convenience store's parking lot, and scowled. Was she going to run into Pete Marcella, the owner's rather unpleasant son? She'd met him two years before. The young man had big plans for his future, hoping to open a recycling business. He had convinced his father to support his ambitions by putting multiple recycling containers outside their store, and they didn't give plastic bags to customers who only purchased one or two items. It probably saved them money, as well as helping to keep the local environment tidy. There was nothing wrong with that, but Pete had been so insufferably smug about it all.

Tricia's cell phone trilled and she retrieved it from her purse, instantly recognizing the number. "Hello, Christopher."

"I wanted to let you know I'm in town. Are you free for dinner tonight?"

Oh, dear. He'd been serious when they'd spoken the day before.

"Not really," she lied.

"How about tomorrow?"

"My former assistant is getting married. The rehearsal and dinner are tomorrow night."

"How about lunch?" he asked in what sounded like desperation.

Tricia mulled it over. She'd just as soon have a tooth drilled as have lunch with him, but finally acquiesced. "Okay. Where and when?"

"I'm staying at the Brookview Inn. One o'clock?"

"All right. See you there," she said and rang off.

Tricia replaced her phone and got out of her car, berating herself for again forgetting her hat. The wind was brisk and relentless. She hurried into the store, grateful to shut the door behind her and let the warmth envelop her. The first thing she noticed was that the store was meticulously clean. The floors looked freshly mopped, and there wasn't a speck of dust on any of the shelves or other displays. She found the items she needed with no trouble, plucking them from the shelves. She looked up and spotted a security camera trained in her direction.

There was no monitor near the young man who stood behind the counter, selling lottery tickets to a customer. She was grateful it wasn't Pete. Since she wasn't a regular customer at the store, only using it when she was too lazy to drive the extra five minutes to the large grocery store in Milford, Tricia was unsure if the senior Marcella had an office on site. Juggling her purse, the creamer, and the sugar, she wandered the aisles, noting the location of several more strategically placed cameras. Surely Marcella would be monitoring them, watching out for shoplifters from his office as he worked on paperwork and made calls to his suppliers. As she passed a wall of refrigerator cases, she came upon a door marked EMPLOYEES ONLY. Should she go inside or ask the counter clerk if the boss was in? Instead, she decided to test the door handle. It turned, and she quickly ducked inside, emerging into a short hall that separated a storeroom and another smaller room, its door ajar. A sign said MANAGER.

Tricia knocked on the door and pushed it open. "Mr. Marcella?"

John Marcella sat behind a cluttered desk, peering at a computer screen. He looked up and over the reading glasses perched on the bottom of his nose. "Ms. Miles," he said flatly, obviously not overjoyed to see her.

"Can we talk?" she asked.

Marcella waved a hand to indicate she take the folding metal chair that sat before his desk. She sat down, the cold metal sending a chill through her. "What exactly do you want?" he asked.

"I was hoping you'd tell me about your friendship with Stan Berry."

Marcella suddenly looked weary, and his voice reflected his state of mind. "We weren't friends. I met him through the Chamber and we talked a few times at Chamber breakfasts. We had similar ideas about what the Chamber ought to be doing for its members. He approached me about a week ago with the idea of opposing Bob Kelly and asked me if I'd second his nomination. It's as simple as that."

"Did he actually think he could win?" Tricia asked.

"I doubt it. Bob Kelly might be a miserly landlord, but he *has* done a lot for the village. He might have favored the booksellers, but the rest of us wouldn't still be in business if his efforts hadn't revived the entire village. I think there's enough of us who are grateful for that. He'll probably get elected again. And quite honestly, who really wants to take on that kind of effort?"

"My sister," Tricia reminded him.

He shrugged. "Everyone knows she's just opposing him out of spite because Bob dumped her."

Everyone knew?

"Excuse me, but Bob did *not* dump Angelica—she ended the relationship and had every right to after he—" But she didn't finish the sentence, deciding instead not to air Angelica's dirty laundry.

Marcella waved her aborted explanation aside. "Whatever."

"I honestly think she's got the village's interests at heart," Tricia added.

"Of course you would. And I don't doubt that she could do a good job. She has a reputation for getting things done, and obviously she's a successful businesswoman. But still, how long would she hang in there and work for the Chamber? A year—maybe two—before she moves on to something else?"

True enough. But she *could* get things moving again, and that had value as well.

"Do you know why anyone would want to kill Stan?" Tricia asked.

Marcella shook his head. "I barely knew the guy."

Tricia remembered the colorful signs in the convenience store's window.

"It's obvious that Stan did work for you."

"You mean signs?"

Tricia nodded.

"Yeah. But we didn't talk about it. I would e-mail him when I wanted something done, and he'd drop off whatever I asked for, leaving it at the cash desk up front. He'd send an invoice via PayPal and I'd authorize payment. It couldn't have been easier." Or more impersonal, Tricia silently agreed. "Now I've got to find someone else to handle my signage needs," Marcella conceded sourly.

"So you never had any personal conversations with Stan?" Tricia asked.

"Not that I remember."

"Did he ever mention his son?"

Marcella shook his head and again said, "Not that I remember."

That wasn't really all that surprising. Stan hadn't been close to his son, although he'd left him all his worldly goods. Had Stan been close to anyone besides Joelle?

"Did Stan ever mention a girlfriend?" Tricia said.

Marcella took off his glasses and shook his head. "Look, I told you we didn't talk much. Now, I've got a lot of work to do. Are we through?"

Tricia rose. She would have liked to interrogate the man a little further, but she could see he was fed up. She stood. "Thank you for your time, Mr. Marcella. Will I see you at the Chamber meeting on Wednesday morning?"

"I'll be there," he said with resignation. "But just long enough to vote. Black Friday might be the best day of the year for *your* sales, but on the day before the year's biggest feast, I'll be selling boxes of stuffing and cans of cranberry sauce like crazy."

Tricia didn't doubt it. "I'll see myself out."

Marcella put his glasses back on and hunkered down to study his computer screen again.

Tricia sidled past the office door and stepped back into the convenience store. The conversation hadn't netted her anything useful. Should she tell Angelica that some Chamber members believed her odds of winning to be nil? No, Tricia decided she'd remain cheerful and positive on that subject, and honestly, she only had to do it for another four days. But she crossed her fingers after she paid for her purchases and walked back to her car. Whether most Chamber members realized it, the future of Stoneham was at stake, and it was Tricia's steadfast belief that Angelica really was the best (wo)man for the job.

The sun had dipped toward the horizon long before Tricia and Pixie finished their decorating. She'd had to restrain Pixie from putting up too many garlands and other decorations from the third and last box of thrift-shop items Pixie had purchased. After all, they were selling books, not ornaments. Still, she was grateful that Pixie cared enough about Haven't Got a Clue's bottom line to invest her own money to insure their seasonal success.

"It's been a long day. Thanks so much for helping me with the decorations."

Pixie positively beamed, her gold canine tooth sparkling as she looked around the store with admiration. "It does look pretty good."

"You must let me pay for all the things you've brought in. It really is my responsibility."

Pixie shook her head. "I'm not sure I want to part with our little angel village on a permanent basis. You have to admit, it's awfully damn cute," she said with pride.

"That it is," Tricia agreed.

"If it's a success, and our customers like it, I could loan it to the store next year."

Tricia smiled. "That seems reasonable."

Pixie stared at the figurines and cardboard houses and churches in admiration. Then she shook herself and looked at the clock. "Time for me to split. I've got a bunch of DVDs from the library that I need to watch before they have to be returned on Monday."

"What are you watching?" Tricia asked.

"*Midsomer Murders*. I hate cops, but I could make an exception for Chief Inspector Barnaby."

Tricia laughed. "I'm sure his wife, Joyce, would have a few choice words about that."

"Wouldn't she just?" Pixie said and untied her Haven't Got a Clue apron. She headed for the back of the store, hung it up, and retrieved her coat. "What have you got on tap for tonight?"

Tricia thought about it. She still hadn't heard from Baker, which left her disappointed. "Nothing special."

"You gonna call your guy?" Pixie asked.

Tricia shook her head. "I don't think it would be in my best interest."

Pixie frowned. "Ya know that song by Simply Red, 'If You Don't Know Me By Now'? Well, it seems to me that your cop friend ought to know *you* by now and stop stringing you along every time a body shows up in this burg. I mean, isn't that what a relationship is supposed to be about—not that I've ever run into anyone who was any better," she amended sadly.

Tricia wasn't sure how to answer, but she sure felt the same way. If Baker hadn't learned to trust her—to know she wasn't capable of hurting another living thing—then he really wasn't worthy of *her* trust or affection.

And hadn't Angelica hinted at the same thing the evening before?

Miss Marple, who'd been listening to the conversation from her perch behind the register, jumped to the cash desk and down to the floor, intercepting Pixie and rubbing her head against Pixie's ankles. "Good night, Miss Marple. See you in the morning," she said, petted the cat on the head, and then headed for the door. "Night," she called and left the store.

With Pixie gone, Haven't Got a Clue seemed unbearably quiet. As though sensing this, Miss Marple jumped back up on the cash desk and rubbed her little gray head against Tricia's arm.

"I love you, too, my dear Miss Marple, but right now I have a powerful need to get out of here."

And where would that be? She could cross the street and immerse herself in the camaraderie at the Dog-Eared Page, or she could go next door and inflict herself on Angelica. Or maybe she just needed to clear her head. A walk in the brisk night air might just do it. She really should do some of her nightly tasks—like vacuum, tidy the cash desk and the beverage station. Instead, she turned the OPEN sign to CLOSED, pulled down the blinds, and retrieved her jacket and hat. Miss Marple protested, and Tricia shook out a few cat cookies into a bowl and left it on the floor. Then she turned off the lights and locked the door behind her.

Night had fallen more than an hour before, and the cold, dark sky was studded with twinkling points of light. She headed north, crossed the street at the corner, and proceeded down Locust Street, remembering what Frannie had said about Joelle and Stan Berry. When she reached Oak Street, she hung a left.

Already some of the residents had decked out their homes with colored lights for the holidays. A large inflatable snowman bobbed in the wind, its mittened hand waving cheerfully as she walked by. Several houses already had decorated

Christmas trees on display in front of picture windows that faced the street.

Tricia shivered in the cold wind, huddling deeper into her coat as she approached Stan Berry's house, noticing that all the lights were lit. Will must have made himself at home. In fact . . . she lowered her head and looked into the lighted garage. Sure enough, she could see Will standing over a large worktable that was covered with papers, studying them. Tricia debated with herself for only a couple of seconds before she strode up the driveway and knocked on the door. Will looked up, squinted until he recognized her, and then motioned for her to enter the shop.

Tricia hurried inside and, thanks to the wind, closed the door behind her with a bang. "I hope I'm not disturbing you."

"Not a bit." Will waved a hand to take in the shop. "I thought I'd do a little cleaning up before I went out for the evening."

"The Dog-Eared Page?" she guessed.

He nodded and gave her a weak smile. "Looks like it's the only game in town."

"You should have seen Stoneham a few years ago when I first arrived. We didn't even have the pub. There was only one place you could go for lunch, and you couldn't get your blood washed, either."

Will's brow furrowed in puzzlement.

"The dialysis center across from the Brookview Inn," Tricia clarified.

"Oh. Yeah." He shook his head. "What brings you out on such a cold night?"

"Restless. I'm around people all day. Sometimes I just like to take a walk so I can think with no distractions." It wasn't exactly the truth, but it seemed an appropriate explanation for the occasion.

Will laughed. "I've done the same thing myself a time or two. But why visit me if you're sick of dealing with people?"

"I don't know. I saw the light on and I guess I was curious about the sign shop and what'll happen to it now that your father is gone."

Will indicated the papers before him. "It was doing surprisingly well, if I can believe his bank statements. I'm even beginning to wonder if I should give up my plans to become a lawyer and take over the business. As it is, it'll take years for me to pay off my student loans."

Tricia looked around the shop. It looked like Will had been doing quite a bit of cleaning, too. A large plastic garbage can was filled to the top with papers and old magazines. Aside from the usual office computer, all-in-one printer, and file cabinets, several unidentifiable machines lined the walls, as well as rolls and spools of colored vinyl on a floor-to-ceiling rack. Long rolls of heavy-gauge white paper hung on the wall, looking like oversized butcher paper. The signs at the convenience store must have been made with it. "You'd really do that?" she asked.

He laughed. "No. But it might pay me to find someone to run it for a while. If I let them live in the house rent-free, I'd get to keep the bulk of the profits. It could go a long way toward paying off my student loans."

"Wouldn't you be able to pay them off faster if you sold the house and the business separately?"

"Maybe, maybe not. I wouldn't mind talking to a financial advisor to find out, though."

Tricia immediately thought of Christopher. Would he

want to take on another client? As he said, he could conduct most of his business on the phone and via the Internet. Maybe she'd ask the next time she spoke to him. Not that she was looking for an excuse to contact him or anything. She frowned. Why was she even thinking about the man who had dumped her?

Because you still love him.

Yeah, and she loved pizza, too, but that didn't hold any deep significance, either. She loved Christopher for the man he *used* to be—not the man he was today. And enough of that! She forced herself to concentrate on the conversation at hand.

"I must admit, I hadn't thought of ever buying a temporary sign for my shop, but something like that might be good for the holiday season."

"Too bad I don't know how to do the work. I'd be glad to give you a freebie so you could tell all the merchants over on Main Street to give them a try."

"How would you find someone to take over the business?"

"First I'd put an ad on Craigslist. They're free, and with so many people out of work, I'm sure it wouldn't take long to find someone who was eager to work for themselves. In fact, I think I'll do that tonight."

"But what if you decide to sell outright?"

He shrugged. "Putting feelers out can't hurt."

Tricia nodded. It made sense.

Will looked around the large room and let out a sigh. It had been finished off and was well insulated. Baseboard heating lined the walls and seemed to be doing an excellent job of keeping the place warm.

Despite Will's efforts, there were still plenty of signs of

its past owner everywhere. Stan senior's Chamber of Commerce placard hung on the wall near a number of framed photos, mostly chronicling the work he'd done. But there was one notable exception. A faded color photograph of a small boy.

"Yup, that's me," Will verified. "I wouldn't have thought he'd hang it out in the workshop. Shouldn't something like that have been kept in the house?"

"Maybe he spent most of his time out here. Or maybe he was thinking that he was working to give you some kind of financial security."

Will looked skeptical. "I'll bet you believe in fairy tales, too."

"Oh, come on. You did tell me he'd left you everything. Why do that if he didn't care . . . or at least feel a bit guilty about the past?"

"Guilt I can believe."

Tricia didn't comment.

"Damn, I'm a terrible host. I didn't even ask if you'd like a cup of coffee or anything."

"No, thanks. If I have coffee now, I'll never get to sleep tonight."

"How about something without caffeine? Say, a glass of wine?"

Tricia smiled and shook her head. "Didn't I already tell you I was seeing someone?"

"Yes. But I'm not asking you out on a date. I'm just offering you a little refreshment."

And people who drank a little too much wine after a long day sometimes made decisions that weren't good for them. "Thanks, but no."

He nodded. "Suit yourself."

The silence between them lengthened.

"I really should be going," Tricia said and turned for the door.

"Feel free to drop by anytime," Will said.

Tricia smiled.

"Wait. I was going to the pub anyway. Why don't I walk with you?"

"Why not?" Tricia said.

"And maybe by the time we get close to the bar, you'll find yourself suddenly parched."

Tricia laughed. The boy didn't give up easily.

"Let me grab my coat and turn off some of the lights inside, and then we can head on out," Will said and bounded into the house. Tricia looked around the shop, her gaze coming to rest on the garbage can and its contents. She cocked her head, looking at the cover of one of dozens of magazines stuffed into the receptacle, and was about to investigate when Will returned. He turned off the shop lights, locked up, and they set off down the driveway. "Which way?"

Tricia pointed south, and they started off. Would Frannie be looking out her window? If so, what would she think of the two of them walking together? Would she dial 911 and report it to Chief Baker?

Tricia didn't care. "Tell me more about your plans," she said, truly interested—and not just because she thought she might wheedle a clue from him. "If you're successful either selling or finding someone to run the business, what will you do with any money you get?"

Will hunkered deeper into his jacket. "What money? A few grand? I suppose I could put it toward my student loans, or maybe toward the principal on my father's mortgage and rent the place out. That, at least, would give me some additional income until I find another job. And while I'm here, maybe I can reestablish ties with my aunt."

"I didn't realize Stan had any other relatives in Stoneham. I thought he came from out of town," Tricia said.

"He *didn't* have relatives here, but I do. She's my great-aunt on my mother's side. I haven't seen her for years, but my mom thought a lot of her—maybe I will, too." He shrugged.

Tricia slowed her pace, while Will charged on ahead. If Will's great-aunt lived here in the village, was it possible she could have had a reason to want Stan dead? The woman would have to be elderly. Could an old woman in her seventies or eighties have had the strength to drive a knife into a man's heart?

But who said a great-aunt had to be elderly, either? Plenty of people had much younger siblings, and that was true a generation or so ago, as well. And some elderly people were pretty healthy, thanks to keeping active. Many elderly people actually lifted weights to keep up their muscle tone. What if Stan's great-aunt was one such person?

Will finally seemed to notice his walking partner was no longer with him. He stopped at the corner and waited for Tricia to catch up. "Everything all right?"

Tricia nodded. "What's your aunt's name? Maybe I know her." Then again, Tricia didn't know a lot of the locals, just those who'd made it their business to patronize the booksellers and other merchants on Main Street—and those that worked there, too, of course.

"Don't laugh, but I called her Auntie Yum-Yum."

Tricia couldn't help herself and giggled. "You're kidding, right?"

Will shook his head. "Hey, I was only four or five at the

time. She used to bake the best bread, cakes, cookies, and pies anyone ever ate. When she came to visit, she never came empty-handed. She was a godsend to my mom and me."

"Did she help you out financially, too?"

"That whole side of the family did. I lost track of her years ago when she moved up here for a job. She was divorced, so I never did know her real name. And now that my mom and other relatives are gone, I'll probably never know."

"That's a shame." If she'd been on better terms with Russ Smith, Tricia might have suggested he write a story about Will looking for his aunt. Russ liked to run human-interest stuff. He said it sold papers—or in his case, advertising, since the *Stoneham Weekly News* was a free rag. She didn't want to talk to Russ—but there was an alternative: Will could ask for himself.

"As you've no doubt noticed, Stoneham is a pretty small village. Talk to the editor at the *Stoneham Weekly News*. If he's intrigued . . ." She gave Will Russ's name and when they reached Main Street, told him where to find the office. "They'll be open at eight o'clock on Monday morning," she said.

"Thanks," Will said gratefully.

They'd arrived at the Dog-Eared Page, which was even more crowded and boisterous than it had been the evening before. "Are you sure I can't buy you a drink?" Will asked.

Tricia shook her head. "Maybe some other time. Good night."

Will nodded. "Good night, Tricia." As he opened the door to the pub, the noise, the light, and the music spilled out onto the sidewalk. For a moment, Tricia regretted turning down his invitation. Then again, she had a hungry cat to attend to, and she still needed to finish her end-of-day tasks in the shop. The door closed and she realized she'd lost another opportunity to spend time with a handsome man.

A much younger, handsome man. A man who couldn't possibly be interested in her in the long haul.

Like Christopher. Like Grant Baker.

Tricia crossed the street for home. As she opened the door to Haven't Got a Clue, she thought about the nearly full garbage can she'd seen inside Stan Berry's shop. There was something odd about the magazine covers that had been piled in it. She wasn't sure what the subject matter was, only that it seemed to be . . . weird. And she wished she could've examined them in more detail.

A sleepy Miss Marple got up from her nest in a chair in the readers' nook, stretching her long back legs.

"Ready for dinner?" Tricia asked.

Miss Marple said, *"Yow,"* rather enthusiastically, and trotted after her.

As Tricia started up the stairs for her loft apartment, she wondered what day the garbage was collected on Oak Street.

TEN

Tricia had read until the wee hours, occasionally looking up and daring the phone to ring, but it had steadfastly remained silent. She wasn't surprised. She really hadn't thought Baker would call.

She slept fitfully and awakened far too early the next morning, but since it didn't seem likely she'd fall back to sleep, she got up and started her day. It was only after nine, and she had already finished her exercise routine, showered and dressed, and breakfasted, when she and Miss Marple headed for Haven't Got a Clue to start their workday.

Tricia had left most of her end-of-day tasks undone the night before, and Sunday was her day to give the shop's washroom a thorough cleaning . . . not her favorite chore.

Since the store didn't open for another three hours, she had plenty of time to do it, too.

She'd just donned a pair of yellow rubber gloves when she heard someone banging on the shop's door. The sign still said CLOSED, but she decided to put off the unpleasant job to see if it was a customer. Instead, Grant Baker stood outside her door.

Tricia peeled off her gloves, then unlocked and opened the door.

"Can I come in?" Baker asked.

Without a word, Tricia stood back, ushering him in. He hadn't arrived bearing gifts, flowers, or even a cup of coffee. Not a good sign.

"I thought we should talk," Baker began.

Tricia sighed and moved to the readers' nook. She didn't feel like standing through whatever it was he wanted to tell her. She took a seat and tossed the rubber gloves onto the big square coffee table.

"I presume I haven't heard from you because you're working on Stan Berry's murder," Tricia said, keeping her tone even.

Baker nodded, taking the seat opposite her. Miss Marple trotted up and jumped onto the table, situating herself between the two human beings. Tricia idly wondered if the cat had gone into protective mode, acting as a feline shield should sparks begin to fly.

"You know the drill. When these things happen—"

"You mean me finding a body?"

He nodded and continued. "I have to be very careful about the way I conduct my investigation. I can't be seen to be playing favorites."

"You've made that abundantly clear on more than one occasion," she said. "How's the case going?"

"We're investigating every lead," he answered evasively.

"And?"

He shrugged. "You know I can't go into details."

"Yes, I do."

Baker eyed her gravely. "And?"

"We've visited this territory before."

"You know our relationship puts me in an awkward position."

"I don't think it's going to be a factor in this case, or in any future cases—should my bad luck hold out and I encounter another crime scene."

"It sounds like you've given the matter some thought," Baker said.

"And not for the first time, either," Tricia admitted. For all the emotion she'd spilled two nights before, she couldn't seem to muster any right then. Not anger, not sorrow, and especially not love or regret.

"I'm sorry to hear that," Baker said, but he shifted his gaze to take in the floor, not her face. He'd been expecting this, too. Maybe he was even relieved. "I guess there's a reason why they say that rebound relationships don't work out."

"It's certainly been my experience," Tricia agreed sadly.

"I guess we both know where we stand."

"I think I've known all along. I just didn't want to admit it," Tricia said with regret.

Baker stood. "I'll . . . I'll give you a call if I need any more information on the case."

"I'll be glad to give you any help I can," Tricia promised.

"Thank you." My but they were being polite, so adult about severing what had been a yearlong relationship. Well, not exactly a year. There'd been plenty of long periods of time when they'd been apart—for various reasons.

"I'll let myself out," Baker said but hesitated. Was he expecting a good-bye kiss?

Finally he turned and slowly walked toward the door. Again he hesitated, but eventually he had to leave. He opened the door and carefully closed it behind him.

"Good-bye, Grant," Tricia said and reached across the table to pet Miss Marple.

"*Yow,*" the cat said in what sounded like resignation.

"I feel the same way," Tricia admitted. She stroked Miss Marple's sleek gray fur and noticed she'd been sitting next to a small, bristled Christmas tree, no more than seven inches high, which looked as though it might have ducked behind the cat to try to hide itself from her—and with good reason, too. It looked like it had been sat on more than once. The ribbons that decorated it had once been red, as evidenced by the dark color in the creases, but had faded to a sad faded pink. The gold star that topped the tree had started to peel, revealing a white plastic core.

Tricia picked up the pathetic little tree. She'd have to speak to Pixie about trying to sneak in sad, worn-out ornaments and scattering them around the shop. The figurines and the little cardboard houses were adorable. This tree was just pitiful. In the event that Pixie might love the thing, she decided to put it behind the cash desk and return it to Pixie when she came into work that afternoon. Sundays were usually Pixie's day off, but Tricia had too much to do that day, what with her lunch appointment with Christopher and the wedding rehearsal later that afternoon. Pixie and Mr. Everett could handle the store and she wouldn't have to worry about a thing.

Worry? At that moment she still couldn't seem to muster any emotion except perhaps revulsion. After all, she still needed to clean the washroom.

Tricia had completed her chores and had settled down in the readers' nook to enjoy a quiet cup of coffee and to start to reread John Dickson Carr's *The Plague Court Murders*, when the shop door opened and a pink-cheeked Pixie arrived, all bundled up, holding a thin brown paper bag and humming a Christmas tune.

"Good morning, Tricia," she called as she closed the door behind her. She aimed straight for the readers' nook and set down the bag, before whipping off the red beret from her head and unbuttoning her big furry coat. "Beautiful day, isn't it?" she said brightly.

Tricia looked over toward the shop's big display window. She hadn't even noticed that the sun was shining brightly. "You seem pretty chipper. What's the occasion?"

"Just glad to be alive. You know, back in my old life, there were a few times when I wondered if I'd ever make it to this age. And while my mirror isn't thrilled with what it reflects, I'm not gonna complain. At least, not today. Is that coffee hot?"

"I just made it."

"I'll hang up my coat and join you for a few minutes, if you don't mind."

"Not at all."

By the time Pixie had hung up her coat and poured herself a cup, Mr. Everett had arrived. "Good morning, ladies," he said in greeting and unzipped his jacket. "It looks like it'll be a fine day for bookselling."

"Hang up your coat and I'll fix your coffee," Pixie called happily. "I've got a surprise for the two of you."

No doubt it was in the bag she'd put on the coffee table.

Tricia smiled. She'd had her doubts when she'd first hired Pixie, but the three of them made a great mystery-selling team.

Once Mr. Everett had settled in one of the nook's chairs, with his coffee cup in hand, Pixie picked up the bag and withdrew what looked like a thin, but rather large rectangular box wrapped in cellophane. "Look what I got for us."

"What is it?" Mr. Everett asked, craning his neck.

"Is that an Advent calendar?" Tricia asked. The illustration depicted a stately Victorian mansion. Each window in the charming home was shuttered.

Pixie nodded. "Behind every one of these windows is a little piece of chocolate in the shape of a toy. See"—she pointed to one of the perforated cutouts—"behind this one could be a miniature train. Maybe there's a tin soldier here. This one might be a little bell. . . ."

"Yes, I see," Tricia said, before Pixie pointed out each and every one of them, speculating on its contents.

"I figured the three of us could take turns opening one a day right until Christmas. I got it all figured out who should start, too." She looked directly at Tricia. "Since the shop isn't open on Christmas day, you can open that door. But that means you also get to be first, too."

"Oh, Pixie, it's okay if either one of you wants to—"

"No, no—it's gotta be you. Thanks to you, Mr. E and I have great jobs, with benefits. We have fun working every day. You deserve the extra piece of candy." She eyed Tricia from her toes to the tip of her nose. "Besides, you could stand to wear a few more pounds. You make the rest of us feel like lardos."

"Ms. Poe!" Mr. Everett protested.

"Okay, compared to you"—she looked at Tricia—"*I* look like a lardo."

Tricia's mouth dropped, and she wasn't sure what to say in her own defense. She didn't mean to be so much thinner than Pixie. Then again, she *did* work at it.

"It's still more than a week until the first day of Advent; perhaps we should put the calendar away until then," Tricia suggested.

"But we have to figure out where we're going to hang it so everyone who comes in can enjoy it, too. Not near the radiator or where the sun can melt the chocolate. That would take away all the fun."

Tricia forced a smile for Pixie's sake. After her conversation with Baker, she simply was not in the mood to have fun. She looked at the clock. "I'd better put some money in the till. We're due to open in a few minutes."

She left Pixie and Mr. Everett and walked purposefully toward the cash desk. Miss Marple was already stationed on her perch behind the register, ready to start her usual day of rest.

As Tricia counted out the cash, she heard laughter coming from the readers' nook. Pixie had taken the seat Tricia had vacated and she and Mr. Everett were sharing a story and a laugh. Tricia almost wished she hadn't left them. She could use a good laugh about now.

She raised the blinds, turned the CLOSED sign to OPEN, and Haven't Got a Clue was officially open for business.

Tricia glanced at the clock. She still had almost an hour before she was to meet Christopher. Unless they had an influx of customers, she could probably get in three or four more chapters of *The Plague Court Murders* before she had to leave for the Brookview Inn.

Pixie and Mr. Everett finished their coffee, rinsed their cups, and donned their Haven't Got a Clue aprons, ready to begin their workday. Mr. Everett had commandeered the lamb's-wool duster and started on the back bookshelves. Pixie wandered up to the cash desk.

"I don't mean to be nosy," she said, her voice sounding deadly serious, "but . . ."

Tricia had known that a *but* was coming.

"Why don't you like Christmas, Tricia?"

The question caught Tricia off guard. "I do like Christmas. Everybody does."

"You coulda fooled me. You don't like to decorate. You don't want to eat the great food. Your sister said you don't even put up a tree or anything."

Angelica had told Pixie about Tricia's lack of a Christmas tree?

"I figure your heart had to be broken at Christmastime. Why else would you be such a Scrooge?"

"I'm hardly a Scrooge," Tricia cried, taken aback.

"Well, maybe not, but you *have* had your heart broken—haven't you?" Pixie asked, her voice filled with sympathy.

Tricia averted her gaze. Yes, but it wasn't what Pixie thought. Her heart had been broken on more than one unhappy Christmas. And the fact that she hadn't spent Christmas with her parents in a very long time weighed heavy on her mind . . . not that it seemed to bother them. And now that Grant Baker was going to be out of the picture, too . . .

"You're right, Pixie. Not all my holidays have been happy ones."

"You should talk about it. If you don't want to tell me, you could tell a shrink. They're good at unraveling all that kind of crap."

"I don't think I need . . . unraveling. I just like to spend the holidays in quiet contemplation. And have dinner with my sister and some friends," she amended. "That's what we've done for the past two years, and it was very nice."

"Well, if you want to talk, I'm sure I can get my shrink to squeeze you in. She mostly works with ex-cons, but I'm sure she'd make an exception for anyone I recommend."

So not happening, Tricia thought but said, "That's very thoughtful of you, Pixie. Thank you."

Pixie nodded, smiling . . . like she'd just done a good deed and expected a reward.

Tricia changed the subject. "Let me also thank you again for agreeing to work on your day off. Mr. Everett and I—"

"I know, I know—got that wedding rehearsal thing to go to in the afternoon where that guy died. Creepy, huh? Just think, Ginny and her hunk tying the knot—starting their new lives where a guy ended his." She shook her head at the irony.

"Yes, well, I hope you won't be too bored if it gets slow."

"Wouldn't bother me a bit," she said cheerfully. "If it's slow, I'll just read. If it's busy, I'll have fun talking to people about the books. Win-win situation, as far as I can see."

"Thank you."

"Yeah, this has gotta be the *best* job in the world."

Tricia smiled. "I'm glad you think so." She looked up at the clock. She wasn't due to meet Christopher for almost fifty minutes, but Antonio had invited her to look at the inn's holiday decorations, and she wondered if Eleanor had calmed down since the murder two days before. Tricia was sure she could find enough of interest to kill time until her luncheon . . . date.

No, she and Christopher were not going on a date. They were meeting for lunch. The man had broken her heart before—she wasn't about to let him do it again.

"Did I mention an old friend of mine is in town for the day and wants to have lunch with me?"

Pixie shook her head.

"I'd best be on my way."

"So soon?" Pixie asked.

"I'm afraid so." Tricia headed for the back of the store, grabbed her jacket, collected her purse and keys, and made a dash for the exit. She wanted to get out of there before Pixie pried any more of her secrets from her.

ELEVEN

Tricia trotted down the sidewalk, heading for the municipal parking lot. Despite the cold, if she'd been in a better state of mind she might have walked the mile or so to the Brookview Inn, but she felt depressed and decidedly lazy after what she'd already endured that morning. She knew there were others who had real problems—life-threatening ailments, job losses, bankruptcies—to contend with, and in comparison her mild depression was a selfish indulgence. But she could only wear the skin she'd been given, and knew (hoped?) that her feelings of malaise would be short-lived.

Minutes later, she pulled into the Brookview Inn's parking lot, got out of her car, and walked around to the front of the building, and her spirits immediately rose. As Antonio had promised, the inn looked absolutely lovely. Outside, all the windows were bedecked with fresh pine wreathes, and each wreath sported a perky red velveteen ribbon. The front porch rail and banisters had pine boughs twined around them, with twinkling white lights and sparkle-flocked pinecones interspersed here and there.

The inn's interior had also been transformed. A ten-foot artificial tree stood in the middle of the lobby. It must have been decorated with close to a thousand tiny white lights that made it glow, while gold ornaments and a gold ribbon garland adorned its branches. Tricia stood there for a long moment, admiring the tree. Was this what Pixie wanted for Haven't Got a Clue? No, this tree was elegant. Pixie was willing to settle for bright and gaudy.

Then it occurred to Tricia why the inn's tree appealed to her. It was reminiscent of the trees her mother had decorated when she was a child. Or rather, that the decorator her mother had hired had put up in their library—where she and Angelica were forbidden to enter without being accompanied by a parent far into their teens.

Tricia made a slow circuit around the tree. It reminded her of the last time she'd had a Christmas tree in her own home. She'd finished decorating it hours before that last annual Christmas party she and Christopher had thrown for his colleagues and important clients—except Christopher hadn't been there. An hour before it was to start he'd told her he wanted a divorce, and then abandoned her to "think things over," leaving her confused and distraught while having to deal with his guests.

She sighed. Suddenly Pixie's bright and gaudy version of celebrating the holidays seemed a lot more honest and appealing.

A familiar voice broke her revelry. "Pretty, isn't it?" Eleanor called.

Tricia shook herself out of the dazed moment and quickly moved to join the inn's receptionist. "The entire inn looks lovely."

Eleanor beamed. "Ms. Ricita chose everything. Not that it's all that much different than what we've had in the past. She just refreshed the look in a new way."

"Nicely refreshed," Tricia agreed. She studied Eleanor's face. "How are you doing?"

The smile quickly vanished, leaving Eleanor's face once again drawn and worried. She obviously hadn't fully recovered from the shock of Stan Berry's death. Eleanor sighed. "Not well. These last few days have been very upsetting. And the fact that poor man was killed with my own letter opener." She shook her head, and her eyes filled with tears. "Mr. Barbero says there was nothing I could've done to stop it from happening, but for some reason I can't help but feel responsible. I mean, who uses letter openers these days? I should have been using one of those cheap envelope slitters. Goodness knows, Bob Kelly has given me three or four of them over the years." She opened her desk and pulled one out, showing it to Tricia. It was imprinted with Kelly Realty information.

"No one blames you," Tricia said kindly, although she had to admit if the circumstances were reversed she might very well feel that way.

"I only stepped away from my desk for a few moments that morning. I swear."

"Where did you go?"

"Into Mr. Barbero's office. That must have been when someone lifted my letter opener."

"What did you go into his office for?"

"You know, at this point I'm not sure. I was either looking for the new menus for the dining room or needed to get his calendar to make an appointment. I couldn't have been gone for more than a minute—probably even less."

"Do you remember who was milling around the lobby?"

"So many people had just left the dining room, it seemed like a mad exodus. It's all a blur to me. I mean, this happens all the time. I just don't pay attention to the people who come and go."

Tricia couldn't imagine working in a fishbowl like the inn's reception desk had to be. Except for those renting the bungalows out back, everyone staying at the inn came in and went out through the lobby. That, in itself, had to be awfully distracting. Those looking to book a reservation in the dining room came to or called the inn's main telephone number, which Eleanor answered during her shifts. And how many people interrupted the poor woman's work with questions, or a request for a new toothbrush or some other forgotten personal item? She herself had relied on Eleanor a lot during the three weeks she'd lived at the inn during the worst of Haven't Got a Clue's renovation.

Eleanor sighed. "I'm sorry. I've been so preoccupied with my own troubles, I never bothered to ask why you're here."

"I'm having lunch with a friend."

Eleanor looked behind Tricia. "It wouldn't happen to be that hunky Mr. Benson standing across the lobby, would it?"

Tricia looked over her shoulder to see Christopher standing to one side of the entrance. He was wearing a winter jacket, scarf, and hat, so he must have entered after she did. She turned back to Eleanor. "As a matter of fact, yes."

Eleanor's smile was crooked. "Does Chief Baker know about you and your . . . *friend*?"

"Yes, he does," Tricia said and yet for some reason she felt herself blush, as though meeting Christopher was some kind of betrayal. She'd known him far longer than she'd known Grant Baker, and why shouldn't she share a meal with her ex-husband? Baker had often done that with his ex-wife—and not all that long ago, either. Tricia hadn't kicked up a fuss, and nobody seemed to think anything of it. Was it because Mandy Baker had been ill? Everyone, including herself, had admired the way Baker had supported his ex until she'd recovered. Christopher didn't look the least bit sick. In fact, since they'd split, he'd lost weight, had taken up exercise in the fresh air, and without the stress of his former job now looked his age, instead of ten years older. Besides, soon the entire village would know that she and Baker were no longer an item, but she wasn't about to announce the news to Eleanor.

"I'd better scoot," Tricia said, while Eleanor beamed. Would the whole village soon know about her lunch date with Christopher? She could have explained her past relationship with Christopher but resented the fact that she would even consider doing so.

Tricia hurried across the lobby.

"Tricia, my love," Christopher said and held out his hands to her, captured them, and then kissed her on the cheek. Tricia felt the blush return.

"Let's get in the dining room fast," she said, not bothering to even say hello. As she'd hoped, Christopher was amiable and willingly followed her.

They were met at the door by Henry, who checked them

in, grabbed a couple of the leather-bound menus, and led them to a table near the kitchen. "Is there a better seat than this?" Tricia asked, noting the dining room was half empty.

"Oh, certainly," Henry said. He apologized and led them back to the windows that overlooked Stoneham Creek. "Better?"

"Yes, thank you," Tricia said, as Christopher helped her off with her coat and then pulled out her chair before he removed his coat, hung it on the back of his chair, and then seated himself.

"Darlene will be your server today," Henry said with a smile and handed them the menus. "She'll be here in a few moments to take your drink orders."

"Thank you," Christopher said.

"We haven't had time to chat in quiet a while, Henry. How are things?" Tricia said, not entirely sure why she'd asked. Or maybe she just wasn't eager to talk to Christopher.

"Lately, or since Friday?" Henry asked.

"In general," Tricia clarified. "In fact, since the new management took over the inn. Are you okay with the changes so far?"

Henry's eyes brightened. "We were all pretty worried when Nigela Ricita Associates came in like gangbusters, taking over the day-to-day operations, but I have to admit they gave the place a new lease on life. Gave us all raises, too. It sure is a relief to know I'm not going to be let go just because I'm old."

"That would be discrimination," Christopher pointed out.

Henry shrugged. "It happens. Some places just change the job titles, or say you lack training without offering it to you."

"I guess we'll be seeing each other later today," Tricia said.

For a moment Henry looked puzzled, but then he smiled. "Yes, at the wedding rehearsal. I was honored that Mr. Barbero asked me to be his best man."

"Surely you don't call him that when you're off duty."

"Yes, I do—out of respect. He is my boss. But I imagine I could call him Antonio when it comes time for me to give the wedding toast." He smiled. "You folks look hungry. I'll send Darlene right over to take care of you," he said with a smile, and turned to head back to his station. Tricia watched him go. When she turned back she found Christopher staring at her.

"Sweet old man," he commented.

"Yes, he is."

Christopher leaned forward. "How come the groom has an employee—one who won't even call him by his first name—for a best man? Doesn't he have any friends?"

Tricia shrugged. "He works a lot of hours, not unlike what you used to do. Besides, his boss, Nigela Ricita, seems to be a bit of a slave driver. That said, she sure inspires a strong sense of loyalty among her employees." She straightened in her chair and picked up her menu. "So, how are you today?"

"Peachy," Christopher said. "It's you I'm worried about."

"Me?"

"It seemed like you were in a hurry to sit down, and then you start shooting the"—he paused—"bull with the host. What's going on?" Christopher asked Tricia as he grabbed the linen napkin that had been artistically stuffed into his water glass, shook it out, and placed it on his lap.

"Oh," Tricia said dismissively. "The woman at the receptionist's desk is a very sweet lady, but she's also a terrible gossip. I'm sure our meeting for lunch is going to be all over town within minutes."

"So what? It's not like we're meeting in my room."

"I wouldn't be surprised if that's the story that goes around the village." She thought better of that statement. "I'm sorry. That wasn't fair to Eleanor. But she will be telling everyone she knows about us. Especially since you kissed me. I wouldn't be surprised if she's talking to Grant right now."

"Did you tell him we were having lunch together?"

"I can have lunch with anyone I please." She didn't want or need to go into the details of what had transpired earlier in the day.

Christopher opened the menu and shrugged, making no reply.

Tricia set her menu aside and took in the dining room's decorations. Like the outside of the inn, it, too, was festooned with greenery, gold bows, and ornaments. Even the table had a vase with a red carnation and a sprig of fresh pine. Everything was simple yet dignified. Why couldn't Pixie understand that that was the atmosphere Tricia wanted to convey?

Christopher set his menu aside and gazed at Tricia. "Well, here we are."

"Yes." Why did she feel so awkward sitting across from the man she'd once vowed to love until death did them part? "I was wondering . . . what have you got to tell me that's so important?"

Christopher looked surprised. "Nothing. I just thought it would be nice to spend a little time together, maybe reminisce, and share a little holiday cheer."

"It's not even Thanksgiving yet, let alone Christmas."

"That's true, but I'm not likely to make it south again before the spring—so it's now or never."

"You know I never could understand why you—who loved the excitement of the city—would choose to run away to the mountains and hibernate."

"It was the noise, too many people squeezed into too little space, and corporate edicts to lie to clients became too much to bear. I was suffocating. I needed to leave it all behind."

And he had, ditching Tricia along with everything else. She didn't feel like pursuing that conversational thread any further.

"How did the interview go?" she asked, glancing down at the list of specials on her menu.

"Terrific. I got the job and start tomorrow."

"Then are you heading back north today?"

Christopher shook his head. "Have laptop—can work. Besides, I'll be meeting with my new management team over the next few days. Also, as long as I'm down here, I'd like to visit Miss Marple again. I think it's great that she hasn't forgotten me."

"She's a very intelligent being," Tricia agreed.

Darlene appeared with a pitcher of water and filled their glasses. She set it down on another table and took out her order pad and stood before them. They waited for her to speak, but her attention seemed to be focused outside the window on the brook, which rushed madly past.

"Miss?" Christopher prompted.

Darlene shook herself and gave a nervous laugh. "My apologies. Our specials today are . . ."

She rattled off the list of entrées, but still seemed distracted. So much so that Tricia asked, "Are you okay?"

"Yes, of course. Well . . . no. Since Friday, the police have interrogated everyone on staff about—"

"The murder?" Tricia asked.

Darlene nodded. "We're not supposed to talk about it to customers." But it was obvious she wanted to.

"Who said you're not to say anything?"

"Trish, give the woman a break," Christopher cautioned.

She ignored him. "Is that what Chief Baker told you, or was it Antonio Barbero?"

"Both."

"Surely Stan Berry wasn't known to any of the staff," Tricia went on.

"Not as far as I know," Darlene said, keeping her voice quiet, her eyes wandering the room to see if anyone was watching them and listening.

"What kinds of questions are the staff being asked?" Tricia pressed.

Christopher snatched his napkin from his lap and tossed it onto the table. "Tricia, stop it."

"Stop what?" she asked.

"Interrogating the poor woman. You can see she's been traumatized."

"That's okay," Darlene said kindly, "everybody in the village knows Tricia is a frustrated investigator."

"No, I'm not," Tricia protested without thinking.

"What can I get you to drink?" Darlene asked.

"I'll have a scotch and water and Tricia will have a glass of Chardonnay."

"I prefer to order my own drink," Tricia said and turned her attention back to Darlene. "I'll have a gin martini up, with olives."

"You don't drink martinis," Christopher accused.

"Yes, I do." Or at least she did since Friday night.

Christopher frowned. "I'm beginning to think you're not the girl I married."

Tricia's expression mirrored his. "First of all, I'm a woman, not a girl. Second, you ceased being the man I married a long time ago."

Darlene backed up a step. "I'll get your drinks," she said and fled.

"I apologize," Christopher said. "I simply meant you're different. More confident, and certainly more somber."

"Christopher, I found a man murdered on Friday morning. Things like that tend to take the joy out of one's life."

"And now you're driven to find out what happened to the guy?"

"Something like that."

He nodded and reached out to rest his hand on hers, his touch electric. "For what it's worth, I'm proud of you. I always knew you had more potential and that your job at the non-profit was holding you back."

"Then why didn't you encourage me to go out on my own years ago—or when I lost my job?"

He answered without hesitation. "Because I was a selfish bastard."

That admission gave Tricia pause.

Christopher continued, "You weren't on my radar. I had my career, an attractive wife, and a pretty shallow existence."

"And you figured all this out while living alone in the mountains?" she asked.

"I was starting to figure it out when I left you. I've often wondered what my life would be like now if I'd taken time to think it all out before I took off—and where we'd both be now if I'd asked you to go with me."

"We'll never know," Tricia said and pulled back her hand. She really didn't want to continue to talk about the past. It was over. Finished. No going back now. But there was an unfinished piece of business that needed clarification.

"A couple of months ago, someone sent me some souvenirs of the past. A cocktail napkin from—"

"The Elbow Room," Christopher supplied. "I took you there the night you lost your job at the nonprofit. We drank to the future."

"And a scarf—"

"It was a birthday gift from your mother. It arrived two weeks after your birthday and you were so upset you tossed it in the trash. But I insisted you wear it at least once. You humored me—"

It all came back to Tricia. She'd found out that her mother's housekeeper had actually bought the scarf—her mother had been too busy with charitable responsibilities to shop for her second daughter. How ironic was that? Her mother sought to help others—make them happy—but she hadn't the time or the interest to do that for Tricia. And now that the long-submerged memory had resurfaced, when she got home the scarf would go back in the trash once again.

Tricia found herself breathing deeper than she had before, trying to control her temper. "Why did you send it and the napkin with no explanation and no return address? Were you trying to scare me?"

Christopher took umbrage. "Of course not. At the time I hoped it might help us rekindle what we once had."

"By sending me unpleasant reminders of our past to-gether?" she asked, hurt.

"I didn't think—and . . . to be honest, I don't have many reminders of our past together. I can't even find one picture of us together."

Of course not. He'd jettisoned all of that stuff in his haste to escape from her and the life they'd shared for over nine years.

"Trish, I came back East because I love and miss you. I hoped that I could make it up to you somehow. That maybe we could get back to—" He stopped as, tray in hand, Darlene approached their table, first setting out napkins and then placing their drinks in front of them.

"Ready to order?" she asked hopefully.

Tricia studied Christopher's face. A face she still loved but not in the same way. She loved him from a time long since past. When their future had looked so bright. At that exact moment all she felt was an intensifying anger.

"I don't know about you, but I've lost my appetite." Tricia pushed her chair back, intending to stand, but Christopher caught her hand once again.

"Please don't go."

Tricia pulled her hand away from his. "You're about four years too late with that request."

She grabbed her coat and purse and left the dining room. Alone once again.

Tricia drove back to the village with her hands clutching the steering wheel in a death grip. How dare Christopher hint at a reconciliation between them when he was the one who had broken them apart in the first place? And he'd admitted that he was a selfish bastard. Yes, that perfectly described him—he'd been selfish in the past, and he was being selfish now.

Tricia pulled into the Stoneham municipal parking lot and was surprised to see Bob Kelly standing in its midst. As

she pulled into her usual spot at the far end, she noted that
he was standing next to Angelica's car. What on earth was
that all about? Since Tricia had read so many mysteries during the course of her life, she immediately assumed the worst.
Was he about to pour—or had he already poured—sugar
into Angelica's gas tank? Was he going to let the air out of
her tires? Would he key the paint or windows, gouging them
with an X or worse?

She got out of her car and marched over to join him, just
itching for a fight. "Bob!" she called smartly, startling the
man, who suddenly looked like a deer caught in a car's
headlights.

"Tricia?"

"Yes, that's my name," Tricia said. "What are you doing
here?"

"Uh . . ." Bob's jaw dropped. "Nothing. I was . . ."

Tricia could envision his mind racing to come up with a
plausible explanation. "Doing what?" she pressed.

"Uh . . . wondering if I should petition the Board of Selectmen to put a new coat of blacktop on the municipal lot.
It's kind of patchy in spots."

A blatant lie—the lot had been upgraded earlier that
spring. Tricia decided not to press the point, even though it
was far too late in the season to do that kind of upkeep, and
decided to deal with Bob using a completely different approach. "Are you okay, Bob?"

"Okay?" he repeated, confused.

"Yes. I know Stan Berry's death has Angelica completely
devastated." Okay, that was a total and complete lie, but Bob
didn't need to know that.

"Really?" he asked, sounding suspicious.

"Yes, and I'm sure you must feel the exact same way."

"Oh . . ." Bob seemed to shake himself. "Yes. Yes, Stan was a good pal—a worthy opponent. I-I, too, am devastated by his loss."

Devastated? Hardly, but Tricia didn't press the point. "Do you have any theories about what happened?" she asked.

Once again, Bob looked momentarily blank, and then his capacity for bullshit took over. He really was a master. "Someone had to have had a grudge against the poor man. It certainly wasn't me. I welcome anyone to challenge me as Chamber president. After all, my first concern is and always has been for the welfare of every business owner here in Stoneham."

Oh, yeah—sure. *Not!*

"May I ask why you're standing next to Angelica's car?" Tricia asked.

"Was I?" Bob said and laughed.

"You weren't thinking of sabotaging it, were you?"

"Tricia! I'm hurt by your accusation."

"And I'm worried about the car's paint, gas tank, and tires."

"How could you think I'd even contemplate damaging another person's car? I have a reputation to uphold."

"Yes, you do. And getting arrested for petty vandalism sure wouldn't help you win reelection, especially if you damage your surviving opponent's property."

Bob bristled. "I wasn't going to touch Angelica's car, and I resent the accusation."

"No accusation—just a warning."

"You think because you have Chief Baker in your pocket that you're immune from suspicion, but that's not reality. I find it just a little funny that you keep stumbling over bodies."

"It's just my bad luck," Tricia said.

"And that of the victims," he countered and shook loose the ring in his hand and stuffed it into his jacket pocket.

"What kind of a man stands over his ex-lover's car with a menacing look on his face?" Tricia challenged.

Bob blinked, the epitome of innocence. "Menacing? Me? You've got me all wrong, Tricia. I've always had Angelica's best interests at heart."

"Is that so?"

"Why, of course. Just because she turned on me like a snake has no bearing on the affection I still feel for her."

"Give me a break. You're as angry as hell at her for challenging you for the Chamber presidency."

Bob shook his head, his expression bland. "I have nothing but love in my heart for Angelica . . . and I will take her back in a second—as soon as she comes to her senses and gives up her delusions of grandeur, that is."

Well, if that wasn't a classic case of projection . . . Tricia shook herself, lowering her voice. "I've never had a very high opinion of you, Bob, but now you've sunk to a new low."

"Frankly, my dear, I don't give a damn what you think," he said smugly. "I intend to win the election and grind Angelica into the dust—or at least the snow. Get it? It's winter."

"I get it, Bob, but I don't get you and I hope I never do."

"You're just a spoilsport—you *and* your sister."

Tricia frowned. Bob sounded just like a schoolyard bully, and she would not dignify the slur with a reply.

"And don't go on about what a saint Angelica is. As far as I'm concerned, she's stacked the deck in her own favor," Bob continued.

"And how's that?"

"She owns a stake in the Sheer Comfort Inn. I'm sure that's an automatic vote for her."

"The manager of the inn can vote any way she pleases," Tricia pointed out.

Bob rolled his eyes. "Yeah, right."

Tricia didn't reply. Instead, she made a point of walking around Angelica's car, noting any imperfections in the paint before she turned back to face Bob. "Should this car suffer any unfortunate calamities—such as scratches or gouges, I'd have to inform Chief Baker that I found you standing over it ready to key it."

"I think you're mistaken," Bob said calmly.

"And I think you're a fool to stand here in broad daylight contemplating vandalism in front of goodness knows how many potential witnesses."

"Vandalism? Me? You've got that all wrong, Tricia. I just happened to note a small stain on the tarmac. I was worried Angelica's car might be leaking oil or transmission or radiator fluid. It might be best if you inform her that her car needs servicing. I'm sure she's probably just as suspicious as you and wouldn't see my actions as that of just good citizenship."

Tricia realized she was wasting her breath talking to this idiot. "Good-bye, Bob," Tricia said and stalked away.

"Aren't you going to say *may the best man win*?" Bob hollered.

Tricia didn't bother to look back as she called, "Sometimes the best man for the job *is* a woman."

TWELVE

"You're back early. How did lunch go?" Pixie called brightly as Tricia entered Haven't Got a Clue.

Tricia glowered at her and headed for the back of the shop where she hung up her coat. Contrary to what she'd told Christopher, she *was* hungry, and opened the door to the stairs marked PRIVATE and headed up to her loft apartment. Unfortunately, the cupboards—and fridge—were bare, so back down the stairs she went, grabbed her coat once more, and went across the street to Booked for Lunch.

The joint was jammed, with Angelica dressed in her waitress uniform, helping her tiny staff serve customers. Tricia hung her coat on a peg and took the only empty seat at the counter, wedged between a bald, aging biker in black leathers and a teenager with pink hair furiously texting.

Angelica swung around to the back of the counter and slid the decaf coffeepot back into its home base warmer, and bent down to access the small fridge under the counter. She fished out a plate wrapped in plastic and sat it before Tricia. "I take it your lunch with Christopher didn't go well."

"Looks like you anticipated it," Tricia said and removed the wrap from her tuna plate.

"I thought we should be prepared—just in case."

"Wait a minute. How did you know I was having lunch with Christopher? I didn't tell anyone."

"Everybody in the village knows about it."

"Eleanor?" Tricia guessed.

Angelica nodded and glanced at the biker. "Can I warm up that coffee for you?"

His mouth was full, so the guy simply nodded, and Angelica refilled his cup and produced a couple of containers of half-and-half from her apron pocket. She turned back to Tricia. "So what did he say that sent you running?"

By the time Tricia had finished her story—in between stops and starts while Angelica refilled another six or seven cups of coffee and cashed out customers—the café was beginning to empty out.

"I can't remember a time in my life when I've felt so unhappy and unsettled. And I know I'm being a total bitch, but I don't know what to say—how else to feel." She fought the urge to cry once more; that another meltdown might be only moments away.

Angelica eyed those remaining in the café and leaned in closer. "Honey, don't be so damned hard on yourself. You have this mistaken impression that you have to be perfect—and let me tell you, only God has that distinction." She patted Tricia's hand. "Christopher was a rat to send you those trinkets from the past. But you know what? He's just a dumb man. Very smart when it comes to financial affairs, but kind of clueless when it comes to the personal kind."

"You can say that again," Tricia said and took a sip of her coffee.

"If nothing else, cut the guy some slack for finally realizing how incredibly stupid he was to cut a stand-up chick like you out of his life."

The ghost of a smile touched Tricia's lips. "A stand-up chick?" she asked, amused.

"Hell, yes!" Angelica's smile was mischievous. "You could have wallowed in self-pity when Christopher left you, but instead you looked at it as an opportunity to do what you always wanted. And the lovely settlement you got made that entirely possible."

"You're being very kind," Tricia said, unable—or maybe unwilling—to give herself the same consideration.

"Not at all. You know, it seems like we all go through some kind of midlife crisis. This is yours."

Tricia sighed. Maybe she'd been too hard on Christopher. If what she felt was the same as what he'd been through, it was hell. But despite her mixed feelings, reconciling was completely out of the question.

"It's been a terrible day all around," Tricia said finally. "And that's not all. I think I saved your car from being keyed by none other than your opponent."

"Bob? You can't be serious," Angelica said, perturbed.

Tricia swallowed her last bite and nodded. "Deadly serious."

"Why, that jealous rat. Speaking of the election, have you been talking me up to the other Chamber members?"

"Only John Marcella."

Angelica frowned. "He isn't likely to vote for me."

"No, he's not."

Tricia sipped her coffee, only then remembering her conversation with Chief Baker. "With everything else that's gone on today I forgot to mention that it's now officially over between Grant and me."

"Well, that was a given," Angelica said. "So, who'll be your date at Ginny's wedding?"

"Good grief. I forgot all about that. I guess I'll have to go stag."

"You'd better let Ginny know, in case she needs to have Joelle amend the reception seating chart. Although since the Brookview is doing the catering, and Antonio is the manager, they won't get socked for the cost of a no-show like at most receptions."

"That's true." Tricia thought about the situation. Now that she was an unattached woman, she wondered if Will Berry would still be in town the following Saturday. He'd asked her out twice and she'd had to turn him down. Now . . . why not at least entertain the thought?

"That's an awful wistful smile for a woman who's had two men disappoint her in the past five or six hours. What—or who—are you thinking about?"

Tricia hadn't even realized she'd been smiling, and she schooled her features. "Nothing—and no one—in particular," she lied. She looked up at the clock. Pixie and Mr. Everett had been manning the store without her for hours. If the business at Booked for Lunch was any indication, they were probably just as busy.

"I've got to go," Tricia said and slipped off the stool. "Thanks for lunch—and the chat."

"You're welcome. And don't forget the rehearsal dinner is at my place," Angelica said.

"I won't." How could she? Everyone she'd be with would be heading there, too.

"And feel free to bring a date," Angelica called after her.

"Yeah, right," Tricia said but once again thought of Will Berry.

And smiled.

Business *had* been booming when Tricia returned to Haven't Got a Clue, but it wasn't anything that Pixie and Mr. Everett couldn't handle, leaving Tricia free to catch up on her paperwork.

Things had calmed considerably by late afternoon when it was time for Tricia and Mr. Everett to leave for the wedding rehearsal. Rather than take two cars, Tricia had invited Mr. Everett to ride along with her. Pixie waved good-bye as they left the shop.

If Tricia thought the Brookview Inn's decorations looked pretty during daylight hours, she was even more delighted to see them in twilight's glow, lit up, and twinkling.

"I don't think the inn has ever looked lovelier," Mr. Everett said in admiration as they strode up the front walk. He was just as impressed with the decorations inside, as well.

Joelle Morrison was on hand, checking her watch and tapping her foot at their being all of two minutes late. "Hurry along—hurry along," she cajoled, ushering Tricia and Mr. Everett into the dining room. "The waitstaff will soon need to get the room ready for the dinner service."

Antonio stood to one side of the room, with his arms

crossed over his chest. "We cannot proceed without the bride, who called to say she won't be here for at least another ten minutes," he said, but Joelle didn't seem to be listening.

Mr. Everett made a beeline for his wife, while Tricia set her purse down on the table nearest Antonio and shrugged out of her coat, setting it on the back of one of the chairs. "What's with Ginny?" she asked.

Antonio shrugged. "She said they were very busy at the store. It seems people are already madly shopping for Christmas. But that will give us time to talk," he said and pulled out a chair, offering her a seat.

She took it and he sat down beside her, but instead of initiating conversation, they watched Joelle flutter about the room, with a clipboard in hand and a terse expression. Antonio shook his head. "I fear that woman will have a stroke before the ceremony on Saturday. She worries far too much and always over the most insignificant things."

"I guess that's what you're—or rather your stepmother—is paying her for. Speaking of worry, has the investigation into Stan Berry's death adversely disrupted the inn's routine?"

"Not as much as I'd feared, although my staff has been questioned again and again—especially poor Eleanor."

Tricia nodded. "It was just her bad luck to have owned the murder weapon. I didn't see her at the reception desk when we came in. Is she okay?"

"Just—how do you say?" He thought about it for a moment. "Rattled. I let her go home early—with pay. Do not inform Nigela," he cautioned with a smile.

"Speaking of Eleanor, what do you think of her as an employee?"

"The inn is lucky to have her. She misses nothing. She is the eyes and ears of the place. She's been here so long, knows all the workings, and can anticipate trouble before it happens."

That didn't jibe with what Eleanor had told Tricia earlier that day. She'd said she was so *used* to people coming and going that it was all a blur to her. Of course, maybe she was so upset the day of Stan Berry's death that she misspoke. That her personal property had been responsible for a death had to be more than a little jarring.

Tricia frowned, upset with herself for doubting her friend; she seemed to be upset far too often these days. And yet could Eleanor really be considered a friend? Except for the time she'd stayed at the inn, they'd only ever chitchatted when Tricia came to dine or had time to kill before a meeting. And yet, Eleanor seemed more than just an acquaintance. She'd gushed that she'd entered the pie contest at the Milford Pumpkin Festival the year before—and she'd proudly framed her blue ribbon and hung it in her office, along with her bowling trophies and other certificates. Was it possible Eleanor was Will Berry's aunt?

No. Will had said that his great-aunt had been a fine baker, but he'd stressed that the woman was elderly. Eleanor was in her sixties, but pretty active—not at all what Tricia would consider elderly. And what possible motive could Eleanor have had to kill Stan, anyway? And surely if she'd had a familial connection, she'd have told Baker about it. Then again . . . Baker had refused to tell her anything about the case.

Tricia frowned. She liked Eleanor, who had always been friendly and helpful to her, and felt ashamed for even considering her a suspect.

"I got to talk to Henry earlier this afternoon," Tricia started.

Antonio nodded. "Another of my valued employees."

"He sang the praises of the inn's new management. You've got a loyal crew."

"Something Nigela has always told me: treat your employees well and they will perform well for you."

Tricia noted motion to her left and saw that not only had her former employee just arrived, but she'd entered the dining room with Judge Hamilton in tow. "Let's get this show on the road," Ginny called, taking off her scarf and jacket and looking as radiant as only a bride-to-be can be. "I'm eager to see what delicacies Angelica has prepared for our celebration dinner."

Since Ginny's parents wouldn't be arriving in town until Friday morning, Joelle snagged Henry to play the dual role of her father and best man. With everyone now in attendance, Joelle got down to doing what she did best—bossing everyone around. She made everyone go through their paces, individually and in group mode. Over and over and over again until they'd performed up to her expectations, which seemed to make Darlene and Henry very nervous—as they were charged with setting up the tables for the dinner crowd.

Finally Antonio announced that he'd had enough, or rather that he was more interested in saying "I do" than worrying whether the bridal party would be standing in perfect formation during the actual ceremony. Joelle pursed her lips but said nothing.

Grace and Mr. Everett were the first to leave. Judge Hamilton was invited to attend the dinner, but had other plans for the evening. Tricia grabbed her coat to leave, with only Ginny and Antonio going over a few last details with Joelle before they, too, would be allowed to depart.

Henry called to her before she could leave. "Ms. Miles,

please give your sister my regrets. I'm afraid something's come up and I won't be able to attend the rehearsal dinner tonight."

"Oh, I'm sorry to hear that," Tricia said sincerely. "I hope it's nothing serious."

"No." But he didn't offer a more detailed explanation.

"Good night," Tricia called as he entered the lobby.

"Good night."

Tricia pulled her coat tighter around her, yanked open the heavy oak door, plunged into the cold, and nearly ran into Will Berry on the inn's porch.

"Oh, hey, I'm sorry," he apologized, reaching out to steady her.

"It's totally my fault," Tricia said and brushed the wind-swept hair from her face. "Did you come to the inn for dinner?"

He nodded.

"Oh, I think I heard that the dining room is booked solid tonight," she fibbed, since they hadn't even set up for, let alone started serving dinner.

"Oh, crap. I'm about sick of diner food."

"Why don't you come home with me?" Tricia suggested.

Will started. "What?"

Tricia laughed. "That wasn't what I meant. My sister is hosting a dinner for friends tonight and one of the guests won't be able to make it. Not only is she a fantastic cook, but she makes enough food to feed an army. There'll be an empty seat, so you won't be putting anyone out. And this will give you the chance to get to know your new neighbors a bit better."

"I'd like that," he admitted. He shrugged. "Okay, you talked me into it. Where are we going?"

"My sister lives above her store, right next door to my place. Why don't you follow me? I'll be parking in the municipal lot, but if you can find a spot on the street, go ahead and take it."

"I will."

Will followed Tricia to the inn's parking lot where they both retrieved their cars. Three minutes later, they met outside the Cookery. Tricia unlocked the door and let them in, leading him through the darkened store and up the stairs to Angelica's loft apartment.

"Come on back," Angelica called from the kitchen as they hung their coats on the rack inside the door. Sarge galloped down the hall to meet them, jumping up and down and wagging his tail so hard Tricia thought it might fall off.

"Well, who's this?" Will asked, bending down to scratch behind the dog's ears.

"That's Sarge. He's Angelica's protector."

"What a big brave boy you are, too," Will said, and Sarge jumped up to lick his face. "Down, boy, down!" Will said, laughing.

"Come on. The kitchen is this way," Tricia said, pleased at the dog's reaction. Sarge didn't take to just anyone.

Mr. Everett and Grace were already seated around the large table when Tricia arrived. "Hello, everyone," she called and the Everetts waved.

"Oh, you took my advice and brought a guest," Angelica said with glee, her eyes wide with delight.

"This is Will Berry. Stan's son. This is my sister, Angelica. . . ."

"Yes, we've met," Will said.

"Oh, that's right. Sorry. This is my friend William Everett and his wife, Grace," Tricia said in introduction.

"I'm so sorry about your loss," Grace said, ever poised.

Will pursed his lips and nodded. "Thank you."

"Henry sends his regrets," Tricia told Angelica.

"Oh, that's too bad. I was hoping to get to know him better," Angelica said. "Ginny had already called to say Joelle gave her regrets." She lowered her voice. "And I can't say I'm unhappy about it. That woman is a pill." She turned to Will. "Can I get you a drink? Wine? Beer? Spirits?"

"A beer would be great, thanks."

"Where are Ginny and Antonio?" Angelica asked. Just then the bell in the shop rang out.

"That must be them now. I'll go down and let them in," Tricia said and hurried back down the stairs to retrieve the guests of honor. Antonio held a big silver platter filled with the most amazing appetizers, courtesy of the inn's chef, Jake Masters, who had once been the short-order cook at Angelica's café. Ginny carried a couple of bottles of champagne—no doubt what Nigela Ricita had given them.

"Oh, that Jake, he's such a sweetheart," Angelica said with approval when Antonio gave her the tray. "And champagne, too?" she said, accepting the bottles. "Domaine Chandon," she said, inspecting the labels, and beamed as she put one of the bottles into the waiting, ice-filled champagne bucket. "Someone has *very* good taste." Ginny put the other bottle in the fridge, while Tricia put their coats away.

Soon, there wasn't an extra inch of space around Angelica's dining room. Tricia hungrily soaked up the low rumble of the various conversations that circled the table. Was this what big family dinners were like? She had to admit this was more enjoyable than the formal dinners where the Miles clan had gathered in restaurants when she was growing up. There was more to a gracious meal than just starched white linens, crystal goblets, and polished silverware, although Angelica's collection was just as lovely. At least if Tricia spilled gravy on the tablecloth, she was fairly sure she wouldn't get scolded.

"More champagne?" Antonio asked and didn't wait for an answer, just refilled Tricia's flute.

"Thank you."

"Nothing is too good for any of us tonight, I think," Antonio said, as he took a step to his right to fill the next glass.

"Much as I love my apartment, it's a bit tight for entertaining," Angelica said.

"No, it is perfect," Antonio insisted. "Just like you, dear lady. Thank you for your generosity by inviting us all."

Angelica positively glowed at the compliment. "Very well, but I'm already planning for future holiday gatherings. And if the guest list keeps growing, I'm going to try to persuade you to let me rent out the Brookview's dining room. If the restaurant isn't serving anyway, you may as well let me take over that lovely kitchen for the day."

"But then you'd be behind closed doors and unable to attend to your guests," Antonio pointed out.

"That's true," Tricia agreed.

Antonio sidled around the kitchen island to refill Angelica's glass.

"What are your Thanksgiving plans?" Angelica asked Will.

"I'll probably go to Shaw's in Milford and grab one of those rotisserie chickens, a box of stuffing, and a can of cranberry sauce."

"I would've thought you'd spend the holiday with your aunt," Tricia told Will.

He swirled the champagne around in his glass and took

a deep swallow and then smacked his lips. "Much better than soda pop," he commented. "I haven't been able to track her down yet."

In a town as small as Stoneham he hadn't been able to find one elderly woman?

"What's her name?" Grace asked.

"You see, that's the problem. Now don't laugh, but I always called her Auntie Yum-Yum."

"Yum-Yum?" Ginny repeated, unable to suppress a smile.

"What else would you call a woman who gave you heavenly baked treats?" he said and took a much more appropriately sized sip of the chilled bubbles.

Ginny shrugged. "Yum-Yum sounds about right. What else can you tell us about her? I'm sure someone at this table must know her. Mr. Everett, Grace, and I have lived in Stoneham all our lives."

"That's right," Grace chimed in. "We all love mysteries"—she glanced across the table—"especially Tricia, here," she said with a grin. She turned back to Will. "There must be other things you remember about your aunt that would give us a clue."

Will thought about it for a few moments. "Well . . . she was kind of fat."

"Fat?" Angelica, who'd been a lot heavier at certain times in her life, blurted.

Will nodded.

"Must have been all those cakes, and cookies, and pies," Ginny said with a laugh.

"In fact, she wasn't just fat, she was morbidly obese. I'm not even sure she's still alive. And if she is, she probably has terrible health problems."

"What did she look like—I mean besides her weight? Do you remember the color of her hair?" Grace suggested.

Will looked thoughtful. "Brown. But it probably wouldn't be that shade anymore."

"I don't know," Angelica said. "The colorist over at the Milford Beauty Salon does a pretty good job. What color were her eyes?"

"I'm not sure I remember. Hazel maybe? Or were they gray?" Will shrugged. "My memories of her are pretty hazy."

"Was she married?" Tricia asked.

Will nodded. "She was once, which is why I don't know her last name. It must have been over by the time I was born, because my mother once warned me not to bring up the subject."

"Who's to say she hasn't remarried in the intervening years?" Ginny piped up.

"True, true," Grace conceded.

Will shrugged. "Would you pass those bacon-wrapped shrimp? They're delicious. What did you put on them?" he asked Angelica. Tricia wasn't interested in the answer, noticing how he'd deftly changed the subject. Did he really want to find this long-lost aunt? Maybe not.

She watched him chew and swallow the appetizer. Was she sincerely interested in Will as a person, or more as a diversion? If she were honest with herself, it would have to be the latter. Unlike Michele Fowler, Tricia really wasn't cut out to be a cougar.

"More champagne, Tricia?" Antonio asked.

Tricia looked down at her glass. She hadn't remembered draining it. "Why not?" she said and held it out to be refilled once more.

"Let's toast to the happy couple," Angelica said. "And then let's eat."

All the glasses were refilled, and it was Mr. Everett who stood and raised his glass. "To Ginny and Antonio. May this be but the first of the happiest days of your lives, for I'm sure, as with Grace and me, the best is yet to be."

They all reached across the table to clink glasses. Tricia let her gaze wander in Will's direction. He winked at her.

And just what, if anything, did that mean?

THIRTEEN

Tricia drank far more of that lovely champagne than she should have and, if pushed, might admit to having just a slight headache the following morning, but it was well worth it. The feeling of love, appreciation, friendship, and camaraderie that had flowed in Angelica's small apartment the previous evening had cheered Tricia more than anything that had happened in the years since her divorce and move to Stoneham. Yes, despite the headache, she was feeling pretty chipper.

After following all her morning rituals, Tricia and Miss Marple descended the stairs to Haven't Got a Clue and started their workday. But all too soon a knock at the shop door caused Tricia to look up from her paperwork. The store wasn't slated to open for another hour; still she peeked outside the big display window's blind and saw her former assistant standing before the shop's door. Tricia hurried to let her in. "Good morning."

"And the same to you," Ginny said and proffered one of the cups of the Coffee Bean's best brew that she held.

"What a nice surprise," Tricia said, taking the coffee and ushering her in.

Ginny laughed. "Just trying to repay the favor." She shrugged out of her jacket and they both sat down in the readers' nook. Miss Marple deigned to join them, sitting atop a pile of crooked back issues of *Mystery Scene* magazine.

"That sure was sweet of Angelica to host our rehearsal dinner last night. The food was out of this world."

Tricia smiled, happy to hear that her sister's efforts had been so appreciated. "Nobody plays hostess like Angelica, that's for sure."

"I'd like to do something special to thank her. Is there anything she needs or wants?" Ginny asked.

Tricia shook her head. "I have the same problem when it comes to Christmas shopping for her."

"I was afraid you'd say that," Ginny said and took a sip of her coffee. "But then I seem to be drawing a blank a lot lately."

"What do you mean?"

"After dinner last night, I wracked my brain trying to think of anyone who fit Will Berry's description of his aunt."

"I've been trying to think of every elderly woman I know in the village. All I come up with is Grace and Stella Craft— the high school English teacher who taught Zoë Carter and Kimberly Peters."

"And me, too," Ginny piped up. "Neither of them is terribly overweight, either."

"Do you know if Stella has any relatives?"

Ginny shook her head. "Haven't got a clue." Then she laughed. "I mean, who gets friendly with—let alone hangs around—their old high school teachers?"

"You've got a point. Yet you've lived here all your life. Who do you know who fits the overweight elderly lady criteria?"

"That depends on your definition of elderly—and overweight. You mentioned Grace, and I know she's in her late seventies, but I don't think of her as elderly because she's so active. When I think of elderly, I think of someone with one foot in the grave and the other on a banana peel."

Tricia had to admit she felt pretty much the same. She wondered about Mrs. Roth, Jim Roth's mother. He'd owned History Repeats Itself and had died in an explosion the previous spring, but she quickly discarded the idea. That elderly lady was English. She wasn't overly heavy, either. And she'd told Tricia she had no living relatives—at least in this country.

Tricia changed the subject. "How much do you know about your wedding planner?"

Ginny frowned. "I'm not sure I know what you mean."

"Frannie told me that until recently, Joelle and Stan Berry were lovers."

"Get out!" Ginny cried in wide-eyed surprise.

Tricia nodded. "Honestly. So, I take it she never mentioned him to you."

"Not a hint." Ginny shook her head. "With her thorny personality, I didn't think Joelle could handle friendship with another woman, let alone a relationship with a man." Her eyes widened. "You don't think *she* killed Stan, do you?"

"I don't know. But being dumped is a terrible blow to the

ego." *And don't I know it.* "It's possible she could have been angry enough to . . ." She didn't finish the sentence. "Then again, she's so self-confident and sure of herself, she's just as likely to move on without a qualm."

"That's true," Ginny conceded. "But if she *did* kill Stan, I hope they don't catch her until after the wedding. Much as I wish I could've done more myself, without her help and guidance, this wedding just would not happen on time."

"Oh, come on, you wouldn't want a murderer working on your wedding," Tricia chided.

"As long as she doesn't kill us or any of our guests. . . ." Ginny glanced at the clock. "Look at the time! I've got to get to work before I lose my job."

"Fat chance of that happening. In another five days, you'll be the boss's stepdaughter-in-law."

"If she can't be bothered to come and meet me, she's not likely to let me keep my job if the business tanks," Ginny said sourly. She drained her cup but didn't toss it. Tricia knew she'd use it throughout the day and only reluctantly throw it away when it was no longer useful, making sure it went into the recycle bin. "Gotta fly. Talk to you later," Ginny said and stood, donning her jacket once more. "If you think of any way Antonio and I can thank Angelica, please let me know."

"I will," Tricia promised, following her to the exit. "Thanks for the coffee."

Ginny waved as she opened the door, letting in a fierce wave of chilled air. Tricia hurriedly closed the door behind her.

Tricia started back toward the cash desk where she'd been working but paused to look at the blind cord. With Ginny gone, the shop seemed cold, lonely, and a little depressing.

It wouldn't hurt to open the shade and let in the daylight. Tricia pulled on the cord, and as she did she saw Frannie Armstrong walking up the sidewalk, heading for the Cookery. She was just the person Tricia needed to talk to, and she waved to get her attention. Frannie waved back but seemed in a hurry. Tricia scooted to her door, opening it and letting in another blast of cold air. "Frannie, have you got a minute?"

"A minute," Frannie said and stepped into Haven't Got a Clue. "What's up?"

"This is going to sound really odd, but I was wondering if you could tell me when the garbage is picked up on Oak Street."

"That *is* odd," Frannie agreed, "but I've known you long enough not to question those kinds of information requests— because I know you're not likely to tell me anyway. The trash gets picked up tomorrow."

"Do most of your neighbors put out their garbage cans the night before?"

"Yes. The truck comes early—between seven and eight." Perfect.

"Anything else you want to know?" Frannie asked.

"Um . . . if I wanted to visit your street tonight—"

"After dark?" Frannie asked. She knew Tricia well enough to guess what was in the offing.

"Possibly. Would you mind if I parked in your driveway?"

Frannie's grin was positively evil. "Why, of course not. But you know you're going to have to eventually spill the beans as to why."

"Eventually," Tricia promised.

Frannie nodded. "Did I just see Ginny leave here?"

"Yes. She wanted to know if there was something she could give or do for Angelica as a thank-you for the rehearsal dinner last night."

"How'd it go?"

"Everybody seemed to enjoy themselves. And the food was to die for."

"Oh, good. I can't wait until Saturday and the wedding." She shook her head wistfully. "Little Ginny getting married. I'm bringing plenty of hankies because I'm liable to cry my eyes out through the whole ceremony."

Tricia smiled. "I may join you."

Frannie laughed.

"By the way, do you know of anything Angelica would like or need? Ginny wants to repay her for her kindness. I'd like to know, too. Christmas is coming and Angelica is the hardest person on earth to buy for."

"Don't I know it? Last year I ended up giving her flowers for Christmas. She seemed to like them, but they're only a memory after a couple of days."

Flowers would be an appropriate gift from Ginny, but Tricia wanted to give her sister something more long lasting. Maybe jewelry. Angelica loved jewelry, and she could wear just about any metal or stone and look fabulous in it. Yes—she'd find time to go to Nashua and one of the more exclusive jewelry stores sometime during the next couple of weeks.

"I'd better get going," Frannie said and opened the door, letting in more cold air. "Time waits for no man—or woman. See you later, Tricia."

"Have a great day," Tricia said and decided she'd don another sweater before the store opened for the day. The forecast hadn't called for balmy temperatures and she hoped the door would open many times to let in potential customers.

As she headed for the back of the store and the pegs that held her jacket, hats, and extra store sweaters, Tricia pondered her plans for the evening—half-baked though they might be. What she needed was an accomplice, and she knew just the person to ask.

Pixie arrived early for work, once again wearing what looked like a bearskin fur coat, this time with a lavender beret covering her pompadour. She carried yet another large, beat-up cardboard carton. Tricia sighed, wondering what else Pixie could have possibly found in the way of inappropriate decorations. "Good morning," she called in what she hoped was a cheerful voice. "What have we here?" She indicated the box.

"Hey, boss lady, just a little something to celebrate the season." She didn't stop, and kept moving deeper into the store.

"Oh, Pixie, you really mustn't spend your hard-earned money on Haven't Got a Clue. Honestly, we've already got everything we need to decorate for the holidays."

Pixie dumped the box on the readers' nook table. "It's not for the store, it's for you."

"Me?" Tricia echoed.

"Uh-huh. After our talk yesterday, I kinda felt sorry for you. I figured you might need something to make up for all the unhappy Christmases you've endured."

"Oh, but you shouldn't have," Tricia said politely and with a little dread.

Pixie wriggled out of her big heavy coat, tossing it onto

one of the upholstered chairs. "Go on, open the box," she encouraged.

Tricia braved a smile and lifted the folded-in tabs. Whatever was in the box was swathed in wads of crumpled tissue paper. She fished them out to find that something else had been wrapped in the same tissue.

"Go ahead, tear the paper," Pixie encouraged.

Tricia did as told and ripped at the tissue to find . . .

"It's a—"

"Baby doll," Pixie cried in delight.

Tricia pulled the large, heavy vinyl doll out of the box. It wasn't new—probably forty or fifty years old—and dressed in a little sailor suit, but it was in remarkably good shape. The head was also molded vinyl, the brown hair coloring embedded in the same material.

"Oh, my," was all Tricia could think to say.

"Do you like it?" Pixie asked, her eyes shining with delight.

"It's-it's . . ."

"Pretty darn cute, huh?"

Pixie was older than Tricia by at least ten years. Did this doll represent the kind of toy she'd had as a child—or, perhaps, had coveted?

"Cute about sums it up," Tricia said. *Not.*

Pixie clapped her hands enthusiastically. "I just knew I'd find Sarah Jane a loving home."

"Sarah Jane?" Tricia asked.

"I named her after a character from *Doctor Who.*"

"Doctor what?"

"No, *Who.* She was the fourth doctor's traveling companion—probably the favorite of all time. Of course we're talking vintage *Doctor,* here."

Tricia had no idea what Pixie was talking about and wasn't about to ask. Instead, she knew what she must say next. "Thank you, Pixie. It was so thoughtful of you to give me this . . . gift."

"You need something to love. You can love Sarah Jane when the old cop boyfriend isn't around."

But I have Miss Marple to cuddle with during those times, she didn't say. And the old cop boyfriend was a boyfriend no more.

Tricia gazed at the doll's plastic blue eyes. They blinked if you moved the doll up or down. It had plastic filament eyelashes. In its day, it must have elicited many squeals of little girl delight.

The shop door opened, allowing several customers to enter. Tricia scooped up the wads of tissue, returning them to the carton, while Pixie grabbed her coat. "I'll take that box out back to get it out of the way." She took it from Tricia and headed toward the rear of the store.

Tricia moved Sarah Jane, placing her in one of the upholstered chairs and quickly walked away, feeling like a heel because the doll did not inspire love—it was nothing she would have wanted as a child, and it was nothing she wanted as an adult, either. She felt angry and ashamed for feeling that way, too, because if ever a doll needed love, Sarah Jane was it.

"Can I help you?" she asked the two women who stood in the entry, surveying the store.

"I'm looking for a book by John Dickson Carr. *Dark of the Moon.*"

"If we have a copy, it'll be over here," Tricia said and led the woman over to the side shelves. The other customer wandered off to browse.

Mr. Everett burst through the door. "Please forgive me for being late, Ms. Miles. But like Bob Cratchit in *A Christmas Carol*, I was making rather merry last evening."

Tricia smiled and looked at the clock. It was exactly ten o'clock. "No need to apologize; you're right on time."

He took off his cap and jacket and hurried to hang them on a peg at the back of the store. Tricia had no time to even station herself at the cash desk before the door opened once again. Arms laden with what looked like quite a heavy box, Angelica backed into Haven't Got a Clue. "They've arrived!" she called cheerfully, changed direction, and headed straight toward the readers' nook.

"What has arrived?" Tricia asked.

"My rulers. And they're just darling." She dropped the box, which made a loud thump. Angelica immediately noticed Sarah Jane sitting in the chair—her expression one of surprise. She was about to say something when Tricia grimaced and mouthed, "It's from Pixie."

Angelica nodded in understanding and turned back to the carton on the table.

Their customers forgotten, Pixie and Mr. Everett gathered around as Angelica pried open the interleafed box top. She grabbed a handful of rulers and passed them around.

"I don't think I need more than one," Tricia said as she glanced at the slogan printed on the wooden ruler. As she'd threatened, the rulers said: *Angelica Miles. Entrepreneur. Author. Leader.* And under that, *A vote for Angelica Miles is a vote for progress.* It then gave the Chamber of Commerce web URL.

"Why so many? The Chamber only consists of about sixty members."

"The minimum order was five hundred," Angelica

explained. "You can give them out to your customers, as well as any Chamber members you happen to come across in the next few days. I imagine Frannie will be giving them out at the Cookery for the next six months."

The bell over the door sounded and Tricia looked toward it to see her two customers making a hasty exit through it.

"You aren't going to visit them all individually?" Tricia asked, chagrined.

"Of course I will. But you know what they say, it takes seven repetitions before someone's brain will process a sales pitch."

Again Pixie and Mr. Everett looked at one another. Mr. Everett was the first to speak. "They're very nice. Thank you. And thank you again for a lovely dinner last evening."

"Oh, you're more than welcome," Angelica said and smiled.

"Now, if you ladies will excuse me, I need to dust the back shelves," Mr. Everett said and escaped.

"I'd better go stand behind the cash desk. You never know when our customers might want to cash out," Pixie said. The store was now empty, but she scurried across the carpet, leaving the sisters to themselves.

Angelica wore a wad of rubber bands around her wrist like bracelets, and began counting out rulers in bundles of five.

"I'll echo Mr. Everett and say that was some dinner you put on last night," Tricia said.

"Three, four, five," Angelica counted and snapped one of the rubber bands around the rulers. "Not bad, if I do say so myself. The prospective bride and groom seemed very appreciative."

"It was very nice of you to throw them the party."

"I figured Antonio wouldn't have time . . . and maybe wouldn't even know the custom. I don't know what the groom's family does in Italy, do you?"

Tricia shook her head. "Do you want help with those?"

Angelica shook her head and continued to count. She snapped a rubber band around another bundle and eyed the doll once more. "What's the story?" she whispered.

Tricia sighed. "Pixie seems to think I need something to love."

"And she brought you *that*?"

"Her heart was in the right place."

"I think I'd rather love a prickly cactus," Angelica hissed and began counting rulers once again.

"Ange, I never got a chance to actually talk to you last night, but I was wondering what you were doing this evening."

Angelica wrapped a rubber band around another bundle of rulers. "Not much. I'll probably work on the new cookbook manuscript for a while. Worry a lot about the election. Maybe polish the silver again. Why? What did you have in mind?"

"When I was over at Stan Berry's house on Saturday, I noticed that Will had tossed out a lot of weird-looking magazines. I wanted to get hold of one to see what his father might've had to hide."

"Why didn't you just ask him about it?"

"He covered one of them up when I was there the other day. It was obvious he didn't want me to see what he was throwing away."

"And now you want to Dumpster dive for a copy?"

"I'd hardly call it Dumpster diving. I just want to grab one before they're recycled."

"And how do you know you can dig through his garbage tonight?"

"Frannie said most of the neighbors put out their trash the night before. What better time to go digging? That way no one will see me—us."

"Uh-huh," Angelica said, her expression sour. "Why can't you just go alone?"

Tricia squirmed inside her sweater set. "I always thought you enjoyed these little investigative forays."

Angelica scowled. "Why don't you just admit you're a chicken?"

"I am not."

"You are, too," Angelica asserted and counted out another bundle of rulers. "Tell you what, if you help me distribute these rulers, I'll go with you tonight."

It wasn't much of a deal, but reluctantly Tricia agreed. After all, she'd anticipated this was in the offing.

"Excellent. I have a list right here for you." Angelica dipped a hand into the box and brought out a piece of paper.

Tricia scrutinized the names. Quite a few of them were members who rarely, if ever, came to the monthly meetings. And as she studied the addresses, Tricia thankfully noted that Angelica had kept the not-so-easy-to-get-to locations for herself and had given Tricia the names of members who were situated on or near Main Street. That was one blessing. Distributing the rulers—and trying to cajole less-than-enthusiastic Chamber members to attend the meeting—was sure to eat up most of the morning, if not half the afternoon. But then, it would also give her an opportunity to speak to half the Chamber members and ask what they remembered about the day of the murder. Sort of a win-win situation.

"Okay."

Angelica's mouth quirked into a smile.

Set up! She'd known Tricia would be looking for an excuse to talk to the other merchants and had conveniently given it to her.

Touché.

Angelica counted the bundles of rulers, and then removed four of the rubber bands that had been constricting the blood flow to her fingers. "Here. Help me do another eight and that should be enough for you to work with. Of course, if they want more—I'd be glad to supply them."

Tricia refrained from rolling her eyes—but only just. She grabbed a bunch of rulers and began counting. In the back of her mind, she was already thinking what questions she would ask her fellow Chamber members about Stan Berry and hoped she didn't run into his killer.

FOURTEEN

Tricia spent several frantic hours chasing down the Stoneham Chamber of Commerce members who rarely made an appearance at Chamber meetings. Most of them were polite and at least listened to her pitch to come to the special Wednesday morning meeting to participate in the Chamber elections while not promising to accept her invitation. Getting past the receptionists at the local doctor and dentist offices proved impossible, but she left Angelica's rulers and business cards and hoped for the best.

It was nearing the lunch hour when she returned to Haven't Got a Clue and hung up her coat. As she approached the cash desk, the shop door opened and a deadly serious Joelle Morrison entered the store. For someone who worked in the bridal industry, where the end result was supposed to be lives merrily on their way to happily ever after, plus-sized Joelle's personality seemed more suited to that of a frenetic undertaker. Did the woman ever crack a smile?

"Joelle, good to see you again," Tricia lied but smiled brightly just the same.

Joelle sighed, as though the weight of the world rested on her shoulders. "I realize that you're a frightfully busy person, Ms. Miles, what with running your own business and all, but I'm afraid you have been sorely neglecting your duties as Ginny Wilson's maid of honor."

Tricia frowned. She'd hosted a shower a month before, given Ginny the gift of an espresso maker, which Antonio seemed over the moon about, and had helped Ginny pick out her dress. What more was she supposed to do?

She asked.

"The wedding is only days away, and you've shirked your responsibilities when it comes to Ginny's emotional well-being." Emotional well-being? Tricia was the one who seemed to be living through one emotional crisis after another. Ginny had visited Haven't Got a Clue just that very morning and had seemed perfectly fine.

"How's that?" Tricia asked.

Pixie sidled closer, not bothering to hide the fact she was eavesdropping.

"This is a very emotional time for the bride, making her feel completely vulnerable. She needs everyone around her to bolster her confidence, to make her feel like she's the most important person in the world."

"What a load of bullsh—"

"Pixie!" Tricia admonished.

Joelle turned a jaundiced eye on Pixie but spoke directly

to Tricia. "Do you always allow your employees to listen in on personal conversations?"

"Pixie, would you mind?" Tricia asked, making sure her voice was gentle and without reproach.

Pixie glowered but turned and walked a few steps to her left, stopping at one of the bookshelves. She made a show of tidying, but Tricia had no doubt she intended to continue to soak in the rest of the conversation.

Joelle turned back to Tricia, reminding her of an old-time schoolmarm who expected her to shape up—and right now!

"I've spent a good deal of time with Ginny these last few days, and she didn't seem to need any bolstering. She's a pretty confident young woman."

Joelle shook her head and tsked loudly. "She's horribly depressed over the fact that her soon-to-be mother-in-law has not committed to attending the wedding."

"Oh, that. She'll get over it," Tricia said confidently.

"Ms. Miles, how can you totally dismiss what to Ginny is an earthshaking problem?"

"Joelle, if this was the biggest problem Ginny was going to face as a married woman, I might have a bit more sympathy. But her family will be there, as well as all her friends, and it will be a lovely day. It should be Antonio who's heartbroken, and he seems to be shouldering the burden just fine. Once Ginny gets caught up in the festivities she'll forget all about it and have a wonderful time."

Joelle shook her head sadly. "I think you're terribly wrong, and I only hope Ginny won't hold it against you in years to come."

Tricia doubted that. A glance at Pixie confirmed she seemed about to comment again, but a stern look from Tricia made her look away.

"By the way, I had the good fortune to meet your ex-husband yesterday at the Brookview Inn," Joelle said

"Oh?" Where was this conversation thread going?

"He's a real charmer. Whatever possessed you to let that man get away?"

Tricia's jaw dropped, but she quickly recovered. No way was she going to go into the details of her failed marriage, consequent divorce, and current feelings about Christopher with Joelle Morrison.

"Is there a chance you two will get back together?"

Tricia blinked, surprised. And yet something told her it might be best to play along if she hoped to get useful information out of Joelle. "We haven't discussed it." But, boy, was Christopher going to get an earful the next time their paths crossed.

"I wonder, when you and your ex were married, did *you* have the wedding of your dreams?" Joelle challenged.

"Yes, and I can tell you that in retrospect I spent far too much time worrying about the colors, the dresses, the shoes, the flowers, the cake, and everything else that goes along with the supposedly perfect wedding day. None of it means a damn thing if the marriage doesn't last," she said bitterly.

"I'm beginning to see *why* your marriage didn't survive," Joelle said with disdain.

"When things don't work out, divorce is sometimes the only answer. Surprisingly enough, the condition is *not* fatal."

"Ain't that the truth," Pixie said under her breath but still loud enough for Tricia to hear.

Joelle continued to ignore Pixie. "I'm very sorry you feel that way. Every bride deserves her day. I'm deeply disappointed you can't find it in your heart to make Ginny's wedding day as special as it can possibly be."

Tricia sighed. Why was it everyone on earth could pull a guilt trip on her and it would work? "I'll try harder, Joelle," she said, if only to shut the woman up.

Joelle straightened her shoulders, her smile one of triumph. Tricia wondered if her next question would wipe the look from Joelle's face.

"I understand you've recently suffered a loss," Tricia began.

Joelle looked wary. "I don't know what you mean."

"I don't mean to be nosy, but I understand you and Stan Berry were good friends."

Joelle exhaled loudly, her lips a flat line of annoyance, or was it chagrin? "The past tense is correct. But we parted on good terms."

"You were at the Brookview Inn the morning Stan was killed. Did you speak to him?"

"I believe we said hello to one another but that was the extent of our contact," she answered stiffly.

"Do you mind if I ask why you were at the inn?"

Joelle bristled. "If you must know, I had to speak to Antonio. I'd finished the wedding reception's seating chart and wanted to get his approval. Unfortunately, he was busy with the Chamber of Commerce breakfast. I hung around and waited, but I had another appointment, so I never did get to talk to him that morning."

"Were you in the building when Stan was found dead?"

"No!" Joelle's eyes widened in irritation. "Ms. Miles, I realize your life revolves around mysteries, but let me assure you that I harbor none."

That seemed unlikely. The fact that Stan had been attracted to Joelle and had presumably bedded her, too, hovered in the realm of the impossible, and yet they had had some kind of oddball relationship. Could Joelle actually have a personality that she hadn't shown to Tricia or Ginny? If she and Stan had been together for a year or more, she must have had some qualities other than organization that she showed to a minority of the people she interacted with.

The shop door opened, admitting a couple of potential customers.

"If it'll make you feel better, I'll talk to Ginny, but I truly think she'll be just fine," Tricia said.

"I hope you're right, Ms. Miles. And by the way, if you and Mr. Benson decide to retie the knot, I hope you'll consider me to take care of the details. A woman as successful and career-oriented as yourself cannot afford to forsake her business when there's another who can take on the details and plan the most recent happiest day of your life."

"I honestly don't think it'll come to that."

"Perhaps," Joelle said, threw her head back, and sniffed. She pivoted and, without a word, stalked toward the exit. Her head was held so high, though, that she failed to see the door swing open and walked right into the customer who entered through it.

"Excuse me," the man said, ruffled.

Joelle threw her head back further and exited the shop.

The man timidly entered the store, trying to look invisible.

Pixie abandoned the pretext of working and joined Tricia at the cash desk. "That dame is a ditz," she declared. "And full of crap, too."

Tricia shook her head. "Poor Ginny. I wouldn't be surprised if it was Joelle who was making her feel miserable about Nigela Ricita being a no-show at the wedding. It's not like Ginny to act this way."

"From what I've seen, Ginny is a stand-up chick. She'll be fine. And everybody knows the honeymoon is way more enjoyable than the wedding, anyway."

The comment made Tricia smile. Angelica had described her the same way just the day before. "Unfortunately Ginny has to wait a couple of months for that."

"Hey, she's got Mr. Eye-talian stud in her bed every night. That's where the *real* fun is."

Tricia wasn't going to dignify that remark with a reply, but she nonetheless had to stifle a smile.

"And what about that ex-husband of yours? *Is* there a chance you two *could* get back together?"

"Perhaps. When hell freezes over," Tricia added.

Pixie snorted with laughter. "So when do I get to meet him?"

"He seems to have talked to just about everyone in the village. I'm sure he'll eventually show up here, too. He's threatened to come visit Miss Marple."

"Is he a hunk?" Pixie asked, waggling her rather bushy eyebrows.

Tricia thought about Christopher, who only seemed to get better looking with age. "I guess you could say so."

"Yeah, but if he left and broke your heart, he must be a real jerk."

Christopher, a jerk?

Maybe.

Tricia didn't want to discuss him—and especially not with Pixie. "I find talking about the past very difficult."

"I'm sorry," Pixie apologized. "But you know, you're a real nice person. I'm sure you're gonna find Mr. Right one day."

"Really?" Tricia asked, and then realized just what Pixie was saying. Had word gotten around the village that she and

Baker had called it quits? She decided not to comment. And honestly, she wasn't all that broken up about it. Right now she was more interested in finding happiness in the simple things of life. A nice meal, a good glass of wine, and spending time with her sister and friends. Maybe one day she'd consider Christopher her friend once again, but for now he was persona non grata.

"It's time you and Mr. Everett went to lunch," Tricia said.

Pixie looked up at the clock. "So it is. We're snagging his missus and heading over to Milford and the Mexican joint. You want we should bring you back some enchiladas or quesadillas?"

Tricia thought about the fat content in both entrées and shook her head. Now if they'd been heading to the Indian restaurant in Merrimack, she could've rattled off any number of items she'd accept from the take-out menu—most of them low fat and vegetarian. "Maybe next time."

Pixie nodded, content with that answer. "Come on, Mr. E. There's a fajita with my name on it just waiting for me."

Mr. Everett hurried to the back of the store, grabbed their coats, and joined the woman by the readers' nook. "I wish you could join us, Ms. Miles. It's a shame we can't all have lunch together."

"I promised we'd have brunch together soon. Let's make it Sunday, if that's okay with you, Pixie?"

"I'd love it. And as it's my day off, I'd have time to shop here in Stoneham."

"I'd enjoy it, too," Mr. Everett said as he zipped his jacket.

"Then it's settled," Tricia said. "Enjoy your lunch!" she called as her employees headed out the door. Chances were, they'd be back late, but she didn't mind. It was a blessing they got along so well.

As Tricia returned to the cash desk, she found Angelica's bundles of rulers and the list of Chamber members she still needed to visit. It had been a while since she'd spoken to Chauncey Porter. This was one visit she was actually pleased to make, and she might as well fit in lunch, and a trip to the bank, on the outing, too.

That settled, she set it aside and looked around the empty shop before she picked up her copy of *The Plague Court Murders* and enjoyed the guilty pleasure of reading on the job.

And then the phone rang.

Tricia set her book aside and picked up the receiver. "Haven't Got a Clue. This is Tricia. How—?"

"Tricia, it's Grant."

Tricia closed her eyes and sighed. "I thought we'd said everything we needed to say yesterday."

"I still have some questions for you about the investigation."

"Couldn't you assign one of your officers to ask?"

"I *am* the officer in charge of the investigation," he said with an edge to his voice.

Tricia sighed again, hoping he not only heard it but got the message behind it. "When do you want me to come to the station?"

"I thought we could talk about it over lunch."

"That sounds more like a date than an interrogation, and I thought I made it clear—"

"You made yourself perfectly clear. This is purely business. But we both have to eat and I will have to insist that you pay for your own meal."

"Oh, all right. But Pixie and Mr. Everett have gone out to lunch and won't be back for at least an hour—maybe more."

"Then meet me at the Bookshelf Diner at two thirty. Okay?"

"Okay."

Baker hung up and Tricia put the receiver back in its cradle with far more force than she had intended. She picked up her book, but the mood had been broken. Instead, she left the cash desk and headed for the beverage station, intending to give it a good scrub. That way she could work out her frustration before meeting Baker. Getting together for lunch didn't seem like a very good idea. But on the off chance he might tell her something useful about the murder, she was willing to at least go through the motions. And she *did* need to eat.

Grabbing the antibacterial spray bottle, she squirted the counter and began to clean. Goodness knows, she didn't have anything better to do.

Pixie and Mr. Everett returned to Haven't Got a Clue earlier than Tricia had anticipated, and in great spirits. It turned out that Mr. Everett was a fine baritone and he and alto Pixie shared a love of holiday standards. They came in singing "Winter Wonderland" and were just starting a rousing chorus of "Jingle Bells" when a trio of customers arrived and thankfully ended their recital. But it did remind Tricia that she should dig out the Christmas CDs, and she sighed when she realized they'd be listening to them beginning on Black Friday straight through until Christmas Eve.

Tricia took that opportunity to run her errands before she met with Baker. Since the Armchair Tourist was closer than the bank, she went there first.

The bell over the door tinkled cheerfully as Tricia entered Chauncey's store. Unlike other times when she'd visited,

there were actually customers browsing the shelves, while
Chauncey rang up a sale. Earlier that year, Chauncey feared
he might be forced into bankruptcy, but since diversifying
his product line, business had picked up. Tourists bought
items they'd forgotten when packing, and the villagers who
needed advice or travel supplies made the Armchair Tourist
the first stop on their journey.

Tricia patiently waited until Chauncey had a few free
moments to talk.

"What can I do for you today, Tricia?"

"Hi, Chauncey. Looks like business is booming."

"It sure is," he said with a grin. "Thanks to you." He
cocked his head and winked at her.

Tricia grimaced and shook her head, embarrassed. "Let's
not go there."

"But I'll never be able to repay you for your kindness. If
you hadn't cosigned for the loan I took out from the Bank
of Stoneham, I'd be living in my car right now, a victim of
bankruptcy."

"You don't owe me anything," she said. "You've already
paid off the loan—and six months ahead of schedule, too."

"If you and Angelica hadn't advised me on how to maxi-
mize my business—"

Tricia shook her head. "Angelica gets full credit for that."
She was the one who'd encouraged Chauncey to branch out.
Tricia had only helped him secure the loan to do it.

"I'm grateful to both of you. Now, what brings you to my
fair shop this lovely day?"

Lovely? The sky was overcast, but Tricia envied his ability
to see beyond the gloomy weather.

"I brought you these." She withdrew a bundle of Angelica's
rulers from her coat pocket.

Chauncey took them from her, removed the rubber band, and laughed. "Angelica doesn't need to bribe me to vote for her for Chamber president. I'd vote for her dog before I'd vote for that miserable skinflint Bob Kelly. The way he's raised my rent year after year, I'd almost think he was trying to put me out of business."

Tricia said nothing. She wasn't about to bad-mouth Angelica's opponent—at least not until after the election. If Angelica won, she hoped Bob would quietly fade into the woodwork, although she suspected that if he lost he'd become an even more painful thorn in Angelica's side.

"Other than that, life seems to be treating you well these days. You look terrific," Tricia said.

"And I feel great. My doctor took me off all my meds. I'm saving a small fortune because of it, which is how I paid off that loan so quickly. But even better, I've finally got a love life."

Tricia fervently hoped he wasn't going to go into intimate detail about his relationship with Eleanor. Chauncey must have read her mind, for he laughed.

"They say finding love late in life can be the sweetest, and I agree. I wish Eleanor and I had found each other a lot sooner. We'd have been happier and healthier much longer."

"Then things are getting serious between you?"

Chauncey motioned her closer and lowered his voice. "I'm thinking about popping the question on Thanksgiving."

"So soon?" The two had only been dating for five months.

"At our ages, why wait?"

Why, indeed.

"I know you won't say a word. I want this to be a surprise. I've already picked out a ring and everything."

"My lips are sealed," Tricia promised.

"And I hear that you might soon have some good news?"

"Oh?" Tricia asked and couldn't think of what he might be referring to.

"I met your ex-husband when he came into my shop yesterday."

Tricia frowned, more than a little annoyed. "It seems he's been making the rounds."

"He said he'd moved to the White Mountains to be closer to you."

"Did he really?" He seemed to have told plenty of people that—and before he'd said it to her.

"Yes. I thought it rather sweet."

"That's Christopher all right." Sickeningly sweet.

The shop door opened, letting in a couple of customers. "I'd better get going. I've got another errand to run. See you at the Brookview on Wednesday for the election."

"I wouldn't miss it," Chauncey said and gave her a wave as she exited the shop.

Damn Christopher. He had no business talking about her to her friends—and for him, mere strangers. Then again, that might be exactly what he wanted: an opportunity to engage her in conversation.

Tricia plunged ahead, fighting the north wind as she headed for the Bank of Stoneham. What was with the men in her life? Were they determined to drive her crazy? She had a feeling she might find the answer to part of that question when she met Grant Baker for lunch.

FIFTEEN

The Bookshelf Diner was located halfway between Haven't Got a Clue and the Stoneham police station, which had made it a convenient place for Tricia to meet Chief Baker for lunch. As usual, she was the first to arrive. Since they both tended to order the same things off the menu, Tricia took it upon herself to order for both of them; a julienne salad for herself, and a cheeseburger and fries for Baker, hoping he would arrive before his order got cold. Tricia sipped coffee while she waited.

She was on her second cup when Baker finally arrived, a little out of breath. He sat across from her, without stopping to give her even the briefest of kisses.

"Did you jog all the way?" she asked.

"Just most of it. It's my exercise for the day," he said. "Did you order already?"

She nodded. "If I know you, you'll eat and run. It can't be good for the digestive process."

"I don't suppose it is," he said and reached for his water glass to take a sip.

"Have you made any headway on the investigation?" Tricia asked, as though their conversation earlier that day hadn't happened.

"Not yet. That's why I want you to tell me once again everything you remember before and after you found Stan Berry dead. Every detail—no matter how small."

Tricia sighed but granted his request. It was better than rehashing why their relationship would never progress. When finished, she asked, "I assume everyone you've talked to is sticking to his or her story?"

"So far," he admitted. "Nearly everyone says they didn't really know Stan Berry and had little to no personal contact with him. How on God's earth did Berry think he had a chance to win the Chamber election?"

"Maybe he figured a direct challenge might jolt Bob into paying more attention to what the members who aren't located on Main Street might want or need, instead of just doing as he pleased."

"Possibly. What about Angelica?" he asked.

"She wants to win but had nothing against Stan. By the way, how would you like a ruler for your desk?" Tricia pulled one out of her purse and handed it to him.

He studied it. "Thank you. I think." He set the ruler on the table. "Why is Angelica wasting her time with a piddly organization like the Stoneham Chamber of Commerce, anyway?"

"She sees it as a learning experience—and as a chance to network. She wants to be the next Martha Stewart."

"So she told me. Do you see Bob Kelly as a viable suspect in Berry's death?"

At least he still respected her opinion on such matters. "Not a chance. He's too arrogant to think someone could get more votes than him. And he'd never do anything that could get him thrown in the pokey." At least she'd always believed that . . . until yesterday. Should she mention the incident at the municipal parking lot? She decided against it. For now.

"He tried to bribe you last spring. And he rigged the Chamber raffle for a free night at the Sheer Comfort Inn," Baker reminded her.

Oops. Tricia had forgotten all about that. "Okay, so he's fully capable of petty crime, but that doesn't make him a murderer."

"I've spoken with everyone who was at the Brookview Inn on Friday. It seems everyone has an alibi for the time of the murder. Each and every story has been corroborated."

"Have you spoken to Joelle Morrison?" Tricia asked.

"She was seen in the Brookview lobby minutes before the victim was found, and the fact that she had recently ended a relationship with the deceased certainly has our attention, but at this point, she is not a person of interest."

So, Baker knew about Joelle. Still . . .

"Oh, come on, Grant, a woman scorned? It's the basis of many a murder mystery. Joelle had the motive, the opportunity, and—"

"And you and Ginny don't like her. That's why you'd be happy to see her arrested for the murder."

"Happy? I barely know the woman. Why would I want to see her arrested?"

"If she was out of the picture, she'd stop harping on you."

How did he know about that? Still, Tricia hadn't consciously thought of that, yet there was no denying his conclusion. Still, she suggested another possibility. "Could a stranger have killed Stan?"

"No one reported seeing a stranger that morning."

"Then you've eliminated the inn's guests as suspects?"

Baker nodded.

The waitress arrived with their lunches, then topped Tricia's coffee cup before leaving them alone once more.

Baker uncapped the ketchup bottle, turned it upside down, and tapped the bottom to speed up the process. It worked too well, with ketchup nearly drowning his fries.

"Tell me again what you observed on the day of the murder," he said.

Tricia was sick of telling the tale and viciously stabbed a grape tomato. "Do you want me to leave out the reason I was out in the inn's lobby? I mean, we are now eating lunch."

"You had to pee. Big deal," he said and took an enormous bite of his burger.

"Yes, well, I went in search of other facilities and spoke to Eleanor about her love life, while she searched for her missing letter opener. She was annoyed that it had been misplaced."

"Would you say upset or flustered, because she might have been trying to cover the fact she'd just murdered a man?"

"No way." Although her eyes and nose had been red. Allergies, she'd said, but she'd seemed fine on Sunday. Had the culprit really been perfume?

"Since when does she even have a love life? I hadn't heard of it." Baker said, shaking Tricia from her memories.

"Oh, come on, it was the talk of the summer. Eleanor and

Chauncey Porter have been going out for months. They started out as diet buddies, encouraging each other to lose weight. Their relationship appears to be on the verge of changing. You should talk to Chauncey if you want to know his intentions. I've been sworn to secrecy."

"I wish everyone involved in this case would unburden themselves to me like they do to you. It would sure make my job a lot easier."

"I have spoken to quite a few of the Chamber members since the meeting," Tricia admitted. "Angelica has me handing out those rulers with her name and campaign pledge." She dipped a piece of lettuce into the small container of dressing that had accompanied her salad. "Have you received the results of the autopsy?"

Baker cut a long fry with his fork and then popped it into his mouth, chewed, and swallowed. "You're the only woman I know who could ask that question while eating."

"I read a lot of murder mysteries, many of them while I eat my breakfast, lunch, or dinner. The fact that we're talking fact and not fiction makes no difference to me."

"Some investigators might find it highly suspicious."

"Do you count yourself as one of them?"

Baker shook his head and picked up his burger once again, but paused to speak before taking another bite. "As suspected, Berry died of a fatal stab wound to the heart. That's why there was so little blood. Otherwise, he was a healthy male of fifty-seven with no clogged arteries and no lesions of any kind."

"Poor Stan," Tricia said and dipped another piece of lettuce into her vinaigrette dressing. "He didn't seem the kind of man who would annoy anyone to the point of murder."

"Everyone's capable of murder," Baker said. "They just

need to have had the right buttons pushed. I'll figure out who killed Berry. It might just take me a while."

"How about DNA evidence? Too soon for a report, I suppose."

Baker nodded.

"Were there fingerprints on the letter opener?"

"No. And the only fingerprints in the washroom belonged to the victim and the janitor, the latter of whom has been exonerated. He'd punched out at eight o'clock that morning. His wife corroborates that he was in bed asleep at the time of the murder. Neighbors say they saw him pull into his driveway at the usual time."

"So, another dead end."

Baker polished off the last of his fries. "Every time you eliminate a suspect, you're that much closer to solving the crime."

Or not, Tricia thought.

Baker wiped his mouth with a napkin. "I'd better get going. But one thing we haven't talked about is Ginny's wedding. I'd still like to go. What do you say?"

"You've got to be kidding," Tricia said.

"Not at all. I had to reschedule half the force to make sure I'd be free. And the Brookview puts on a great dinner. Besides, it'll give me a chance to interact with half the Chamber members. I'm convinced one of them—or a member of the Brookview's staff—is responsible for Berry's murder."

A staff member? He had to mean Eleanor, who was to be a guest at the wedding, accompanied by none other than Chauncey Porter. If they announced their engagement as planned, would Ginny try to toss her bouquet Eleanor's way?

"Meanwhile," Baker continued, "I need to reread all the witness statements we collected after the murder. I might think of something to ask—or, hopefully, catch someone in a lie."

"Good luck," Tricia said. She hadn't yet finished her salad.

Baker tossed a ten-dollar bill on the table and stood. "We are still on for Saturday?" It sounded like a challenge.

"I guess," she said with a shrug.

"I'll keep in touch." And with that, he nodded and left the diner.

Tricia picked at her salad for a couple of minutes, rethinking the conversation, yet she came to no new conclusions. She was surprised when movement in front of her caused her to look up and see Russ Smith hovering above. She frowned. "What are you doing here?"

"Same as you. I came for lunch."

"Not with me."

"You've got that right, but every other table is occupied and you look like you're almost done."

Tricia pushed her nearly empty salad plate aside. "I guess I am now." She reached for her coat, which hung from a peg just outside the booth.

"Don't run away," Russ said and slipped into the booth where Baker had sat only minutes before. "I thought we could talk about the Berry murder."

Didn't any man on the planet want to talk to Tricia about any other subject?

"I don't think Nikki would like it. And speaking of Nikki, is everything on schedule for your wedding on Saturday?"

"Don't bring up a sore subject," he groused.

"Have you canceled?" Tricia asked, surprised.

"No, but I think we should. Of course, we'd lose all our deposits, but then we might actually have a guest list. It was just our bad luck to pick the same weekend as Ginny, and then we didn't get the invitations out fast enough. Everyone Ginny had invited had already accepted by the time Nikki got ours out. As it is, we changed the time, making it earlier in the day. I hoped some of the Chamber members and merchants could attend, but they're reluctant to close shop prematurely the day after Black Friday."

And Tricia could understand why. She started to scoot out of the booth when Russ's voice stopped her again.

"Wait! We haven't talked about Berry's death."

"There's nothing to talk about."

"Oh, come on. You found him," Russ accused.

"And that was the extent of my participation in the investigation."

"Knowing you, I doubt that."

"And just where were *you* when Stan was killed?" she asked.

"Unlike most of the rest of the Chamber members, I never left the dining room. I understand you got Antonio Barbero to call 911."

"And your point?"

"It just seems a bit funny, that's all. You've never been shy about making that kind of call in the past."

"There was nothing funny about it. I'd had too many cups of coffee and needed to go to the ladies' room."

"Uh-huh."

"Why don't you tell me what *you* know?"

Since he didn't elaborate, she figured he knew about as much about Stan's death as she did. Which meant not much at all.

"I really have to leave, Russ," she said, grabbing her purse from the seat beside her. "I've got a business to run. Good luck on your wedding day."

"Thanks. Wish you could be there."

Had Tricia just been insulted? Nikki was terribly jealous that Tricia and Russ had once dated. Nikki had made a point of telling Tricia that she wasn't invited to the wedding, and now that Ginny had stolen Nikki's wedding thunder, she'd been absolutely impossible.

Too bad.

Tricia donned her coat, rummaged in her purse, and left money on the table to pay for her salad. "Good-bye, Russ."

"See you around," he promised.

Not if I can help it.

Despite the fact the Christmas rush hadn't officially started, there sure were a lot of customers visiting the shops on Stoneham's main drag that afternoon, which delighted Tricia. Still, once the day's last tour bus was boarded, sales had slowed to a virtual crawl. It was after four when Tricia noticed a man and woman standing in front of her shop, admiring the figurines in her display window. Pixie suddenly appeared at her shoulder. "Didn't I tell you that people would like those little angels and elves and buildings and stuff?"

"Yes, you did." But was the display bringing in cash-spending customers?

Pixie waved to the couple, who smiled and headed for the shop's door. The bell overhead tinkled as the pink-cheeked couple entered.

"Good afternoon," Pixie called cheerfully. "And welcome to Haven't Got a Clue. Let us know if you need any help finding anything."

"Actually, we'd like to know if the items in your front display are for sale."

"All the books are available for purchase," Tricia said.

"We're more interested in the adorable village and the characters that populate it," the woman said.

"Oh. Uh, they belong to my associate. Pixie?" Tricia turned.

"Gosh, I hadn't thought about selling them," Pixie said, sounding unsure of herself. "As a matter of fact, I just bought them a few weeks ago."

The woman opened her purse and withdrew a business card. "My name is Diane Gunther. I'm curator of the Providence Museum of Kitsch. This is my associate Rodney Adams. We're looking for examples of holiday decorations from the 1950s and '60s. You have a fine collection in your display."

Pixie studied the card. "Thank you. I saw them in a thrift shop. I figured the owner had probably just croaked and her relatives dumped all her junk at the charity store. Those little guys looked like they needed a good home, so I bought them all."

"They really are amazing. Their expressions are incredibly cute," Diane said.

"I particularly like the cardboard village pieces. Our museum has a few pieces, but not in such pristine condition," her associate chimed in.

"Well, I aim to keep them that way."

"Then you really should remove them from the window. Ultraviolet light can be incredibly destructive," Diane pointed out.

"Gee, I hadn't thought of that," Pixie said and bit her bottom lip.

"We're prepared to make an offer, if you'd be interested in parting with any or all of them," Rodney said.

"Sell them?" Pixie said again, as Mr. Everett joined them.

"Would you be insulted by an offer of a thousand dollars?" Rodney asked.

"A thousand dollars?" Tricia and Pixie cried in unison.

"I'm sorry. Apparently we *did* insult you. How about twelve hundred?"

"Twelve hundred?" Pixie practically squealed.

"You drive a hard bargain. Fifteen hundred, and that's as high as we can go."

"I-I-I—" Pixie sounded like a broken record.

"She'll take it," Tricia said, afraid the couple might change their minds if the deal wasn't quickly sealed.

"As it happens, we can pay you in cash, but we will need a receipt," Rodney said. He reached into his topcoat pocket and withdrew his wallet. Opening it, he pulled out fifteen one-hundred-dollar bills, handing them to Pixie, who still seemed unable to speak.

"We've got some boxes and newspaper in the back. I'll go get them," Tricia offered, but Diane shook her head.

"We've got acid-free wrap and boxes out in the car. If you wouldn't mind removing the items from the window, we'll go and get them."

Pixie nodded so vigorously that Tricia was afraid she might give herself a good case of whiplash.

"We'll be back in a few minutes," Diane promised, and she and her associate exited the shop.

Tricia moved to the window and began dismantling the display.

"I can't believe it," Pixie gasped. "Fifteen hundred smackers."

"Can I be nosy and ask how much you paid for the lot?" Tricia asked.

"Seventy-five bucks." Pixie's gaze remained on the crisp new bills in her hand.

"What are you going to do with this windfall?" Tricia asked.

"I have no idea. Maybe buy some new old clothes, or a new TV, or get the muffler fixed on my wreck of a car. Or maybe I'll just stick it in the bank for a rainy day," she said, grabbing her purse from under the cash desk and stowing the money away.

"That would be a wise decision," Mr. Everett agreed. "Do you need help, Ms. Miles?"

"I think Pixie and I can handle it."

"Very well." He turned to Pixie. "Congratulations, Pixie. Imagine all those little Christmas angels charming hundreds of people for years to come." He shook his head and went back to straightening the shelves.

Tricia and Pixie had retrieved just about all the figurines by the time the couple returned. "You'd better let us wrap them," Diane said, and it was obvious by her somber expression that she didn't trust them not to break them and wouldn't take no for an answer. Tricia and Pixie watched as they wrapped each piece with reverent care and stepped aside to let them work in peace.

"Well, we're back to square one," Pixie said quietly. "What are we going to do for our Christmas display?"

"We'll think of something," Tricia said, smiling bravely.

"I still have a couple of boxes of stuff I got from the thrift shop in the trunk of my car that we haven't gone through yet," Pixie offered.

"Uhh . . . well, we could take a look," Tricia said without enthusiasm.

Pixie's eyes lit up. "I'll go get them."

"I don't want to put you to any trouble," Tricia said with dread, but she could tell Pixie wasn't going to be dissuaded. She'd hit pay dirt with the figurines; maybe she figured it could happen again.

"It's no trouble," Pixie said and headed for the back of the store to grab her coat.

Oh, dear. Not again, Tricia thought, unhappy at the prospect of disappointing Pixie by rejecting yet more of her treasures.

The couple up front were wrapping the last of the figurines when Pixie staggered in under the weight of yet another large cardboard carton. She carried it to the now-clear display counter and dumped it. "You guys want to see what else I've got?" she offered.

Diane's eyes lit up, as though anticipating a new prize.

Pixie shucked her coat and opened the carton, dropping it on the floor and started pulling out yards and yards of plastic holly and ivy garland.

"Do you have anything of the same quality as the figurines?" Rodney asked, sounding dubious.

"You never know," Pixie said eagerly, but it was evident to Tricia that the carton was filled with more useless junk.

"It'll be dark soon, and we've got quite a drive back to Providence," Diane told her associate. She turned back to Pixie. "Thank you again for the figurines. You can see them set up at the museum in about a week, after we've cataloged and photographed them."

"Uh, sure," Pixie said.

The two strangers each picked up a box and allowed Pixie to hold the door open for them. "Bye!" she called, looking after them until they were out of sight.

Tricia turned to the junky garland on the counter. At the

bottom of the box was an assortment of plastic and home-made wooden snowmen, their paint scraped and discolored. They *might* be able to use them in the display but only if Pixie was able to repaint them and make them cute once more. Now to convince her.

Pixie approached the cash desk, her grin exposing all her teeth. The gold canine flashed. "Wow—what a piece of luck."

"It sure was," Tricia agreed.

"Do you like the snowmen? I know they're kind of shabby right now, but I did a lot of crafts when I was in stir. I figure I can spruce them up with a little paint and they'll be as good as new."

"Go for it," Tricia said.

"Great." She started tossing everything back into the box.

"I'll be glad to give you a hand taking that box to your car, Pixie," Mr. Everett offered.

"I think I can handle it."

"Since we're due to close in just fifteen minutes, why don't you two go now. I can handle closing up."

"Are you sure?" Pixie asked.

"Positive," Tricia assured her.

"You don't have to tell me twice," Pixie said with a grin. "This will give me time to check out another thrift shop on my way home."

Oh, dear.

"You're free to leave, too, Mr. Everett."

"That's very kind of you to offer, but Grace is meeting me here, and I'm happy to help you with the end of the day's tasks, Ms. Miles."

"Very well."

Mr. Everett held the door for Pixie, who hollered, "See ya tomorrow," before the door closed on her. Then Mr. Everett retrieved the vacuum cleaner and started on the carpet. He was rewinding the cord when Grace arrived, dressed in a dark wool coat with a matching felted hat.

"Goodness, it's cold out there," she said. "I do believe I saw a few snowflakes, too."

That wasn't what Tricia wanted to hear—not with the mission she and Angelica had planned for that evening.

"Tricia, I wanted you to know that I made a few calls this afternoon."

"Oh?"

"After speaking with that nice Will Berry, I wondered if I might play detective and track down his great-aunt."

"Thank you. I'm sure he'd be thrilled."

"Unfortunately, I'm no Miss Marple."

At the sound of her name, Tricia's cat appeared as if from out of nowhere, although Tricia suspected she'd been napping in a carton of old paperbacks under the sales counter.

Grace sighed, her brow furrowing. "No one I talked to can even remember anyone even mentioning Mr. Berry. And, sadly, a lot of our friends and acquaintances have died over the years. It's a shame young Will doesn't even know his aunt's name."

"That does make the task even more daunting," Mr. Everett chimed in. "If we lined up every older lady in the village, would he even recognize her?"

"I wondered that myself."

"We'd better get going, dear." Grace looked back at Tricia. "We're going for the final fitting for William's tuxedo tonight."

"I don't want to disappoint Ginny with pants too long or a baggy jacket," Mr. Everett said somberly. "I'll just get my coat," he said and trotted off to the back of the store.

Grace watched him with pride before turning back to

Tricia. "Aren't we going to look darling in our bridesmaid dresses?" she asked and giggled.

"Definitely," Tricia agreed.

"I thought my days of being asked to stand up for a bride were long past," Grace admitted. "It's going to be a lovely wedding."

"I don't think Joelle Morrison would accept anything less," Tricia said.

"Oh, yes. Joelle," Grace said without enthusiasm.

"Did you get a visit from her, too?"

"Yes, she had the nerve to accuse me of being negligent as to Ginny's emotional needs."

"Same here."

"I've never heard of such a thing," Mr. Everett said, rejoining them.

"I thought about mentioning it to Ginny, but wondered if she doesn't already have enough on her mind," Grace said. "What do you think?"

"I'll think about it, and if the timing seems right, I'll say something."

"Very good."

"We'd better go, dear," Mr. Everett said, clasped Grace's elbow, and steered her toward the exit. "Good night."

Tricia locked the door behind them, wondering if Grace had heard that Joelle and Stan Berry had been lovers. Then again, even if she had, Grace would never mention it. And why was Joelle being such a pill about Ginny's emotional state? Was she projecting her own unhappiness on her client? It must be doubly difficult to be helping brides get ready for their special day when her own hopes for getting married had been so recently dashed. And could that kind of hurt and anger push one to her absolute limits?

Joelle was at the inn just before Stan's death. She had a motive. She might have had the opportunity. Could she have actually killed him?

Tricia glanced at the clock. She'd have to think about the implications while getting ready for her stealth mission to check out Stan's trash cans.

"Let's go, Miss Marple," she said, and the cat bounded ahead of her, heading for the door that led to Tricia's upstairs apartment. She intended to dress all in black, the better to fade into the shadows, and wondered what she'd say to Will if she and Angelica were caught red-handed.

SIXTEEN

Angelica pressed down on the brake, cut the lights, and then backed into Frannie Armstrong's driveway, which was several houses away from Stan Berry's place. She gave Tricia a hard stare. "Are you sure you want to go through with this?"

Tricia pulled the dark knit hat down and tucked her hair up under it. "Yes. If I'd had second thoughts, we wouldn't be here now."

Angelica shrugged. "Well, hurry up. It's cold out here and I have other things I need to get done tonight."

"You didn't *have* to drive me. I could've just walked over here by myself."

"Just go," Angelica ordered.

Tricia opened the car door, slipped out, and quietly shut

the door. She looked at the home's lighted living room window, where Frannie stood watching. She waved, smiling like a lunatic. Tricia's stomach sank as she waved back and then began to jog down the sidewalk. She slowed as she approached Stan's home. There were lights on in the garage once again, but as she'd hoped, the trash was stacked at the end of the drive ready for pickup the next morning.

Two years before she'd almost Dumpster dived with a bunch of freegans, so picking through a garbage can full of papers wasn't going to be a problem. And unless Will had jumbled up the can's contents, the magazines should still be at the top of the pile.

Tricia pulled on her heavy-duty gloves and forged forward. No sooner had she crossed the drive next to Stan's house when a dog started to bark. Loudly.

Tricia stopped dead, unsure what to do. The dog's barking went into overdrive, and the lights went on in the neighbor's house. Adrenaline shot through her, and instead of fight, Tricia chose flight and pivoted, running as fast as she could back toward Angelica's car.

She yanked open the door and hopped inside, breathless.

"Did you get it?" Angelica asked.

Tricia shook her head, gasping. "The dog next door started barking and the lights went on. I was afraid someone was going to come out and catch me rummaging through the trash."

Angelica sighed—loudly. "So what are you going to do now?"

Tricia squinted through the windshield into the darkness. "I guess I'll wait until after midnight and try again."

"Are you kidding?" Angelica practically squealed.

Tricia shook her head.

"What if that dog is still outside? Don't you think that'll be even more suspicious if he barks at that time of night?"

"I'll just have to take that risk."

Angelica sighed again—even louder, if that was possible. "Give me that hat," she said and swiped the knit cap from Tricia's head.

"What are you going to do?"

"Go and dig through Stan Berry's garbage, what do you think?"

"But you don't even know what can to look at."

"So, how many cans are there?"

"Four."

Angelica shrugged, grabbed Tricia's hands, and plucked the gloves from them.

"What if you get caught? What will you say?"

"That I'm a freegan and I'm trying to recycle."

"Ange, if you're seen, it could ruin your chances of being elected Chamber president."

"Oh, Trish, you worry far too much," she said, yanked open her door, got out, and then slammed it.

Tricia winced. How many of the neighbors had heard that?

It was so dark that Tricia soon lost sight of Angelica, who was also clad in black. She found herself counting. She got to sixty, and counted to sixty again. Next she hit the window control, letting it down a couple of inches. No dog barked. That was something in Angelica's favor. Tricia counted to sixty again, and again. A full five minutes had gone by and there was still no sign of Angelica. What could be taking her so long?

Tricia eased the car door open and stepped outside, quickly and quietly shutting the door so that the car's interior light went out. She peered into the darkness, but couldn't see anything but the lights on in the houses along the street. More than a few of them were already dark. People sure went to bed early on Oak Street—but not Frannie, who seemed to wander in and out of her living room to check on the car in her drive.

Tricia wished her watch had a lighted dial. She started counting again. It sure was cold. She rubbed her arms and stamped her feet hoping to keep some of the chill away. Her breath came out in cloudy puffs and she wondered if she ought to go looking for Angelica.

Something touched her shoulder and she yelped—jumping at least six inches into the air.

"Will you be quiet?" Angelica hissed.

"Where have you been?" Tricia grated, wishing her heart would stop pounding.

"Get in the car," Angelica ordered and headed around to the driver's side. Once they were both inside, Angelica dumped several magazines onto Tricia's lap.

"What took you so long?" Tricia asked, not bothering to look at the magazines. There wasn't enough light. She could see that Frannie hadn't abandoned her vigil and was eager to leave the area.

Angelica jammed the key into the ignition, started the car, and pulled away from the curb. "One of the neighbors saw me, asked me what I was doing. I told him I was taking a walk around the block. So . . . I did. I really *do* need the exercise," she said, turned on the headlights, touched her turn indicator, and made a right.

"Did you have any trouble finding the magazines?"

"Nope. They were practically overflowing from one of the garbage cans. I couldn't see what they were about—too dark.

Come on up to my place and I'll fix us both a nightcap and we can page through them."

Nightcap? Tricia hadn't even eaten dinner.

As soon as Angelica pulled into the lighted municipal lot, she looked at the cover of the top magazine. "*Chubby Chasers International?*" she said, reading the magazine's title. The cover model was an incredibly large woman dressed in a neon pink leotard, tights, tutu, and ballet slippers, tottering while striking what Tricia knew from experience was the third ballet position. The unflattering outfit accentuated the woman's excess rolls of fat that hung from her body like mounds of rising bread dough.

"Oh, good lord," Tricia muttered under her breath.

"What?" Angelica asked.

"Never mind. You can look at these rags when we get upstairs. And I think after what I've been through tonight I'm going to need that nice stiff drink."

"Whatever you say," Angelica said.

They exited the car and Tricia found herself holding the magazines close to her chest, lest one of her neighbors see the covers and wonder about her taste in reading. Not that it would happen, of course. Main Street boasted pretty gas lamps, but they were hardly bright enough to read by.

Tricia followed Angelica through the Cookery to the stairs that led to her loft apartment. Sarge started to bark as soon as they hit the first step. "Mommy's coming," Angelica called and the barking went into joyous overdrive. Angelica unlocked the door and turned on the light. Sarge was like a yo-yo, jumping up and down with excitement. It had been less than an hour since he'd last seen his human mistress, but it might as well have been a year. Angelica scooped him up and he licked her face in love and admiration as they trudged down the long hall that led to her living room and the kitchen that overlooked Main Street.

"Mommy will give you a nice treat," Angelica told the dog, setting him back down on the floor, and then opened a glass jar on the counter, plucking out what looked like a piece of jerky. Sarge started dancing around her feet, took the treat, and headed for the little basket she kept for him in the kitchen.

"What've you got there?" Angelica asked as Tricia shrugged out of the sleeves of her jacket.

Tricia tossed the magazine onto the kitchen island. "What do you think of that?"

Angelica's eyes widened and her jaw dropped as she took in the sight of the titanic ballerina on the magazine's front cover.

Tricia took off her coat, settling it over the back of one of the island stools. "How about that drink?"

Angelica started paging through the magazine, her eyes going so wide Tricia was afraid they might just pop out. "Good grief," she cried as she came across a nude shot. The woman on that page sat on a big square coffee table, not unlike the one that took up space in Haven't Got a Clue's readers' nook, only the woman's bottom covered the entire surface of the table as she glanced over her shoulder in what Tricia guessed to be her best come-hither look.

"It's like a car wreck. I can't pull my eyes away," Angelica said in awe as she turned the page to find the same woman lying on a zebra skin rug. Or maybe it was *two* zebra skin rugs. Zebras weren't all that big, after all.

Tricia decided that if she wanted a drink, she'd have to get it herself. She crossed the kitchen, grabbed a couple of glasses from the cupboard, and hauled out a bottle of gin from Angelica's kitchen liquor stash. "I sure hope you have some tonic water. And a lime, too. I've gotten spoiled since the Dog-Eared Page opened."

"Oh, sure," Angelica said, her gaze riveted on yet another mammoth nude model.

Tricia scrounged the fridge's crisper drawer, found the lime, and washed and then sliced it before she fixed them both a drink, pouring the gin into the glasses without the benefit of a shot glass. "Will you stop looking at those pictures," she chided her sister.

"I'm just wondering how we're going to get rid of these things. They're not going out in my trash, that's for sure."

"Too bad we don't have a fireplace. We could burn them and no one would ever know we were the wiser," Tricia said and handed Angelica a drink.

Angelica finally settled on one of the stools and took a sip of her drink. "Whoa! That's pretty strong."

"Sorry. Want me to pour some of it out and top it with tonic?"

"Not on your life," Angelica said and took a healthy gulp. She set the glass aside and turned another page.

Tricia picked up another of the magazines and scanned a few pages before tossing it aside in disgust. "What would make women pose for these demeaning kinds of publications?" she asked.

"Let's see . . . to pay the rent? Put food on the table?" Angelica postulated. "Maybe it was a chance for them to feel sexy? I don't suppose many men ever told them that in person."

Tricia sighed and sipped her drink. Michele over at the Dog-Eared Page made them much better than she did. "So, we know that Stan Berry had some kind of sick fascination with supersized naked women. What does that mean in the grand scheme of things?"

"One man's trash is another man's treasure . . . or fetish," Angelica offered. "Everybody's got stuff tucked away they don't want anyone to know about. I wonder what Will thought when he found the stash."

"And it was a pretty big stash," Tricia said. "It looked like an entire trash can was full of those magazines."

"I didn't have to dig deeply, that's for sure," Angelica agreed. "Do you think Stan's recreational reading had anything to do with his death?"

"I don't see how it could."

Angelica's gaze traveled back down to the magazine in front of her. "Still, maybe you should tell Chief Baker about it anyway."

"And admit I was digging around in Stan Berry's garbage?"

"You didn't dig through it. I did," Angelica reminded her.

"He'd be annoyed no matter what." Tricia shuddered just thinking about the content of the magazines. Why would any man be fascinated at looking at rotund naked women? And what was Stan doing while he studied the nudes within *Chubby Chasers International*'s pages?

She reached around her for her jacket and the bottle of hand sanitizer she kept in its right-hand pocket. "If I were you, I'd wash the island off with some kind of antibacterial cleaner before you put down another fork and knife," she advised.

Angelica looked at her blankly, then her mouth dropped open once again. "Oooh! Give me a squirt of that sanitizer, will you?"

Tricia complied, recapped the bottle, and put it away before taking another large swig of her drink.

Angelica found a plastic grocery bag, used it as she would to pick up Sarge's droppings on one of their walks, and removed the magazines from the island. Tricia picked up their glasses while Angelica found some disinfectant spray and gave the counter a thorough going-over. She deposited the used paper towel into the trash and washed her hands before joining Tricia once again. "Want something to eat?" she offered.

"After looking at those magazines, I've lost whatever appetite I might've had."

"I've seen worse," Angelica said.

Tricia stared at her. "Where and when?"

"A man I dated many years ago. We weren't together long," Angelica deadpanned and sipped her drink.

"I should hope not." Tricia rested her elbows on the island's cool, now germ-free surface. She thought about what she knew about Stan Berry. He lived alone, made signs, and read dirty magazines. Or maybe he just looked at the pictures. Something Will had said days before came back to her. "Do you think it's possible that Will's morbidly obese aunt could have killed Stan?"

"That sounds like a tabloid story: *Revenge of the voluptuous elderly woman.* We don't even know of any extra-sized women in the village."

"Maybe she doesn't live here anymore."

"You're forgetting one thing. Nobody saw an old, really chubby woman in the Brookview the morning Stan died, and no one like that lives here in Stoneham."

"That *we* know of," Tricia stressed, repeating Angelica's

words. "Except, neither does Grace, Mr. Everett, or Ginny, and they've lived in Stoneham their entire lives."

"That's got to be a dead end. And why are you obsessing over this, anyway?"

"Because, dear sister, you and Bob are considered the most likely suspects."

Angelica sighed. "Chief Baker would have to be certifiable to think that. He's been hanging around Stoneham—and my kitchen—long enough to know I'm no killer. Bob on the other hand . . ." She shook her head. "But let's face it, you don't believe Bob killed Stan."

"You're right. In fact, he may have been eliminated as a suspect. I don't think he ever left the inn's dining room during the ten or so minutes when Stan was killed."

"I wouldn't know—because I did," Angelica admitted. "Nature called."

They looked at one another for a long moment.

"I know you and Grant are on the outs, but is there a chance you could ask him?"

Tricia frowned. "I guess so. By the way, we had lunch today."

"And how did that go?"

"Sort of weird. Except for making me pay for my own meal, he acted like everything was fine between us. Is he in denial or trying to win me back? I'm just not sure."

"Men," Angelica said and shook her head. "I swear, if I live to be a hundred, I will never understand them."

Tricia nodded. Baker had blown her off one time too many, and now that she'd told him they were finished, he seemed to suddenly understand just what he might be losing. Too little attention, too late. He'd been married to his job . . . until his ex-wife had a potentially fatal illness. Their marriage had been on the rocks, but he'd put his relationship with Tricia on hold to support his almost ex-wife. Now that Tricia was his almost ex-girlfriend/lover, he seemed willing to put some quality time into that almost-dead relationship, too. Tricia did not want to be the object of Baker's pity or desperation.

"I think I lied," Angelica said, and her stomach growled. "In fact, I know I did, because I'm hungry."

"Me, too," Tricia admitted.

"If you could eat anything in the world right now, what would you want?" Angelica asked.

Tricia closed her eyes and thought about it. "A Belgian waffle with bacon on the side."

"And a mug of hot chocolate?" Angelica asked. Tricia nodded. "Sorry. I don't have the ingredients here."

Tricia sighed, disappointed.

"But I do over at Booked for Lunch."

"Since when do you serve waffles? The place is called Booked for *Lunch*, not Booked for *Brunch*."

"I only make them for certain customers. Now, feel like taking a walk across the street?"

Tricia smiled. "It's not all that far."

Sarge barked. It was obvious he did not want to be left behind again. They put on their coats and Angelica scooped him up as they headed for the door.

They walked across the street in silence. Could Stan's killer actually be an outsized woman? The chances were nil. It would have been such an easy person to pin the murder on . . . if they'd had a clue who the woman might have been.

One thing was certain; very few Chamber members even knew Stan Berry, and therefore they had no motive to kill him. The most viable suspects in the case were still Joelle

Morrison and, much as she didn't want to think about it, Will Berry. Case? The thought amused her. It wasn't *her* case. She was just an innocent bystander. Well, as the person who'd found the body she was more involved than most who'd been at the inn Friday morning, but she knew only a little more than everyone else who'd been at the inn at the time of the murder.

Angelica opened the darkened café, set Sarge down on the floor, and headed for the small kitchen. Tricia took off her coat and put a pot of water on to make the instant cocoa, thinking about the pathetic women in the smutty magazines. Why, next to them she looked like a stick figure. A stick figure who was about to eat a great big waffle, bacon, and down a mug of cocoa.

This was one time she wasn't going to worry about calories, and she positively grinned.

SEVENTEEN

Whether it was the heavy meal or trying to figure out who killed Stan Berry, Tricia found it nearly impossible to sleep that night. She tossed and turned. Turned on the light to read for an hour, then turned off the light to stare at the ceiling for an hour. She did this several times. She must have slept a little, for her alarm clock roused her from a doze, and Miss Marple, who'd had no trouble sleeping through the night, let Tricia know she was ready for a hearty breakfast. Coffee was all that Tricia wanted on that gray, gloomy morning. Better yet, espresso. There was only one place to get it in Stoneham. After showering and dressing, and taking even more care with her hair and makeup than usual—to cover up the dark circles under her eyes—Tricia headed for the Coffee Bean.

She'd timed it right, too—arriving after the locals had gotten their caffeine fixes and before the tourists showed up. "Good morning, Alexa."

"Good morning, Tricia." Alexa and her husband, Boris, had been among the first merchants to open for business in the revitalized village of Stoneham. The Russian couple was known for being opposites. Alexa was usually smiling and cheerful, while her husband tended to scowl and grunt. Thankfully, it was Alexa who waited on the customers during peak hours, and even though this was between rush times, Tricia was glad it was Alexa behind the counter when she arrived.

"What can I do for you today?" Alexa added, with just the barest hint of an accent. Boris, on the other hand, sounded like a villain from a Cold War flick.

"A cup of espresso, please."

"Ah, it's going to be *that* kind of day?" Alexa asked as she prepared the coffee order to go.

Tricia nodded. When she paid for the brew, she handed Alexa one of Angelica's rulers.

"*Was ist das?*" she asked, showing off her ability to speak yet another language. She happened to be fluent in at least four of them. Obviously Angelica hadn't made it to the shop to give the barista a ruler.

"Just a little reminder that my sister Angelica is running for Chamber of Commerce president."

Alexa frowned as she inspected the cheap wooden ruler. "Is that all there is?"

"I'm not sure I understand what you mean?" Tricia said. Had Bob Kelly been by with his own brand of payola?

"Mr. Kelly has offered us a month of free rent—if he wins, that is."

Tricia blinked, her mouth going dry. "A whole month? Has he offered that to everyone on Main Street?"

Alexa shook her head. "Just his tenants. The others will get a free weekend at the Brookview Inn—all inclusive."

Good heavens! "And would that sway your vote?"

Alexa shrugged. "Maybe. Maybe not. But the Chamber and its members might be better off with someone more experienced than Angelica."

"My sister has lots of business experience. She does have two thriving businesses here in the village."

"Mr. Kelly disputes that. He used the word . . . *neophyte*. And since we do not see her accounts—how do we know?" she asked with a shrug.

Tricia wasn't sure how to counter that argument.

"We have done well in Stoneham," Alexa went on. "Mr. Kelly has done a good job bringing people here to shop. Would your sister do the same?"

"I'm sure she will. She has a lot of ideas on how to make us a destination point."

"Will she make the village a safer place to live? There have been too many murders these past few years."

"Um, it's not up to Angelica to improve safety. Presumably the police will work on that."

Alexa's gaze narrowed. "Always it seems that you are at the heart of these crimes."

"It's just a coincidence," Tricia said and gave a nervous laugh. Since she was already there, Tricia decided to push another topic. "By any chance, were you acquainted with Stan Berry?"

"*Nyet.* I saw him at the Chamber meetings, but he was a cheapskate. He never once came into the shop, so we never patronized his sign shop. We go to Milford for our window signs."

"What did you think of his campaign promises?"

"Not good. He would have destroyed the hard work Bob Kelly has done to bring in business. I think your sister would be good for the village, but free rent for a month might be better."

"I'm sorry you feel that way."

Alexa shrugged. "Business is business."

There was no use arguing the point. It seemed Alexa had already made her decision—shortsighted though it might be. Still, Tricia forced a smile and placed her change in the jar marked TIPS. "Thanks for the espresso. See you Wednesday at the election."

Alexa nodded in the direction of the jar. "Thank you. And do not worry, I *will* be there."

Tricia watched for traffic before crossing the street. She waited until she was back inside Haven't Got a Clue before she picked up the heavy receiver on her Art Deco phone and dialed Angelica's number.

"Good morning, Haven't Got a Clue. Is that you, Trish?" Angelica asked.

Thank goodness for Caller ID. "Yes. Ange, have you heard what Bob is offering as a bribe for votes?"

The door opened, and Pixie entered, holding a shopping bag and her vintage alligator purse. Mr. Everett brought up the rear. Seeing Tricia was on the phone, they tiptoed inside the shop.

"What's he giving out? Kelly Realty pens? Those cheesy envelope slitters? Or how about green tote bags with *Kelly Realty* printed on the side?" she said and laughed.

"He's offering a month's free rent to all his tenants!"

"What?" Angelica hollered, forcing Tricia to move the phone away from her ear.

"And a weekend at the Brookview Inn—all inclusive—for those who aren't tenants."

"Oh, my God."

"Look at it this way: Bob probably figures it's a win-win situation. If he loses the election, he's not out a nickel. If he wins, he's a hero."

"But he'd be out at least thirty grand."

"He'd look awfully good pumping thirty thousand dollars into the local economy, whereas your rulers were made in China."

Pixie allowed Mr. Everett to take her coat to hang in the back of the store and stood there, eavesdropping. Tricia was too upset to even care.

Angelica's voice was hushed. "Oh, God. What have I done?"

"At least you can't be accused of bribery. I wonder what the state Chamber of Commerce organization would think of his strategy. He's also telling the members that you're a neophyte. That you can't do a good job because you've been in business only a couple of years."

"But I'm doing well with the Cookery, Booked for Lunch, *and* my writing career. Bob only has his real estate firm to worry about, and since he's the only Realtor in town, he doesn't have any competition."

"Yeah, and I'll bet he's telling people you'll be too busy with your own businesses to care about theirs."

"I'm doomed," Angelica moaned.

"Don't give up yet. I'm sure we can spin this to make Bob look bad."

"I don't know. I mean, the thing that puts me off on our

whole political system is all the mudslinging and negative campaigning. It makes me never want to vote again. I refuse to sink to that level."

Tricia felt her throat constrict. "I've never been as proud of you as I am right now. You deserve to be the next Chamber president, and if you aren't elected, the members deserve what they get."

"Oh, Trish, what a beautiful thing to say. Thank you." Angelica sniffed. Could it be she was fighting tears?

"Okay, I need to open the store. We'll talk later today."

"Yes. If not lunch, then later."

"All right. Bye." She replaced the phone in its cradle and looked to see Pixie standing in front of her.

"I kinda heard what you said," she admitted. "Ya know, I used to know some pretty tough characters. Some of them still owe me. I could have someone take Kelly out."

"Kill him?" Tricia asked, horrified.

"Nah, nothing that dramatic. Just rough him up a bit. Break a leg or two. Make him see reason—back off on his attempted bribery."

"No, thank you. Angelica is determined to run a clean campaign."

Pixie shrugged. "Then I hope she won't mind losing."

Mr. Everett cleared his throat. "I'm afraid I have to agree with Ms. Miles. It's only proper that Ms. Miles—your sister," he clarified, "conducts herself in a manner that fosters pride in the proceedings, and the office where she hopes to serve. And while your sister and I have had our differences in the past, I do believe she is the best candidate for the job. I'm only sorry I'm no longer a member of the Chamber of Commerce so that I could vote for her."

"Thank you, Mr. Everett."

"I still think taking that bastard Kelly out is the best way to go . . . but what do I know?" Pixie groused and sauntered away, heading for the beverage station, where she found the coffee hadn't been started. She frowned, snatched up the empty pot, and headed for the washroom to get some water.

"I'd best get started on the back shelves," Mr. Everett said and headed off in that direction just as the phone rang. Now what?

"Haven't Got a Clue. This is Tricia—"

"Hey, ex-boss. Are you available for lunch today?" Ginny asked.

Tricia smiled. "I'm pretty sure I could be. Where and when?"

"The Bookshelf Diner—not to cheat Angelica out of our patronage, but because it's so small, we're not likely to get in and out in a timely manner."

"I know. She has lamented that problem since the day she opened."

"And it's too bad, because I'd prefer to go there."

"I can pull some strings. I've got an in with the owner."

"That's true."

"If we meet at one fifty, they'd still serve us."

"Works for me. See you there." Ginny broke the connection.

Tricia replaced the receiver once again. Lunch with Ginny was the perfect opportunity to broach the subject of Tricia's apparent maid-of-honor deficiencies. She had a feeling she knew what Ginny's reaction would be, but still, she felt she had to mention it.

Pixie returned, the coffeepot full of water. "I noticed Sarah Jane is still sitting in the readers' nook," she said and moved behind the beverage station to start the brew.

Oh, dear. Tricia had forgotten about the world's ugliest doll. Pixie paused in her prep, expecting a comment. Tricia couldn't seem to come up with one.

"You know, I was wondering if we could use Sarah Jane in our holiday decorating."

"Oh?" Tricia said, too stunned by the suggestion to offer any other remark.

"Yeah. Remember Nancy Drew number twenty-four?"

Tricia's mind raced. It had been a long time since she'd read any Nancy Drew mysteries. "Uh . . . *The Clue in the Old Album?*" she guessed.

Pixie's eyes lit up. "Exactly!"

"Refresh my memory. What does a doll have to do with the plot?"

"Well, there's an old album, a lost doll, and don't forget the missing gypsy violinist."

Tricia had forgotten all three. "What did you have in mind?"

"We could dress Sarah Jane in a red outfit with a cute little hat, and have her hold a copy of the book."

"Do we even *have* a copy of the book?" Tricia asked.

"Oh, sure. I saw one up in the storeroom last week."

"Where would we get a Christmassy outfit, and what if Sarah Jane proves to be such a great sales tool that the book flies out the door?"

Pixie shrugged. "There's gotta be a million more doll-based mysteries. I could Google it. I'll bet we could sell a lot of them, and if not dolls, then mysteries set at Christmastime."

So far Pixie was batting a thousand. "Okay. If you can find an outfit at your favorite thrift shop, I'll pay for it."

Pixie grinned and nodded. "Man, what a great team we make!"

Tricia allowed herself a small smile. "That we do."

While Pixie finished setting up the beverage station, Tricia turned to adjust the blinds, noticing a familiar figure making his way down the sidewalk across the street: Christopher. She moved to her left and away from the window, just as he stole a glance at Haven't Got a Clue.

Tricia frowned, wondering just what her ex-husband was up to now.

EIGHTEEN

 Ginny was late. But then, she often was. A few stragglers sat nursing coffee at Booked for Lunch, but things would be different the next week when the holiday shoppers came out in full force and Stoneham would see almost as many visitors as they did during the summer or the fall leaf-peeping season.

No sooner had Tricia sat down when Bev, the waitress, showed up with the coffeepot and poured. "Good afternoon, Tricia. The usual?"

She nodded "I'm meeting Ginny Wilson. You can bring mine with Ginny's order."

"Sure thing." Before Bev could return the pot to the coffee station, Ginny arrived, sans coat, hat, or gloves.

"You'll catch your death," Tricia admonished her.

"Coming from you, I take that as a threat," Ginny said with a laugh and scooted into the booth. "But the truth is I ran out the door because I was afraid of getting sucked back into work. Brittney needs to learn to run the shop without me. That won't happen if I'm always standing next to her telling her what to do all the time."

Bev poured Ginny's coffee and placed a couple of creamers on the table. "Do you know what you want?"

"Chef's salad, please, with raspberry vinaigrette on the side. I've got a special dress I need to get into on Saturday."

Bev nodded and headed for the kitchen.

"Sorry, I'm late. In addition to walking Brittney through every sale, I've been working on my window display. I want everything to be perfect on Black Friday."

"I should think you'd be more concerned with the wedding plans for Saturday."

"I'm trying *not* to think about it too much. Thanks to Joelle, it doesn't even feel like my own wedding. It's more like she's staging a performance. My job is to show up in costume, recite a few lines, dance when told, eat when told, and cut the cake when told. Joelle has everything planned to the minute. Oh, how I wish I'd refused the gift of her services."

"It's too late for that," Tricia said.

"I've actually wondered if I should have postponed the wedding. What was I thinking planning it for the first week of real Christmas sales? And even worse, Stan Berry's death."

Tricia sipped her coffee. "It's not like Stan's ghost is going to show up to ruin the festivities."

"I know, but when my folks find out, they'll be basket cases."

"You haven't told them?"

Ginny shook her head. "My mom looks for bad omens, and a murder just a week before the ceremony is just the kind of thing that cranks up her creep-out factor. I don't suppose there's any news on an arrest in the case."

"Not so far. According to Grant, everybody's got an iron-clad alibi."

"Then it must have been a stranger who killed Stan. Antonio says a lot of people come into the inn from the dialysis center across the street. They drive their loved ones to Stoneham, and while the patient gets treatment, the relatives go to the inn for lunch or dinner, or for just a cup of coffee."

"Grant didn't mention anyone like that as a suspect, and he's thorough. I'm sure he's already checked that out."

"Which means it had to be one of the Chamber members. Maybe even someone who's coming to *my* wedding!" Ginny frowned. "Now *my* creep factor has risen another eight or nine notches."

Bev arrived with their lunches and discreetly moved to tidy the café's counter.

Ginny picked up her fork. "What do you think of Will Berry?"

"I hope you didn't mind me bringing him to the rehearsal dinner the other night."

Ginny shook her head. "The more the merrier. Besides, he's kind of cute. Not nearly as handsome and marvelous as Antonio, mind you, but he must have no trouble getting dates."

"He asked me out," Tricia admitted.

Ginny leaned forward, her eyes widening in surprise. "You're kidding. You're old enough to be his—his . . ." She paused, as though realizing she was about to make a major faux pas. "His older sister."

"Nice save," Tricia said with a smile. "But you're right. I told him I was seeing someone."

"If Chief Baker hasn't solved the murder by Saturday, does that mean you'll have no date to bring to the wedding?"

Tricia sampled her tuna salad. "He says he's made arrangements with his staff to insure he gets to come. But he's blown me off so many times, I never get my hopes up. If he's free, he'll come. If he's not, you'll have paid for an extra dinner and I'll have to apologize for him." She wasn't ready to tell Ginny the truth.

"Don't worry about it. We already figured on a no-show number. Antonio says it happens with every wedding."

"And what if you get more guests than sent in an RSVP?"

"Somebody has to eat tuna." She looked at Tricia's lunch and laughed. "Maybe that person will be you."

"Thanks a lot." Tricia sipped her coffee. "By the way, I spoke to Russ Smith yesterday. He's a bit annoyed that, thanks to your popularity, his wedding to Nikki is getting short shrift when it comes to wedding guests."

Ginny bristled. "It's not our fault they chose the same wedding day as us, or that we got our invitations out earlier than they did. Although when I tried to order the wedding cake from the Patisserie, Nikki was downright rude to me. So much for trying to patronize local businesses. The Milford bakery was very happy to take my order."

"Poor Nikki."

"Poor Nikki?" Ginny echoed. "What about poor me?"

"First of all, you've got Antonio. Nikki has Russ," Tricia deadpanned.

"Oh, you're right. I hadn't thought of that."

"She's sure to feel slighted that the majority of her friends and colleagues will be at your wedding, not hers."

"This *is* her second marriage," Ginny pointed out. "By all rights it *should* be low-key with mostly family and close friends attending. This is our first and *only* wedding. Why shouldn't we go whole hog?" Which seemed to negate what Ginny had previously said about wanting a no-nonsense celebration of the day.

"No reason that I can think of," Tricia said.

Ginny picked at her salad, looking grim.

Tricia changed the subject. Well, not entirely. "I spoke with Joelle yesterday. She seems to think I'm shortchanging you as your maid of honor."

"How?"

"She said you were under a terrible strain and that I should do more to keep your morale high."

"Good grief. Is that why everyone keeps asking me how I feel and if I'm okay? Yeah, I feel stressed, but it's my own fault—not yours or anyone else's. I'd better give Joelle a call and straighten her out. I know she reports to Nigela, but this is *my* wedding, and I don't want her alienating my friends. Bottom line, this wedding is one day in our lives. And if it's *too* perfect, we'll have no funny stories to tell our children in the days to come."

"Then I'm glad I mentioned it," Tricia said with amusement.

Ginny took another bite of her salad, chewed, and swallowed. "Were you aware your ex-husband has been in town visiting all the merchants on Main Street?"

"Don't tell me he visited you, too?" Tricia asked, and why did she feel so uncomfortable hearing that statement?

Ginny nodded. "You never mentioned what a hunk he is."

There was that word again. "The subject never came up. What was he doing in the Happy Domestic?"

"He bought a clock. The better to mark the time without you?" she asked.

"I doubt it." Tricia turned her attention back to her food. With so much gabbing she hadn't made much of a dent in her tuna salad.

Ginny's familiar ringtone blasted from inside her purse, and she quickly grabbed the phone, studying the number. "Oh, dear. It's Brittney. I can't even get away from the store for half an hour without her experiencing—or creating—some kind of crisis."

"You'd better take it," Tricia advised.

"I've a mind not to—but then she might abandon the store completely to come here and drag me back. Honestly, I don't see how she's going to handle everything on Saturday and Sunday when I'm otherwise occupied."

The phone went silent. "I'm sure Mr. Everett wouldn't mind spending a few hours over there on both days. After all, the wedding isn't until evening."

"That's a good idea. I'll give him a call when I get back to the store. Honestly, I don't know what I'd do without my friends. You guys have been like family to me."

Tricia couldn't help but smile, but before she could say something, Ginny's phone started up again. She signaled Bev. "Check, please. And could I have a box to put my salad in?" She looked back at Tricia. "I'm sorry. I've got to go."

"Don't worry about it."

Ginny tossed some cash onto the table, tossed what was left of her lunch into the take-out box Bev supplied, and practically flew out the door. Bev set the check down on the table but paused to speak. "I met your husband this morning," she said cheerfully.

"*Ex*-husband," Tricia emphasized.

"Isn't that just a formality? Although I had thought you were still going out with Chief Baker."

Tricia opened her mouth to answer, but then decided not to.

"Can I freshen up that coffee?" Bev offered.

Tricia sighed and shook her head. She was going to have to speak to Christopher. And soon!

The afternoon shadows were lengthening. Darkness came far too early this time of year and seemed to smother the joy out of life. Already Tricia found herself counting the dreary weeks until spring would arrive, bringing with it crocuses, daffodils, and tulips. Pixie had offered her a plastic pine wreath for the shop door, which she had politely declined. Maybe next week she'd buy a fresh one, and hope it lasted until the last days of the holiday shopping season. The scent of fresh pine might inspire shoppers to spend their hard-earned cash . . . those who weren't allergic, that is.

Tricia was still thinking about what color bow would best suit a wreath when the shop door opened, the little bell over it jingling merrily, but the expression on the face of the woman who entered was anything but happy. Joelle Morrison's head hung, and she seemed to shuffle across the carpet, slowly making her way to the cash desk where Tricia stood.

"Good afternoon, Joelle. Is there anything I can do for you?"

Joelle's gaze seemed to sink lower. "I'm here to . . . to . . ." She didn't seem able to finish the sentence.

"Yes?" Tricia prodded. She wasn't about to cut the woman any slack. Not when she'd made her own, plus Grace's, and especially Ginny's life, miserable for the past month and more.

"That is . . . I may have overstepped my bounds when I . . . spoke to you about . . ."

Pixie wandered up to join them. "You mean when you bugged the hell out of half the town, nagging them to be more supportive of Ginny when she doesn't need it?"

Joelle turned so sharply Tricia was afraid she might fall over. "I believe I'm talking to Ms. Miles," she grated, "not you!"

"Pixie, could you give us a few minutes?" Tricia asked kindly.

"Sure thing," Pixie said and turned away, her expression smug.

Joelle watched until Pixie had gone to the readers' nook to straighten up the magazines before she spoke again. "At any rate, I wanted to apologize."

"Apology accepted," Tricia said gravely. Okay, she *would* cut the woman some slack after all.

Joelle nodded and started to turn for the door when Tricia's voice stopped her. "I wonder if you could answer a few questions for me."

Joelle looked back, her expression wary.

"Why did you and Stan Berry break up?"

"That's really none of your business, Ms. Miles."

"Perhaps not, but you *do* realize it makes you a suspect in his death," Tricia said, sounding concerned.

"I've already spoken to the Stoneham police chief. I see no reason to bare my soul to you."

"I'm sorry you feel that way. I thought *we* were becoming friends."

Joelle's eyes widened. "You are *not* my friend. You are the business associate of one of my clients."

"Oh, well, if that's all I am, then when I need the services of a wedding planner, I guess I'll consult the Internet to find one." If everybody thought she was about to renew her vows with Christopher anyway, it might not hurt to play it up.

Joelle blinked, taken aback. "But I thought you said it was unlikely."

Tricia shrugged.

Joelle straightened, schooling her features. "I would hope you'd give me the opportunity to help plan your remarriage."

"As you say, it's only business. Although perhaps I would become friendly with the person who would work to make my wedding day perfect." *That's laying it on thick,* Tricia thought. But Joelle's resolve appeared to be crumbling.

"I suppose I *do* become more than a business associate to my clients. There *is* a strong element of trust involved."

"Yes. Ginny told me that she trusts your judgment implicitly." *Not!*

"Ms. Wilson has been a joy to work with," Joelle replied stiffly. Probably not when she'd chewed her out an hour before, insisting she apologize to both Tricia and Grace.

"Since I've already had a big church wedding," Tricia went on, "I'd be looking for something completely different." *And* with *someone completely different.*

"I can certainly understand that," Joelle said.

How much more chitchat was necessary before Tricia could steer the conversation back to Stan? But then Joelle gave her the opening she'd been looking for.

"I had thought I'd be planning my own wedding . . . that is until just a few weeks ago," Joelle admitted.

Tricia donned her most sympathetic frown. "You must have been devastated when . . ."

"When Stan and I decided that our fundamental differences made it impossible for us to continue seeing each other."

If Joelle had been planning her wedding, Tricia was pretty sure she wasn't the one to initiate the breakup.

"You see, Stan thought of himself as a free spirit," Joelle continued.

Free from making a commitment, Tricia automatically assumed.

"He'd been married before, and unhappily so . . ." Joelle went on.

Because he hated being tied down and forced to support his child.

"Sadly, I couldn't be the woman that would make Stan happy."

Since no woman in her right mind wants to look like Stan's fantasy woman.

"Did you argue about it?' Tricia asked.

"Once or twice," Joelle admitted.

A lot!

"Did Stan find a new someone?"

Joelle shrugged. "But as I said, our split was mutual, and I wished him well."

Like hell! You were as mad as hell. But angry enough to kill? Now that's another story.

"I'm so sorry, Joelle. It seems the road to true love can be full of potholes. Christopher and I still have some things to work out before we . . ." She let the sentence dangle.

It would be a cold day in hell before she would take Christopher back, not that he had come right out and said he wanted to come back—although he did seem to have some kind of agenda working. And whatever it was, she wasn't going to get suckered into it.

Joelle reached into her purse and withdrew a business card. "I do hope when the time comes to make decisions about your upcoming nuptials that you will consider my services."

Tricia graciously received the card. "I certainly will."

Joelle managed a weak smile. "I must be going. I have other errands to run."

"It's been very nice talking with you today, Joelle. And if I don't see you before Saturday, have a nice Thanksgiving."

"You, too," Joelle said and made a hasty exit.

Pixie practically flew across the store as though she'd been catapulted. "What was that cock-and-bull story you handed that broad all about?"

Tricia didn't answer right away; instead she gazed out the window, watching Joelle jaywalk across the street and head straight for the Everett Foundation offices, where she no doubt had a second apology to deliver.

Tricia turned back to Pixie. "I don't know what you mean."

"About getting remarried. I'm sure if that was true, you'd have said something to me and Mr. E long before now."

"You've got that right. And no, I'm not planning to get married anytime soon. To Christopher or anybody else."

"Things a little chilly with the chief?" Pixie asked, her eyebrows rising so high they were in danger of being swallowed by her hairline.

"Chief Baker is always a little distant during these kinds of investigations." Why should she spill the beans that they'd broken up—especially as they were going to make one last appearance as a couple at Ginny's wedding?

"Uh-huh," Pixie said and frowned.

The door opened again, this time admitting an older couple. Pixie shifted into customer service mode and turned toward them, offering to help them find a title among the shelves. They took her up on it, and she led them back to one of the bookcases on the north wall.

Tricia picked up her book and looked at the words, but

couldn't seem to make herself read. Her conversation with Joelle hadn't strengthened or weakened her suspicions that she could be a viable suspect in Stan Berry's death. Joelle had admitted that she'd spoken to Baker—of course she had, she'd been seen at the inn just minutes before his death—but had she told him of her relationship with the dead man? Should Tricia volunteer that information?

She'd think about it for a while. After all, what was the hurry? Nothing would bring Stan Berry back from the dead.

Turning back to her book, Tricia allowed herself to become lost in the adventures of Sir Henry Merrivale and was startled to look up and see Pixie standing before her all bundled up and ready to face the cold. "Oh, my. I guess I lost track of time."

"That's okay. Mr. E vacuumed while I cleaned the coffee station. I even swished the brush around the toilet bowl so you wouldn't have to."

"Thank you, Pixie."

Pixie shrugged. "All in a day's work," she said. "Besides, it's a lot better than some of the jobs I had while in stir. That laundry room"—she threw her head back and rolled her eyes theatrically—"you wouldn't believe the stench. What some of those inmates were up to—"

"I wouldn't even want to imagine," Tricia said, hoping she'd cut off a vivid recitation on the subject.

"So, do you think we'll be busy tomorrow?" Pixie asked.

"We were last year—and the year before," Tricia said.

"Go figure. So no closing early the night before a big holiday?"

"Do you have somewhere to go?" Tricia asked.

"I'm not much of a cook, but I promised I'd bring the Jell-O salad to Angelica's on Thursday."

"Jell-O doesn't require cooking," Tricia pointed out.

"Easy for you to say. I never really had a kitchen until I rented my current crib. A microwave and a hot plate were all I ever had before. Now I have a real stove and fridge. Geez, the place is practically paradise."

Michele Fowler had once driven Pixie home and had confided that the ex-con's apartment occupied a tiny portion of a run-down Victorian home. But, compared to prison, it had to be a virtual palace.

A smiling Mr. Everett strolled up to join them. He had already donned his jacket and cap. "What a wonderful week this is," he said. "I can't remember such a whirlwind few days packed with so many social occasions."

"What are you bringing to Angelica's Thanksgiving feast?" Pixie asked.

"My carving knives. I was trained as a butcher long before I owned my own grocery store. I've been recruited to carve the turkey. Grace is going to make her family's favorite— green bean casserole."

Tricia smiled. "I have a feeling this is going to be one of the best holidays I've had in a long, long time."

Pixie positively giggled. "Me, too. How about you, Mr. E?"

Mr. Everett's smile was faint but sweet. "It's been a long time since I felt part of a big family. Last year was nice. This year is . . ." He paused. "Marvelous. Thank you, Ms. Miles— and your sister—for welcoming Grace and me into your fold."

Tricia's throat constricted. She did not want to start crying. "We've still got a full day ahead of us before the holiday."

"Yeah, but coming here every day ain't like *real* work," Pixie said, smiling. "It's a treat. I feel like I've died and gone to heaven."

"Yes, well, you haven't. So go home and rest up, because tomorrow promises to be a very busy day."

Pixie saluted. "Yes, ma'am." She turned to Mr. Everett. "Let's hit the trail."

"And by the way, you might have to open for me tomorrow," Tricia called. "The Chamber election is tomorrow, and if it runs late . . ."

"Not to worry," Pixie said as she headed out the door. "We'll be okay."

"Good night, Ms. Miles," Mr. Everett called and shut the door behind them.

Well, that was a nice ending to the day, Tricia thought as she looked around at the tidy store. Once again she shook her head in wonderment at her good luck in finding Pixie, someone she was sure would never work out, becoming such an asset to the business.

Tricia turned the OPEN sign to CLOSED, pulled down the blinds, and was about to head upstairs to her loft apartment when the phone rang. She picked up the receiver. "Haven't Got a Clue."

"Tricia? It's me—Christopher. Are you busy?"

Tricia exhaled a long breath. Just the man she didn't want to speak to. But now that he was on the phone . . . "Christopher, what have you been telling the people of Stoneham?"

"What do you mean?"

"I've been getting reports from all over the village that you're going around hinting to people that you and I are about to reconcile, and you know that's absolutely not true."

"I never said anything of the kind."

"Then what have you been saying?"

"That we were married and I've come back to the East Coast to be near my family."

"We are not family."

"I didn't say we were. It's not my fault if people think that we'd make a perfect couple."

"How could they make that assumption without some input from you?" she asked.

"Wishful thinking?" he suggested.

"Christopher, you know I'll always love you, but I am no longer *in* love with you."

"I know that. I'm sorry if people got the wrong impression."

Did she believe him?

"And why are you calling now?" she asked.

"I want to apologize for the other day."

Tricia sighed. This was her day for apologies. And he was doing it again. Trying to worm his way back into her heart. But, she decided, she could forgive—as long as she didn't forget what he had done in the past. "Apology accepted. Anything else?"

"Are you free for dinner?"

"No."

"That was a pretty fast answer. Don't you even want to think about it for a while?" he asked, sounding hurt.

"No."

"Well, how about joining me for a drink?"

"No! If people see us together they're going to get the wrong idea."

"But it's not as if we hate each other. You just told me you still loved me."

Again Tricia sighed. "Did you hear the rest of the sentence?"

"Yeah, yeah. You're not in love with me anymore."

"And you're not in love with me, either."

"Who says?"

"The State of New York's divorce court."

"Oh, yeah. Well . . . I may have made an error."

"That's too late to correct now."

"What about later?"

He'd just crossed the line. "I'm hanging up the phone right now. Have a nice evening. Have a nice life."

"But I haven't even—"

She didn't hear whatever else he was going to say, because she'd replaced the receiver in its cradle once more.

Miss Marple jumped onto the counter from her perch behind the register. *"Brrrpt?"*

"I have no idea what that man's plans are, and we're not going to find out."

Miss Marple rubbed her head against Tricia's shoulder. "I know you love him and want to see him again, but we can't encourage him."

Miss Marple began to purr, as if begging her to reconsider.

"No. And why is it whenever I say that word no one believes me?"

The purring became even louder.

"Come along. I'm going to feed you and then I'm going out. And I'm going to turn off my cell phone so that my evening isn't interrupted." She started walking toward the back of the store. That was all the encouragement Miss Marple needed to jump to the floor and follow.

Ten minutes later, Tricia had fed her cat, changed clothes, spruced up her hair and makeup, and headed out the door, determined to have fun. She just hoped Christopher wasn't in a mood to track her down.

NINETEEN

The lively sound of Celtic music reverberated through the Dog-Eared Page and could be heard halfway down the block. What a change from years past when Stoneham rolled up its sidewalks every evening by seven. The Dog-Eared Page had brought new life to the village, and Tricia was not immune to its lure.

She entered the warm and inviting pub, noting that every stool at the bar was occupied, as were most of the tables. She hung up her coat and threaded her way around the other patrons. The music was too loud for her to say hello or converse, so she waved to her friends and acquaintances. The table farthest back had only one person seated: Will Berry. Tricia used hand signals to ask if she could sit down. Will grinned and gave her an enthusiastic thumbs-up.

No sooner had the band finished their tune than they started another. A waitress with a tray came by, delivering a beer to Will. Tricia had to practically scream to put in her order for a glass of Chardonnay.

She was sipping the last of her wine when the band finally took a break.

Will stuck a finger in his right ear and wiggled it. "My ears are ringing."

"Mine, too," Tricia agreed and found herself speaking far too loudly—but then so was everybody else in the cozy pub.

"Same here," Baker said and slipped into the chair next to Tricia. She hadn't seen him approach. Was her evening to be dominated by men whose attentions she no longer desired?

"It's a surprise to see you here, Mr. Berry," Baker said, his tone just a tad condescending.

"Why?"

"When we last spoke, you indicated you'd be leaving town soon."

"Not all *that* soon. Besides, I'm beginning to see the appeal of this quaint little village. It's no wonder my father enjoyed living here." Not that he'd patronized the Dog-Eared Page, at least not that Tricia had ever noticed.

"Have you made any progress in locating your aunt?" she asked Will.

He took a sip of the beer he'd been nursing and shook his head. "I haven't had much time to look. I spent most of the day trying to find someone to manage dad's business. If today was any indication, it's going to take a lot longer than I thought."

"Have you given any more thought to running it yourself?" Tricia asked.

"Yeah, but I'd still need someone to show me the ropes."

"Most sign shops are closed on the weekends. Maybe you could pay a sign shop owner from Nashua to teach you. You wouldn't be poaching their customers."

"Good idea," he said. "But I've still got probate to contend with. All dad's assets are frozen. It's a major pain in the ass. I even considered closing up the house for the winter and worrying about it all in the spring. That would give me time to tie up my own loose ends."

Baker had been listening with rapt attention. Had Will made it to the top of his suspect list?

"There's just one problem," Will continued.

"Oh?" Baker asked.

Will faced him. "Yeah. I thought my dad owned his house, or at least that he had a mortgage on it. But it turns out it's leased. Bob Kelly wants me to clear out the place by the end of the month."

"Is he forcing you out?" Tricia asked.

"He says he's willing to release the estate from the terms of the lease."

Tricia remembered something Stan said just minutes before he died—that Bob kept raising the rent, making it hard for the merchants to compete.

"When did your father sign the lease?" Tricia asked.

"A month ago."

No wonder Stan was bitter. Bob's motivating force in life was the acquisition of money. Did he want to cancel the lease for fear the rent would be late—or that he might not get it at all? She glanced at Baker. "Can Bob do that?"

Baker nodded. "When I was in the Sheriff's Department, we handled a lot of evictions. As the person who signed the lease is now deceased, Mr. Kelly is within his rights to ask that the premises be vacated."

"But he's giving me less than two weeks," Will protested.

Baker merely shrugged.

"Oh, there you are, Tricia dear." No mistaking that voice. "Do you mind if I join you?" Angelica asked.

Tricia had a feeling Baker was about to say no, so she spoke first. "Of course not, Ange. Please, sit down." She hadn't meant it to sound imperative.

Angelica flopped down on the remaining chair at the table. "What a day I've had. It's a good thing the Chamber election is tomorrow. I don't think I could handle another day of campaigning. Does everybody have one of my rulers?" she asked, already dipping into her purse and withdrawing a bundle. She handed one to both Will and Baker.

Baker's eyes narrowed as he inspected the ruler—his second one. He soon turned his attention back to Angelica, his expression reminding Tricia of a dog tracing a scent. "Just what *have* you been up to?"

"Visiting a lot of the Chamber members and handing out my campaign reminders." Will didn't seem to know what to do with his ruler, so he set it on the table. "I'm so sorry your father died, Will," Angelica continued. "If he hadn't, there would have been no need for me to campaign at all."

"Ange," Tricia admonished.

"It's okay," Will said, sounding amused. "She's only being honest. It's kind of refreshing, actually. Everyone else is tiptoeing around the fact my dad was murdered. I *want* people to talk about it. Maybe that would make it easier for the chief here to make an arrest."

"My department is following up every lead we receive," Baker said defensively, but Tricia knew that phrase usually meant the police had run into a dead end. "In fact, one of our leads concerns you."

Then again.

"According to your credit card company, you stayed at the Holiday Inn Express in Merrimack on Wednesday and Thursday nights. The guy working the reception desk described you to a T. You also charged dinners at a family restaurant on both those nights."

Will downed the rest of his beer in one gulp, avoiding Baker's gaze.

"Now, do you want to tell me about when and where you last saw your father?"

Will had the good grace to look embarrassed.

"You can tell me here, or tell me down at the station. It's your choice," Baker said, in a voice that conveyed the full scope of his authority.

Tricia made to stand. "We'd better give these guys some privacy, Ange."

"And miss all the juicy details? Not on your life," Angelica said, her eyes wide with interest.

"It's all right, Tricia. I don't mind if you stay." Will turned his attention to Baker. "Yes, I did see my father before he was killed. We talked."

"Just talked?" Baker pressed.

Will seemed to squirm. "Okay, we argued."

"About what?" Angelica asked.

"Excuse me, but Mr. Berry is talking to *me*. I'll ask the questions," Baker barked.

"Okay, okay—then get on with it," Angelica said, annoyed.

All eyes turned to Will. "We argued about why he left my mother and me. But it was a good kind of discussion. It finally cleared the air between us."

Baker's expression was skeptical. "And isn't it funny that

you inherit your father's entire estate when you have all those student loans to repay."

"I'm not the only person on the planet with loans to repay. And my father's estate isn't all that big," Will countered, his turn to sound defensive.

"Did you know its worth *before* he died?" Baker asked.

Will seemed to squirm once again. "No."

"I'll ask again; where were you on Friday morning when your father was killed?"

"Driving around the area. The only thing I killed that day was time."

"Do you have any witnesses?" Baker asked.

Will shook his head. "None."

So Will *could* have had a motive for murder, but Tricia didn't believe it. Or was it that she didn't *want* to believe it? And had he lied about the job at the law firm? Pixie suspected as much. Will said he'd quit when his employer wouldn't give him the time off to take care of his father's affairs—but he'd already been in the area two days before Stan's death. Why?

Will stood. "Unless you've got any more questions, it's time for me to call it a day." Baker sat back in his chair, letting his hand come to rest on the service revolver at his side. Will swallowed and turned his attention to Angelica. "Good luck with the election tomorrow."

"Thank you."

"Good-bye," Tricia said, her tone neutral.

Will nodded before making his way through the pub. They watched as he claimed a jacket from a peg near the door and then exited the bar.

Angelica looked down at the table. "Oh, darn. Will forgot his ruler!" She shrugged, scooped it up, and put it back in her purse.

Tricia turned to Baker. "So, are you going to concentrate on Will as your prime suspect?"

"People who lie make very good suspects. And he's lied more than once."

"About what?" Tricia asked.

"His job, for one."

"He didn't work for Weinberg, Metcalf, Henley, and Durgin?"

"Oh, he did, but not as an intern. He's a paralegal and, from what I gather, not very good at his job. Maybe that's why he considered reopening his father's business."

"Was he fired?"

Baker nodded. "Last Tuesday. It's not surprising he came to see his father. He probably hit him up for money."

"Then why did he book a hotel room in Merrimack? Why not stay with Stan?"

Baker shrugged. "I've already said too much."

Angelica picked up where he left off. "My guess is they really did argue and Stan refused to give Will any money, and then told him to get out."

"Did Stan really leave everything to Will?" Tricia asked.

"He told the truth about that. Still, I haven't finished making inquiries into his past."

"Have you ruled me out yet?" Angelica asked. "Because I have enough to worry about with the election, preparing a sumptuous Thanksgiving dinner, and getting my hair done on Saturday before Ginny's wedding. I do not need to be considered a murder suspect, as well."

Baker's expression was impassive. "I haven't made up my mind yet."

Angelica frowned. "You know, Trish, what good is having a cop for a boyfriend if he isn't willing to give you and yours the benefit of the doubt? But then, I guess as you two aren't together anymore it's just something you'll have to spend the rest of your life wondering about."

Baker shot Tricia an annoyed expression. Was he really surprised she'd spoken to Angelica about their so-far unannounced separation?

Tricia shrugged, looking as innocent as she could under the circumstances.

"Ladies, I have a job to perform." Baker turned back to Angelica. "I'm sorry if it inconveniences you in any way."

"Oh, lighten up, Grant," Angelica said. "You're off duty. Order a drink and relax."

"I agree," Tricia said. "You remind me of a clock wound tight. One false move and your mainspring is going to explode and spew shrapnel."

"It's my nature. You can't change your nature."

"Maybe you should just unburden yourself about the case. As you've said before, reading as many mysteries as I have, I could've no doubt aced the police academy exam. If you need someone to talk to about suspects, feel free to bounce ideas off me."

He scowled, annoyed. "You know I can't do that."

"So who do you talk shop with?" Angelica asked and signaled the waitress.

"My second in command. He makes a great sounding board."

Angelica gave her drink order, but Tricia and Baker declined another.

"I'd better get going," Baker said. But no sooner had he said that than his cell phone rang. Baker stuck a finger in his free ear—the better to hear the person calling. "Okay. No, I know the address. Thanks." He slapped his phone shut.

"What was that all about?" Tricia asked.

"Looks like I'll be making a detour before I go home—*alone*—for the evening," he told Tricia.

"Where to?" she asked.

"Stan Berry's house. Young Will just called it in. The place has been burgled."

He got to his feet, reaching for his wallet to pay his bar tab.

"Can I come, too?"

"What for? To offer the boy comfort?" Baker asked.

"You never know," Tricia said.

"Why not?" Baker said and tossed six dollars on the table. Obviously he wasn't going to pay for Tricia. She pulled a ten out of her wallet, left it on the table, and made to follow.

"Call me later, Trish," Angelica called out, then grabbed a ruler from her purse and waved it in the air. "Hey, as long as you're going to see Will, you can take him his ruler!"

There was only one reason Tricia could think of for Baker to allow her to accompany him to a crime scene: he wanted to get back in her good graces, and was willing to stretch police department rules to do it. That said, she knew enough to keep out of his way—and that of the patrol officers already on the scene, but she also made sure she stayed near enough to hear everything that went on.

"Long time no see," Baker told Will as he entered the brightly lit garage that had served as Stan Berry's business—apparently the scene of most of the destruction.

"Believe me, I would have much rather come back to dad's house and found everything in order instead of virtually destroyed," Will said bitterly.

"Can you tell if anything was taken, or was it strictly vandalism?" Tricia asked.

Baker turned and glared at her. "I'll ask the questions, if you don't mind." She shrugged, and he turned his attention back to Will.

"I didn't know half of what dad owned, and the mess that's left . . . I couldn't begin to guess what might be missing."

"Try," Baker ordered.

Will let out a frustrated sigh and looked around the piles of paper, shattered wood, and glass that had once been his father's livelihood. It looked like someone had smashed it all with a Louisville Slugger or perhaps a sledgehammer. The rolls of vinyl sign material had been slashed multiple times.

"I suppose now you'll tell me I have to get a hotel room until you can finish your investigation," Will said sourly.

"You've got that right. We depend on the county to supply a tech team. It might take a day or two for that to happen."

"If I'd known that, I wouldn't have called you guys."

"You can't file an insurance claim without our report," Baker pointed out.

"Damn."

"Speaking of which, what are the odds of this happening now? You being forced to vacate, the business in ruins—how much insurance did your father have on it?"

"Not nearly enough to replace any of this," he said, his voice unsteady.

For a moment Tricia thought he might cry.

Since it didn't look like Baker was going to cut Will any slack, Tricia placed a hand on his shoulder. "I'm sorry you have to deal with this so soon after losing your father."

Will turned a jaundiced eye on Baker before returning his gaze to Tricia. "Thanks."

"My guys will lock up and seal the house until the tech team can get here. When you find somewhere to bunk, let my office know where to find you."

Will looked resigned to his fate. "I may as well head home."

"Please keep in touch," Tricia said.

"I will."

"Tricia, please wait in the car while I finish talking to my guys. I'll be out in a few minutes."

"Sure," she said.

"I'll walk you out," Will said, grabbing his jacket.

"Thanks."

They left the shambles behind and, as promised, Will walked Tricia to Baker's SUV. "Sorry I screwed up your date," he apologized.

"It wasn't a date. As you saw, he joined us."

Tricia reached out to open the door, but Will stopped her. "I really appreciate it that you came along with Mr. No-Nonsense Cop. I didn't realize until he sat with us at the bar that he was your boyfriend."

"You've got the tense right," Tricia said, repeating what Joelle had said about her relationship with Will's father. "He *was* my boyfriend. The fact is, we broke up yesterday." Will's eyes widened in interest. Was that why she'd told him that—hoping to see his reaction? This was ridiculous. Will was far too young for her, but he sure was cute. Handsomely cute.

She made herself stop that train of thought. Handsome he might be—but he also had a problem with honesty. Still . . . "I meant it when I said I'd like to know how you make out," she said, surprised she'd admitted it.

"I was sure you did. I appreciate your kindness."

Again, Tricia said nothing. Though it was dark, there was

enough light spilling from Stan's garage so that they could see each other's eyes. Will reached out, touched her face, and then he leaned in and kissed her, his lips warm on that cold November night.

Tricia wasn't sure what to do. Was Frannie looking out her window? Had Baker seen them kiss? Did she care? After all, it seemed like eons since Baker had kissed her like that. Will leaned in again and she closed her eyes, enjoying yet another kiss, then she pulled away. "I'm sorry, Will. I like you, but the timing just isn't right."

"I know."

"I think you might be confusing appreciation with infatuation." And what was her excuse? Especially since she wasn't sure she could believe a word the man said. Did he even have an elderly aunt?

"You're probably right." Will reached around her and opened the SUV passenger door. "'Til next time."

"Good luck, Will." Tricia climbed into the SUV and he shut the door. She watched as he turned away, pulled up his collar, and got into his own car. Seconds later, he started it, pulled out of the driveway, and disappeared into the darkness.

Tricia huddled deeper into her coat. Had Baker seen that kiss? *Two kisses,* she reminded herself.

She waited and waited for Baker to return. The cold seemed to seep into her bones. How much longer was he going to be, anyway? Tricia raised her arm, hoping to see the hands on her watch, but it was too dark. She opened the SUV's door and the interior light glowed. It was after nine, she realized, and she still hadn't eaten anything.

It was only a three-block walk back to Haven't Got a Clue. Tricia was temped to get out and go home, but then she saw

Baker leave the garage and head toward her. He got in the vehicle but didn't start the engine. Instead he turned to her. "That was some fond farewell you and Will Berry exchanged."

Tricia sighed. "*He* kissed me."

"And you kissed back."

"I told him he was confused about his feelings, and he agreed."

"Are you going to see him again?"

"If you're asking did we make a date to go out, the answer is no."

"I shouldn't have asked. It's none of my business anymore. But I'd hoped you'd at least show some discretion until after Ginny's wedding."

"I don't need an escort. I'm fine going on my own."

"Well, I'm not. I intend to go."

"As my date, or as the chief investigator for Stan Berry's murder case?"

"Both."

It was Tricia's turn to be annoyed.

"Any thoughts on the vandalism in Berry's shop?"

"I don't think it was Will."

"When else, then?"

"Bob Kelly?" she asked.

He nodded. "Destroying the business would be one way to make sure Will would leave the place. You did notice that it was only the equipment that was destroyed—not the walls, doors, or windows."

"Yes."

"So, is Kelly capable of doing that kind of damage?"

Tricia thought back to Sunday when she'd seen Bob standing next to Angelica's car, keys ready to gouge the driver's door. "Until recently, I'd have said no. Now . . . I'm not so sure. If the tech team does find fingerprints, which doesn't seem likely, how long would it take to identify them?"

"These things take time. Those TV crime scene shows have the public thinking that we can process this stuff in minutes. It's going to take months—and that's only *if* we get a decent print."

Tricia shook her head. "Poor Will."

Baker cleared his throat, which immediately conveyed his annoyance. "I guess I'd better take you home."

Tricia sighed, resigned. "I guess so."

Baker started the engine and pulled away from the curb. They rode the three blocks in silence.

Baker pulled up in front of Haven't Got a Clue. "If we don't see each other before the wedding, I'll see you at the Brookview on Saturday evening."

It seemed he intended to be her date in name only, as now it looked like she was going to have to supply her own transportation. Well, so be it.

Tricia opened the passenger door but hesitated. She looked back at Baker, whose face was impassive. He didn't lean across the armrest for a good-night kiss, and neither did Tricia. She sighed and opened the car door. "Good night."

"Good night."

Tricia closed the car door and the SUV pulled out into the street. Baker hadn't even waited to see if she got into the building without incident. Tricia pulled out her cell phone and pressed Angelica's number. She answered right away.

"Where are you, Ange? At home or still at the Dog-Eared Page?"

"Home."

"Can I come up?"

"No reconciliation with Grant, eh?"

"Of course not."

"Okay, I'll get out the wine. Should I get out the tissue box, too?"

"No, but I hope you've got something in your fridge to munch on. I'm hungry enough to eat my foot."

"Now that I'd like to see. Come on up and please do tell all."

"See you in a minute," Tricia said and closed her phone. She had a few other ideas on how to spend the rest of the evening and just hoped she could convince Angelica to be her ally in crime.

TWENTY

Angelica topped up Tricia's wineglass. They'd
spent the previous twenty minutes rehashing the
events of the evening, coming to no real conclusions. Angelica had seemed upset to think Bob might be
responsible for the destruction at the sign shop. She'd truly
been fond of the jerk.

"Why is it that you and I are so unlucky in love?" she
asked.

"Maybe we're cursed," Tricia said and spread some Brie
on yet another cracker. "And speaking of lost loves, for some
reason Christopher has visited just about every merchant on
Main Street—and for all I know, beyond—to tell them I'm
his ex-wife, but making it sound like there's a chance we'll
get back together."

Angelica looked up from the papers spread before her. "You keep saying no way, but is there any chance you might?"

"No way, although the Stoneham gossip hotline has been buzzing like crazy with that news. And then Grant caught me kissing Will Berry. No doubt Frannie saw it, too. She probably was on the phone spreading the word before I even got back in Grant's car."

"Sorry about that. I love Frannie—but not always her mouth," Angelica said. She studied the seating chart in front of her. "If Grant isn't coming for Thanksgiving, I'll have to have a seating contingency plan. How about I invite Christopher?"

"Were you actually listening to me just now, or was I talking to myself?"

Angelica shrugged. "It was just a thought."

Tricia grabbed another cracker and nodded toward the seating chart Angelica was working on. "Can't people just plunk themselves in any chair?"

"Oh, no. The table must be balanced," Angelica insisted.

"Or what? Will it fall off the face of the earth and spin off into space?"

Angelica glowered. "Be serious."

"I'd rather think about something else. Like who besides Bob would've ransacked Stan Berry's business?"

"His killer, of course. Or his competition," Angelica said logically.

"Stan didn't have a competitor here in Stoneham."

"Didn't Will say he'd been contacting competitors?" Angelica asked.

Tricia didn't answer and instead took a bite of cracker.

Angelica made another notation on the pad before her and then set her pen aside. "Just think: twelve hours from now I could be the new head of the Stoneham Chamber of Commerce."

"And if you win, what will you do first?"

"Nothing. I wouldn't officially take the office until January first. That gives me a full five weeks to figure things out."

"Do you think Bob will immediately raise the rent on the Chamber's office building?" Tricia asked.

"In a heartbeat. I've got a list of things to do and one is to find a new home for the Chamber. Too bad there's no separate entrance to the second floor of this building, otherwise we could house it in my storeroom."

"Would you want Betsy Dittmeyer on the premises five days a week?"

"No, but there's a rumor going around that if Bob loses the election, Betsy might quit the Chamber and go work for him."

"And who's spreading that rumor?"

"Frannie, of course," Angelica said.

"Would you hire someone else?" Tricia asked.

"Definitely, but I'm not sure the job warrants a full-time person. I'd have to wait and see."

Tricia ate the last of her cracker and sipped her wine. "Just think, Stan's murderer could be casting a ballot for you tomorrow morning."

"I don't think so. More likely he or she would vote for Bob—and he can have that vote as far as I'm concerned."

"Why would the killer destroy Stan's business after they'd killed him? Do you think someone doesn't want Will to inherit?"

"What about Joelle?"

"For what reason?"

"Spite?"

Angelica shook her head. "I don't think anyone even knew Will existed until he showed up on Saturday."

Tricia glanced down to see Sarge looking at her with pathetic eyes. She broke a cracker into quarters, dabbed a little Brie on it, and held it out for him. Sarge sat up, looking hopeful. Tricia tossed it and Sarge caught it, gulping it down.

"Please do not feed my dog from the table," Angelica said.

"But he's hungry."

"I don't want him pestering my guests on Thanksgiving."

"Sorry, boy," Tricia apologized and grabbed her glass, taking another sip. "Okay, we know Stan Berry lived and worked in Stoneham for three years, but hardly anybody seems to have known him. By most accounts, he kept to himself. Why would someone kill him on the day he announced he'd run for Chamber president?"

"Maybe Betsy did it," Angelica said. "She seems to adore Bob. Maybe she wanted to eliminate half the competition."

"Then isn't it more likely she'd get rid of you—especially if she thinks of you as competition? But even that doesn't wash. She wasn't even at the Brookview last Friday," Tricia pointed out. She shook her head. "It all boils down to Will. I mean, he did admit that he and his father argued."

"But why would he destroy his father's business? After probate, he could have sold it to help pay off his school loans—if he in fact has them. It makes no sense that he'd wreck the place."

"Who says the crimes are related?" Tricia asked.

"You mean it's just a coincidence that someone trashed the place?"

"I suppose it could be."

"And pigs fly," Angelica said and drained her glass. "If

Will Berry killed his father, he might kill again. You ought to strongly discourage him from contacting you."

"Can I help it if I'm incredibly desirable?" Tricia deadpanned.

"Which brings me back to my original question. If we're such hot babes, why are we so unlucky in love?"

"I guess we make up for it in other areas. We're both successful businesswomen."

"And genuinely nice people," Angelica added.

"And our beauty is only surpassed by our modesty," Tricia said.

"That's a given," Angelica agreed, smiling. She poured the last of the wine into her glass.

Tricia sighed and shook her head. "I've got a bad feeling about tomorrow."

"Are you trying to jinx me?" Angelica asked and took a big gulp of wine.

"I'm *not* a jinx. But I feel like something life altering is going to happen. I just don't know whose life will be affected."

"If I win the election, it would certainly alter my life. And if I lose . . ."

"Will you be crushed?" Tricia asked.

Angelica shook her head. "No. Just disappointed. But while you've got a bad feeling about tomorrow, I've got a good one."

Tricia finished her wine, feeling like she ought to cross her fingers. "Now to see whose premonition comes true." She dusted her fingers of all cracker crumbs and got up from her stool. "I've got another favor to ask."

"And that is?"

"Come with me to the Brookview tonight."

"What for?"

"To poke around."

"I repeat. What for? Do you know how late it is?"

"That just means less people around watching us."

"What if they throw us out? What's our excuse going to be for being there?" Angelica asked.

"The wedding, of course—or the election. Either way, we're going to be there on both occasions. You're starring at one event, and I'm the featured act at another."

"Sideshow, more like."

"The dresses are actually quite nice. I daresay Grace and I could both wear them for other occasions."

"At least Ginny was kind to you in that respect. Just make sure you and Grace don't show up at the same gathering when you wear them."

"So, will you go with me?" Tricia asked.

"What good would that do?" Angelica asked.

"I don't know. Maybe we'd see something the police and Sheriff's Department missed."

"Such as?"

"That's it. We wouldn't know unless we looked."

"The scene of the crime was a restroom. Stan died almost immediately, so there was little or no blood. The cops would have been over that restroom not only with a fine-tooth comb but a vacuum, too."

"Then maybe I need to walk through the lobby. It might refresh my memory as to what I saw on Friday morning."

"You think you'll remember something of grand proportions?" Angelica asked.

"Maybe."

"I doubt it. And besides, you were there twice on

Sunday," Angelica said. "Shouldn't that have jarred your memory?"

"Why don't you want to go?" Tricia asked.

Angelica shuddered. "Because it's night and it's cold out."

"You have to take Sarge out in the cold anyway. You could kill two birds with one stone."

"The Brookview doesn't allow pets. Just service animals."

"That's never stopped you from stashing Sarge in your purse. He likes to go to new places and see new things."

"Why don't you want to go alone?" Angelica asked.

"I don't know. Maybe it's the notion of there being safety in numbers."

"Do you think the killer will return to the scene of the crime and come after you?"

"Not really. I mean, there *are* other guests at the inn, as well as the staff."

"As far as I know, the only staff on duty at night is at the reception desk. Besides, from what I heard, a number of the guests were freaked enough to check out early after hearing of Stan's death."

"Yes, but there are sure to be new guests there now who have no idea that a murder took place on Friday."

"And why is that? Because all traces of Stan Berry's death have been obliterated, and his body removed?"

"Okay, you've made your point. There is no good reason to go back there."

"Especially as you're going to be there tomorrow morning, anyway. Why not just go earlier if you want to have another look around?"

Tricia sighed. "I suppose you're right."

"Of course I am. Although if you need a breath of fresh air, Sarge wouldn't complain if you took him out about now."

Sarge knew the meaning of the word *out* and instantly jumped to his feet, looking eager to answer the call of nature.

"Oh, all right." Tricia looked down at the dog. "Walkies?"

Sarge barked and trotted down the hall to where his leash was stashed.

"I'll be back in a few minutes," Tricia said, and followed the dog's path. She snagged her coat, clipped the leash on Sarge's collar, picked him up, and headed down the stairs. Tricia disabled the alarm and went out the back door to the alley. She set Sarge on the ground and he immediately trotted over to his favorite spot by a stand of dying poplar trees. Tricia let the pooch sniff to his doggy heart's content. Her mind was back at the Brookview Inn, going over the events that had led to Stan Berry's death. That is until Sarge stood at attention and began to bark.

Tricia's head snapped around, and she looked for the cause of the dog's concern but instantly relaxed when she recognized the silhouette that approached.

"Is that you, Tricia?" Chauncey Porter called over Sarge's ferocious barks.

"Sarge, hush!" Tricia ordered, but while the command instantly worked for Angelica, it didn't bring her the same results. "Sarge!" It wasn't until she lifted him up that the dog went silent.

"Hi, Chauncey. Taking your evening constitutional?"

"It's the best way to keep the pounds off," he said with a laugh. He stopped in front of Tricia, offered his hand, and let Sarge sniff it. The dog licked Chauncey's fingers, apparently deciding he was friend and not foe. "What a nice little dog you are." Sarge cocked his head to one side, looking incredibly cute.

"And why are you out here instead of Angelica?" Chauncey asked.

"I was feeling restless. I have to admit, I always feel this way after there's been an unexplained death in Stoneham," Tricia fudged.

Chauncey frowned and nodded. "Yes. Me, too. I'll feel better once Chief Baker makes an arrest."

"So will I."

Chauncey yanked the sleeves of his jacket to better cover his wrists. "Is Angelica ready to win the election tomorrow?"

Tricia smiled. "Raring to go. How's Eleanor? I thought she might be walking with you tonight."

"She's fine, but it's a bit cold for her to walk at night. She prefers to use her treadmill when the temperature drops, but I like to be out and about. I can look at the moon and the stars and can revel in the peace and quiet."

"There is that appeal," Tricia admitted.

Sarge yipped, reminding Tricia that his business was done, that he'd saved the neighborhood from attack, and now it was time for bed.

"I'll see you in the morning," Tricia said.

"I wouldn't miss it. Good night."

"Good night," Tricia said. She climbed the steps to reenter the Cookery, locked the door behind her, and reset the alarm. Then she and Sarge climbed the steps to Angelica's apartment.

"We're back," Tricia called as she hung Sarge's leash on a peg.

"What took you so long?" Angelica called. "I was beginning to worry."

Tricia walked back to the kitchen, with Sarge trotting along behind her. "Sarge and I ran into Chauncey." At the sound of his name, the dog sat down at his mistress's feet and gave a yip of acknowledgment.

"And what did he have to say?"

"Not much. Did I tell you he was planning on voting for you?"

"No, but I'm glad to hear it." Angelica got up from her stool, and Sarge immediately stood at attention. "Come on. Let's go to the inn."

"I thought you didn't want to go out," Tricia said.

"I didn't. But I changed my mind."

Tricia gave her sister a suspicious look. "Why?"

Angelica shrugged. "I've learned to trust you on certain things. Maybe going to the inn tonight you'll discover something the police have missed. Either that, or you'll be able to put this behind you and move on."

"Do you really think I need to move on?" Tricia asked.

Angelica sighed and shook her head. "Of course. But knowing you, it won't happen until Stan's killer is revealed."

"And what if that never happens?"

"Trish, if there's one thing you've become good at these last few years—apart from being an exceptional businesswoman—it's tracking down killers."

"You think so?"

"I know so," Angelica said. She looked down at her dog. "Walkies," Angelica announced, and Sarge shot to his feet and ran for the door once again.

"You're not bringing him with us."

"I'm not going without him. And the Brookview has a nice bit of lawn at the side that Sarge can christen."

"He just came in," Tricia protested.

"If there's one thing dogs are good at, it's producing urine."

"Well, just make sure you bring one of your big purses. He's not allowed at the Brookview."

"I never travel without one," Angelica said as she started down the hall. She attached the leash to Sarge's collar, scooped him up, and stashed him in her big pink purse. "You'd better drive. You've had less to drink than me. And I sure don't want to be charged with a DUI the night before the Chamber election."

"The inn is barely a half mile away," Tricia admonished.

"You drive or you go on your own," Angelica said.

"I'll drive."

"Good. Then let's go. The night is no longer young, and I've got a big day ahead of me."

Tricia took the lead and headed down the stairs, grateful Angelica was willing to indulge her whim. But would she be so tolerant if the evening's jaunt brought nothing new to light?

She'd just have to wait and see.

As expected, the front of the Brookview Inn was lit up like . . . well, a Christmas tree. After Sarge had indeed christened the side yard and was once again ensconced in Angelica's purse, they mounted the steps but paused to take in the sight.

"Boy, this place sure looks pretty," Angelica said in admiration.

"They've done a nice, understated, and dignified job of decorating," Tricia agreed.

Angelica smiled, taking it all in. She might have stood

there for another couple of minutes if Sarge hadn't yipped his displeasure. The poor little guy was probably cold.

The main door to the inn was unlocked—just as it had been during the time when Tricia had stayed there for three weeks while her loft apartment over Haven't Got a Clue was undergoing renovation. They entered the lobby, which seemed overly warm after being out in the late evening air. Every light in the place seemed to be lit. The Christmas tree glowed. There was no one behind the reception desk, and Tricia held her finger to her lips before beckoning Angelica to follow her down the corridor that led to the handicapped restroom where Tricia had found Stan Berry only four days before.

She looked around, didn't see any staff or guests, and opened the door. The light and fan immediately went on, but the small room was empty, and her nose wrinkled at the strong smell of disinfectant.

"Are you getting any kind of creepy vibes?" Angelica whispered.

Tricia shook her head.

They must have stood there, staring at the immaculate toilet, where Stan Berry had met his untimely end, for at least a minute before the sound of someone clearing his throat caused them to turn in alarm.

"Is there something I can help you ladies with?" Henry Dawson asked.

Tricia turned and felt her knees wobble in relief. "Henry, you just about scared me to death."

"I'm sorry," he apologized. "I wasn't expecting to find you ladies here, either."

"What are you doing working at night?" Angelica said. "I thought your post was in the dining room?"

Henry shrugged. "I do a little of everything around here. As it happens, I had a doctor's appointment earlier today. I traded shifts with Raul, the guy who works the reception desk at night. That's the beauty of working for a place like the Brookview. Everyone helps everybody else. We're like family. Now, what are you two ladies doing here at this time of night?"

Angelica turned to look at Tricia, then back to Henry. "She made me come."

Tricia's mouth dropped, but it was true—she had coerced Angelica into accompanying her—so she couldn't deny it. She closed her mouth and wished her cheeks didn't feel so hot.

Henry shook his head and smiled, and then he shuffled back to the reception desk. Tricia and Angelica followed. He didn't speak again until he was behind the counter. "I suppose you've got your little dog in that purse," he said, looking at the pink purse slung over Angelica's shoulder.

As if on cue, Sarge gave a muffled *"Woof!"*

"How did you know?" Angelica asked.

"Everybody knows you carry that little guy around in a purse. He's well behaved, so who's going to toss you out?"

"I don't *always* bring him with me," Angelica defended herself, but now that the dog was out of the bag, so to speak, maybe she wouldn't have to try to hide Sarge so often. She set her purse on the floor, opening the top. Sarge's fluffy head immediately popped out and he stuck out his pink tongue, panting for joy.

"I don't suppose you're looking to rent a room for the night?" Henry asked with amusement. "Or were you just looking for an empty restroom?"

"You caught us," Tricia admitted it. "We only came—"

"To gawk at the scene of the murder?" Henry asked.

"I never gawk," Angelica said in deadly earnest.

"Neither do I," Tricia echoed.

Henry nodded. "Doing a little casual investigating, then?"

"You never know. The police might have overlooked something," Tricia said, although without real conviction.

Henry nodded solemnly. "That's true."

Angelica rested both elbows on the reception counter and looked up at Henry. "You've worked here at the Brookview for a long time—"

The older man puffed out his chest in pride. "I've got a certificate with beautiful calligraphy that proclaims I'm the longest employed person not related to the Baxter family, who owned the inn since 1897, to have ever worked here. Forty-two years. I hope to make it another forty-two years, as well," he said and chuckled. The man had to be in his early seventies.

"You must know an awful lot of secrets about the inn," Angelica said. "Care to part with a few of them?"

"Then they wouldn't be secrets," Henry said, straight-faced.

Angelica smiled and nodded. "I guess you're right."

"But surely there's a lot of history you *can* talk about," Tricia said. "For instance, before Friday, had there ever been a murder here in the inn?"

Henry looked uncomfortable, but nodded. "Back in 1902. It seems a few of the guests had gathered in the front parlor—what is now the guest dining room—for a friendly game of poker. At least, it started out friendly. One of the players was accused of cheating. He denied it, but an argument broke out. Someone pulled out a gun and shot the man."

"Good heavens," Angelica said, appalled.

Henry nodded. "The poor fellow was taken to his room where he died of his injuries several hours later."

"Which room was that?" Tricia asked.

"No record was kept of it. The management of the time was afraid no one would want to stay in a room where someone had died—especially a violent death."

"Is the inn haunted?" Angelica asked, her eyes wide.

"I've never seen a ghost, but that doesn't mean there isn't one," Henry said.

"I'm sure a lot of people would *love* to spend the night in a haunted inn," Angelica said.

"That's why our previous management never said so either way, just in case."

"And the current management?" Tricia prompted.

"I don't believe the subject has ever come up," Henry admitted.

"Does anyone on staff have a theory as to what happened on Friday?" Tricia asked.

Henry shook his head, his forehead furrowing. "Everyone on staff has an alibi. We don't know about the Chamber of Commerce members. We're putting our faith in the new Stoneham police force. That Chief Baker seems quite a competent fellow. We're all sure he'll soon figure out what happened on Friday and bring the guilty person to justice."

"He is a skilled investigator," Tricia said.

"I understand you and he are no longer seeing each other," Henry said.

"Oh?" Tricia said, feigning surprise.

"Yes. Our guest, Mr. Benson, has let it be known that he's your ex-husband. He's hinted that a reconciliation is close at hand." The man sounded positively enthusiastic at the prospect. First Joelle—now Henry had mentioned the dreaded *R* word.

"I'm afraid Mr. Benson is being overly optimistic," Tricia said sourly.

"Then I feel very sad. The two of you are such nice people. Nice people deserve to be happy."

And nice Christopher had broken nice Tricia's heart by being not so nice—or considerate—when he'd let his own needs surpass those of a wife who'd adored him. But Tricia had no intention of sharing that piece of her once-broken heart with Henry. Instead, she steered the conversation back to the matter at hand. "So what's the Brookview scuttlebutt about Stan Berry's murder?"

"None of the workers here at the inn know the majority of Chamber members, except for you two ladies, of course. You've both stayed here at the inn for extended periods of time, and none of us believe either of you could have done such a heinous act."

"Well, thank you very much," Angelica said and sounded offended.

"If it's any consolation, Ms. Miles," Henry said, addressing Angelica, "we'd like to see you become the next president of the Stoneham Chamber of Commerce."

"And why is that?" Tricia asked.

Henry looked Tricia straight in the eye. "Darlene and I heard your sister's platform. She gets Stoneham. She understands what needs to be done to take our little village to the next level."

Wasn't that exactly how Angelica had explained her intentions?

"And that is?" Tricia asked.

"Where all the locals have a job. Where the tourist dollars

pay the upkeep of our infrastructure. Where our kids can get a good education. Where everyone who comes to our fair village will fall in love and want to return again and again."

"Oh, Henry, that's *exactly* what I want to happen. This village is not the place I grew up in, but it *has* become my hometown. I only want the best for it—and everyone who lives here," Angelica said, her voice cracking.

Henry's mouth quirked into a smile. "Then perhaps you should run for a seat on the Board of Selectmen."

Angelica smiled—and blushed. "You may have something there."

"Ms. Miles," Henry asserted, "I am seldom wrong."

Tricia had to stifle a grin, afraid it might lead to a full belly laugh. "It's getting late," she said and consulted her watch. Good grief—it was nearly eleven. "We've got a big day ahead of us. We'd better be going."

A soft *"yip"* from the vicinity of Angelica's purse seemed to agree. She picked it up and slung it over her shoulder.

"Thank you for talking with us," Tricia said. "And not reporting us."

"Report you?" Henry said.

"Yes, to—"

Once again, another throat was cleared behind them, and Tricia and Angelica turned to find Antonio standing in the lobby, his suit coat missing, his tie askew, a more-than-five-o'clock shadow darkening his chin and cheeks, and his expression decidedly unhappy.

"Ladies, how may I be of service?"

"Uh-oh," Angelica intoned, once again playing ventriloquist.

"Hello, Antonio," Tricia said, trying to sound cheerful. "How are you this evening?"

"I am fine. Why are you here so late?"

"We're visiting Henry," Angelica said quite cheerfully.

"Henry does not usually work the evening shift," Antonio said. He looked a lot taller than Tricia had ever remembered him being. And, to be honest, a teensy bit annoyed.

"Is that so?" Angelica asked.

"Yes."

"Well, then wasn't it lucky we found him here."

"And why did you wish to consult with Henry?" Antonio demanded. "It is *very* late."

"Oh, sure, yeah," Angelica said. "We were wondering if—"

"The inn was haunted," Tricia finished.

"Yes. We were," Angelica quickly agreed.

Antonio looked skeptical. "Of course the inn is haunted. It is an old building." He threw his hands up in the air. "Okay, it is old for *this* country. Not like in Italia where some buildings are thousands of years old and still in use—and in better shape than many I have seen here in America."

"Have you ever seen a ghost here?" Tricia asked.

Antonio shook his head. "But several of our guests swear they have seen them walking down the corridors late at night."

"Them? Man? Woman? Elephant?" Angelica asked.

"It? Them? I do not know for sure. As long as they do not ask for their money back, I am pleased if they enjoy the idea of a ghost."

"Not Stan Berry's ghost, I take it," Tricia said.

"So far we have had no reports of a ghost in our handicapped restroom. But if we do, I will let you know. Now, ladies, I happen to know you must be here early tomorrow for the Chamber of Commerce election."

"Will you be serving coffee?" Angelica asked.

Antonio shook his head. "Bob Kelly would not authorize the purchase. I should have made it a condition of him using the room, especially since we have had to close the restaurant until at least nine. That will not placate a number of our guests. We will have to offer complimentary continental breakfast delivered to their rooms." He shook his head in disgust. "Very costly. My employer will not be pleased."

"No, I imagine she won't," Angelica said sympathetically. "Will you get in trouble?"

Antonio shook his head. "But I will probably get a lecture. It is a small price to pay to work for such a living legend."

Tricia burst out laughing. "Living legend?"

Antonio shrugged and smiled. "In her own mind, at least." He shook a finger at both women. "You will not tell her I said so."

"Of course not," Angelica said. "Unless, of course, she shows up at your wedding, then that's the first thing I'm going to say." She paused and thought about it for a moment. "Maybe the second."

Antonio shook his head. "Now, ladies, you really must go home. However, if you will wait a moment, I will get my coat and walk you to your car."

"Thank you," Tricia said.

Antonio nodded and headed back to his office.

"Let's take a closer look at the Christmas tree. Maybe I'll get some ideas for the Cookery's decorations," Angelica said, and they moseyed closer to the artificial tree, which apparently the inn kept lit 24/7.

"I'm sorry we wasted a trip down here," Tricia said, as Angelica lifted one of the ornaments and examined it closely.

"Well, we did get to talk to Henry and Antonio. Henry is a dear, isn't he?" Angelica asked. "When we stayed here after I broke my foot, and you would run an errand or go check on your store, he always made sure I had a cup of coffee and a magazine, or the TV remote and the phone nearby. That kind of service is so rare these days."

"Yes, and isn't it lovely that he thinks of his co-workers as family. Even Antonio. I wonder what he'd say about Nigela Ricita? She's supposedly visited the inn on a number of occasions."

"But always undercover, right?"

"I guess. We could ask Henry right now—" Tricia said, but there was no time, as Antonio had returned, looking dapper in his long winter coat and a dark cashmere scarf tucked around his neck.

"Ready?" he asked.

Sarge gave a muffled *"yip"* from inside Angelica's purse, and the three of them laughed.

TWENTY-ONE

The phone rang at exactly six o'clock the following morning, waking Tricia from a lovely dream where she had just repaired the binding on a first-edition copy of the Book of Kells. Okay, somewhere in the back of her mind she knew that there was only *one* Book of Kells, but everything in dreams makes total and perfect sense, and to have the dream shattered irritated her beyond belief.

The phone rang again and she fumbled to pick up the receiver, if only to quiet the offending thing. "Hello," she grumbled and saw that Miss Marple had also been awakened from her slumber, looking quite cross, too.

"Oh, Trish—did I wake you?" came Angelica's wide-awake voice.

"Yes!"

"Oh, well, I'm sorry. Honestly, I am. Only I've been up since four, pacing my apartment. Poor Sarge looks exhausted. He's not used to being awakened at all hours of the night."

"Neither are Miss Marple and I."

"I'm so worried about this damn election."

"Yes, well, there's nothing you can do about it, and neither could I. Couldn't you have just let us sleep until the alarm went off?"

"I'm sorry," Angelica apologized once again. "I just couldn't stand to be alone one more minute."

"You're not alone," Tricia reminded her. "Sarge is with you."

"As wonderful and cute and handsome as he is—he's not a great conversationalist."

By that time, Tricia knew she was never going to go back to sleep. "What do you need?"

"Fifteen minutes from now, I'll take Grandma Miles's peach upside-down cake out of the oven. Wouldn't you just love to have a nice warm slab of it with a wonderful cup of coffee for your breakfast?"

"Make it twenty and I'll join you," Tricia said in resignation. They were, after all, sisters, and they needed to support each other in times of stress. And besides, no matter what, a slice of that upside-down cake would bring back many happy memories. And maybe sharing it would bring Angelica good luck in the election. And yet, Tricia couldn't help but feel that the election would be a big turning point. Not only for Angelica and Bob but the entire Stoneham business community.

"I'll have the table set and the coffee poured when you get here," Angelica said and broke the connection.

As Tricia got ready to leave her apartment, she couldn't

shake the feeling that something really nasty—something life changing—would occur at the Brookview Inn that morning. And yet, she was determined not to share that suspicion with her sister. For better or worse—for all of this—there was nothing she could do to change the events that were about to unfold. She just hoped she was up to mopping up the mess that was to befall them all.

Tricia steered her car toward the Brookview Inn. With her stomach full of a cake she hadn't tasted in decades, as well as the excellent coffee brewed from the Coffee Bean's finest Colombian beans, Tricia listened without interest as Angelica babbled nervously. At least she'd agreed to leave Sarge at home, much to the dog's disappointment. He actually pouted, and Tricia was glad to leave the apartment before he pulled a massive guilt trip on both of them.

Tricia parked in the Brookview Inn's lot for the second time in nine hours. There were still plenty of parking spaces, but that would soon change. Still, with the start of the holiday shopping season only two days away, she knew the other merchants would be as eager to put this election behind them as she was.

They entered the building to find it looking very much the same as it had late the evening before. They seemed to be the first of the Chamber members to arrive, yet the dining room was already fully lighted, and the tables had been set. Despite what Antonio had said the night before, the inn had put on a substantial, complimentary spread of coffee, tea, and a large tray of an assortment of luscious pastries. Tricia wondered what had changed his mind. She meant to ask him, but he didn't seem to be around, and she sure hoped he'd make an appearance before the actual ballots were collected. It would be close, and Angelica needed every vote she could get.

"What do we do now?" Angelica asked, looking pale. Tricia had never known her sister to be so jumpy.

"There's not much we can do but go and sit down and wait for everything to start happening."

Angelica sighed. "I suppose you're right. What will be, will be."

Tricia followed her sister into the dining room. They chose to sit at the same table where they had sat five days before. Angelica took off her coat, settling it on the back of her chair, but she headed for the coffee urns and poured herself a cup. Tricia was not about to drink too much. She had no intention of using the inn's washroom. She didn't want to tempt fate in case there was another body just waiting to be found.

Thanks to all the coffee she'd already drunk, Angelica was definitely wired as the Chamber of Commerce members began to file into the Brookview Inn's dining room some fifteen minutes before the election was to take place. Some of them ignored the sisters, but a few waved and even stopped by to wish Angelica well.

Angelica had placed a folded list of all the Chamber members before her on the table and put a checkmark next to the names of the members as they entered.

"It looks like we're going to have a full turnout," Tricia whispered, but Angelica didn't seem to hear her; her gaze was riveted on the dining room's entrance.

"I'm about ready to jump out of my skin," Angelica admitted.

"We'll know one way or another in just a few minutes."

"Could you get me another cup of coffee?" Angelica asked.

"No. I'm cutting you off."

"How about decaf, then? I'm desperate."

"You will be if you drink anything more. In fact, if you don't want to miss the election, you'd better visit the ladies' room before Bob calls the meeting to order."

"You're right. He'd be just mean enough to lock the doors at precisely eight o'clock, preventing anyone from entering or leaving." She excused herself and headed out the door.

Ginny arrived, looking sleep deprived. "Good morning, Tricia. Point me toward the coffee, will you?"

"Over there," Tricia said. Ginny set her purse on the floor and dumped her coat over the back of a chair and made a beeline for the coffee.

Next to arrive was Michele Fowler. She shuffled up to the table, taking the same seat she'd had on Friday. "Who knew there was an eight o'clock on the opposite side of the day? I haven't gotten up this early since I was at university—and then only reluctantly so."

"You showed up at eight o'clock last Friday."

Michele blinked, dazedly. "I did?"

"You need a caffeine fix. I'll get you a cup."

"Thank you, love. Black would be brilliant."

Tricia got up and headed for the eats table, where Ginny was stirring cream into her coffee. "Looks like there aren't enough napkins," Ginny said. "I'd tell Antonio, but I didn't see him in his office when I arrived."

"He comes in before eight?" Tricia asked.

"Oh, yeah. He's usually here before seven to make sure the breakfast gets off to a good start."

Tricia poured the coffee for Michele. "Would you take this to Michele and I'll go ask Eleanor if we can get some more napkins."

"Sure thing."

Tricia headed for the lobby and the reception desk. As anticipated, Eleanor had already relieved the night clerk and was working on the billing for those who were checking out that day. Tricia had seen the same paperwork when she'd stayed at the inn several years before.

"Hello, Eleanor."

"Good morning, Tricia," said a smiling Eleanor. "All ready to cast your ballot for Chamber president?"

"Am I. I'm absolutely sick of hearing about it from Angelica. By the way, did you get one of her rulers?"

Eleanor laughed and held up two of them. She set them back on her desk and grabbed a pen from the chipped Brookview Inn coffee mug. In among the pens, pencils, nail files, and scissors, was the brass letter opener with the heart on top. The instrument that had killed Stan Berry. Tricia frowned. She didn't remember Baker saying it had been returned.

Eleanor's gaze shifted to the mug. "I see you're looking at my letter opener. I had two of them. They're almost exactly the same." She plucked it from the rest of the office paraphernalia.

"Take a look. There's a flaw on one side of the heart. It probably happened when the piece was cast." She handed the letter opener to Tricia. It was solid brass and quite heavy. The edges were blunt. Whoever thrust it into Stan Berry's chest had to have muscles of steel. Holding the opener made a shiver go down Tricia's spine. She handed it back to Eleanor.

"Was there something you needed?" Eleanor asked.

"Oh, yes. I almost forgot. We've run out of paper napkins in the dining room and I didn't know who to report it to."

"We'll take care of that. Do you want to follow me to the stockroom?"

"Sure."

Eleanor scooted around her desk and headed down the corridor to a door with a sign that read EMPLOYEES ONLY. She dipped into the pocket of her slacks and came up with a key ring. Selecting the proper one, she unlocked the door to a supply room. She had to heft a number of large cartons before she came up with one that held napkins.

"Can I help you with that?" Tricia asked.

"I can manage. I'm used to it. And Chauncey and I have been doing weight training to build our stamina. But if you could hold the door open for me, I'd appreciate it."

Tricia couldn't help but worry as Eleanor trundled down the corridor, hanging on to the large, heavy carton. She marched straight into the dining room, set the box on the floor, and using one of her keys, cut the tape that sealed it. She withdrew a wad of white paper napkins, fanning them out on the table, and then pushed the box under it, making sure the tablecloth concealed it from view.

"I'll let Mr. Barbero know they're under the table. He'll see to it that they're stowed in the proper place."

"Thanks, Eleanor." Tricia turned back to the napkins, taking four or five to share with her tablemates, while Eleanor ducked into the kitchen. Tricia took her seat and passed out the napkins. The dining room had filled up during her absence. "Looks like just about everyone is here."

Angelica had returned to her seat, looking worried. "That's either a very good thing or a very bad thing, depending on how the vote goes."

Eleanor exited the kitchen, holding a tall glass of milk. She gave Tricia a faint smile and paused to let Bob enter the dining room. Betsy Dittmeyer, the Chamber receptionist, brought up the rear.

"What's Betsy doing here?" Ginny asked.

"I believe she's going to tally the votes," Angelica said.

"She's definitely in Bob's court. Someone else should verify the votes," Ginny said.

"How about you?" Tricia asked.

"Brilliant idea," Michele agreed.

"Do I have to nominate myself or something?" Ginny asked.

"I'll do it," Michele said. "If Tricia suggests it, it might look like collusion."

"Agreed," Angelica said.

Bob stood at the podium and consulted his watch. According to the clock on the wall, the time was 7:58—two minutes until he called the meeting to order. Betsy handed him a briefcase and Bob withdrew a gavel. For the first time since Tricia had met him, Bob looked disconcerted. Had it finally sunk in that he might lose the election, or was he worried he was about to be arrested for petty vandalism?

Betsy had shucked her parka and stowed her purse under the table. In one hand she held a small stack of white papers—the ballots—and in the other, pens and pencils. She moved from table to table passing out the ballots and making sure everyone had something to write with.

A few last stragglers entered the dining room, heading first to the table with the coffee and pastries before taking a seat at one of the dining room tables.

Tricia found herself getting antsy. What if Angelica won? Would she be so busy she'd have no time for Tricia? Would she work herself to the point of exhaustion or thrive on a yearlong adrenaline high?

Lips pursed in disapproval, Betsy arrived at their table, handing each of them a ballot. Ginny smiled sweetly and said, "Thank you, Betsy," but like her sister, Joelle, Betsy stuck her nose in the air and moved on. By the time she'd visited every table, it was 8:02. She closed the French doors to the dining room and marched to the front of the room to take her seat.

Bob banged the gavel on the lectern. "I will now bring this special meeting of the Stoneham Chamber of Commerce to order. Our only piece of business today is the election of president of the organization."

Michele stood. "I propose we have a second person count the votes to insure that no mistakes are made. I nominate Ginny Wilson for the job."

Betsy turned angry eyes on her. Apparently she did not care to have her count challenged.

"I'll second that," Antonio said from the side of the room. Tricia hadn't seen him enter the room. Perhaps he'd come in through the kitchen entrance.

"All those in favor?" Bob called gravely. Just about everyone in the room raised his or her hand. "Those opposed?" No one objected. Bob smacked the gavel once more. "So moved. Does everyone have a ballot?"

Tricia looked around the room and saw members with their pens and pencils already marking the ballots.

"Please vote now," Bob said. "And when you've finished, bring your ballots to the front of the room and place them in the ballot box that Betsy has provided."

The ballot box was nothing grander than a large shoe box that read REEBOK on the side.

Tricia marked her ballot, folded the slip of paper, and stood, following the crowd making their way to the front of the room. Beneath her makeup, Angelica had gone absolutely white, and her hand shook as she stuffed her ballot into the box. Ginny did likewise but stood to one side. Tricia and Michele cast their ballots and returned to their table. In less than three minutes, everyone had voted.

Bob was the last to cast his vote. He returned to the lectern and banged his gavel once more. "Betsy, would you please count the votes?"

Betsy lifted the box lid and removed the slips of paper, unfolding them and sorting them into two piles. The Brookview Inn's dining room was absolutely silent as Betsy unfolded each piece of paper, carefully checked it over, and placed it either in a pile to her right or left.

Tricia glanced at her sister. Angelica sat straight and tall in her chair, but the hands on her lap kept twisting, while her gaze remained riveted on Betsy. "Come on," she grated under her breath.

Tricia found herself biting her lip as the feeling of anticipation in the room seemed to intensify to an almost unbearable level.

Tricia turned her gaze back to Bob, whose expression was grave. Until that morning he'd seemed confident that he would once again win the election. Everything about him seemed to say *loser*. His Kelly Realty green jacket seemed a little shabby, and she noted he needed a haircut, too. He'd looked a lot sharper when Angelica was advising him. Since their split, it almost looked like he'd fallen on hard times.

Betsy reached the last folded piece of paper. She eyed the piles and picked up the one on her right, flipped through the sheets and counted them twice. She noted the tally on the top sheet, picked up the other pile of papers and did the same, all the while her face was expressionless. She wasn't about to let anyone know what the outcome was until it was announced. She stood, and Ginny stepped closer to recount the votes. After she'd gone through both stacks, she whispered the results to Betsy, who nodded. Apparently Ginny wasn't about to give away the winner, either, and looked down at the floor, staring at her shoes.

A stone-faced Betsy rose from her seat, walked the six feet to the lectern, and handed Bob a folded piece of paper. The room was silent, save for the sound of the forced-air heating system.

Bob unfolded the paper, his expression stoic. He swallowed and stepped up to the lectern's microphone. He had to clear his throat twice before he spoke. "As everyone can see, the votes were counted, and then counted again to make sure there were no mistakes. It was a close vote. Twenty-six to twenty-three. And the results . . ." He looked around the room, taking in each and every face. Was he trying to figure out who'd voted for whom? And why was he dragging out the results?

"The president of the Chamber of Commerce for the upcoming year will be . . ."

Again he paused.

"Get on with it!" John Marcella called.

"Angelica Miles is your new Chamber president . . . and may God help you all," he said with an edge to his voice.

The room exploded with the sound of both cheers and groans.

"Yahoo!" Ginny hollered and clapped her hands. Tricia, Michele, and several others joined in as Bob banged the gavel and said, "This meeting is now adjourned." Angelica jumped up from her seat as though she'd been goosed. She practically ran to the podium but first stopped to offer her hand to Bob.

He took it, shook it, and quickly yanked his arm back. Grinning, Angelica waved her hands in the air to quiet the room, and, a bit breathlessly, she pulled the lectern's microphone closer to her mouth.

"First of all, I wish my honorable opponent hadn't adjourned the meeting so quickly, so I can only address you unofficially, but I promise to do my best for each and every merchant in the organization. Thank you to those of you who voted for me. And to those of you who did not vote for me, I want you to know that I will earn your trust. Together we'll make Stoneham the prettiest town in New Hampshire, the best tourist destination, and, God willing"—she paused and glared at Tricia—"we'll somehow manage to regain our title of safest village in New Hampshire."

At least that last got a laugh, albeit at Tricia's expense. Meanwhile, Bob kept shaking his head as though in disbelief. Tricia could almost feel the despair dripping from him.

Angelica turned back to her new constituents. "If anyone would like to stay behind to talk, I'd be glad to listen to anything you have to say, and I look forward to serving you as your next Chamber president. Let's make this the best holiday sales season yet—and look for even better days ahead. Okay, everyone, back to work!" she said brightly.

Her impromptu speech received a smattering of applause, but the majority of Chamber members didn't have to be told twice. They shoved back their chairs, got up, and headed for the exit.

Michele turned to Tricia. "Well, I'm glad that's over. That vote was so close. . . . I'm glad it wasn't a tie."

"Me, too," Tricia said.

Michele sat back in her chair, picked up her coffee, and

sipped it. "I wonder what the vote would have been if Mr. Berry hadn't been killed."

"A mess. We'd probably have had to go through a runoff. As it is, I'm surprised Bob didn't even mention Stan." Tricia turned her gaze to the front of the room. Angelica and Bob appeared to be in the middle of a heated discussion. Bob's face was beet red, and he seemed to be holding on to the gavel for dear life. The sight would be comical if the memory of Stan Berry, stabbed to death, wasn't still so fresh in her mind.

"I didn't see Angelica's car in the lot," Michele commented.

"I drove us. But it looks like it'll be a while before she's ready to leave."

"If you want to leave her your keys, I'd be happy to drive you home."

"Thanks, but I'm sure Ange is going to want to crow about her victory. She'd be disappointed if I didn't give her the opportunity."

Michele grinned. "You *are* a good sister. I'll just go up and offer Angelica my congratulations. Ta-ta for now," she said and gathered up her coat and purse and made like a salmon swimming against the current, heading for the front of the room to congratulate Angelica.

Ginny grabbed her coat, said a quick good-bye, and marched over to where Antonio stood at the side of the room. Joelle Morrison had appeared once again. She was probably on site to go over more last-minute details for the wedding on Saturday.

Tricia frowned, wondering if she believed it was Joelle who had dumped Stan or the other way around. But then

half of Stoneham was convinced that it was Tricia who had
let a gem like Christopher get away. Who knew what the
truth was in Stan's case? And though Joelle was pleasingly
plump, she didn't seem to possess the strength or the animos-
ity that could have compelled her to drive a letter opener
into Berry's chest.

Tricia couldn't think of anyone at the last Chamber meeting who fit those criteria. Although Eleanor did say that she
and Chauncey did weight training. Still, Baker had never
even mentioned Chauncey as a suspect. That left Eleanor,
the owner of the murder weapon. But that was preposterous.
Eleanor was one of the sweetest people Tricia had met since
her arrival in Stoneham. And it would have been plain stu-
pidity for her to stab Berry with her own letter opener. And
it was Tricia herself who had established an alibi for the inn's
receptionist. Well, sort of. She'd been present when Eleanor
declared the letter opener to be missing. She'd made quite a
fuss about it. But that was after Berry had already been fa-
tally stabbed. Had she been trying to establish an alibi?

No. After all, what possible motive could Eleanor have
had to kill Stan? He liked his women overly chunky and
Eleanor was not only a few years older than Berry, she was
not in the weight class that attracted Stan. Although . . .
could Eleanor have been obese at one point in her life—just
the kind of woman depicted in the chubby chaser magazines
that Stan collected and enjoyed?

Tricia's musings were interrupted when she looked up to
see Will Berry standing just inside the dining room's main
entrance, motioning her to join him. She got up and joined
the tail end of the line of Chamber members who were
exiting.

"Hey, Tricia," Will called and held up what looked like

a piece of a card. Was that a photo in his hand? She wished the line would move faster.

It took almost a full minute before she reached Will. "What are you doing here? I thought you said you were going home," she said and stepped away from the last of the stragglers.

"I stayed the night here in town with a friend."

A friend? And who could that have been? The only place he'd gone while in the village was to Angelica's for dinner on Sunday night and . . . the Dog-Eared Page. Had he hooked up with a certain older barkeep who enjoyed being known as a cougar? Tricia was too well mannered to ask.

"What's that?" she asked, pointing to the paper he held.

"A picture of my aunt. I almost forgot about it. I found it yesterday while digging through a pile of junk at my dad's house." He handed her the photograph.

Tricia felt the blood drain from her face as she studied the face in the photo, instantly recognizing the woman in it.

No doubt about it. Behind the rolls of fat and the puffy face, the woman was none other than Eleanor McCorvey.

Tricia swallowed and looked out the open doorway where Eleanor had been stationed when she'd arrived at the inn some thirty minutes before. But the reception desk appeared to be abandoned. Had Eleanor recognized her nephew when he'd entered the lobby, and fled before she could be recognized, or had she left her desk to attend to a guest's needs?

"Are you okay?" Will asked, concerned.

"Oh, yes," Tricia said and managed a wan smile. "Um . . . my sister just won the Chamber election."

"Hey, that's great. I'll have to congratulate her and thank her again for letting me crash her dinner party the other night." His expression was expectant. "Well?"

"Well?" Tricia repeated, uncomprehending.

"Do you recognize the woman in the picture?" Will asked.

Of course! she nearly yelled but instead thought better of it. She needed to talk to Eleanor before she introduced Will to his long-lost great-aunt. "Why don't you let me show it around town and if I come up with something, I'll get back to you."

Will shrugged. "Okay. Let me give you my home phone number. If you find her, you can call me, although I'll probably be back as soon as the cops let me back in Dad's house. I still have to clear it out before the end of the month. By the way, I got a call last night. I found someone to teach me the sign business, that is if I can salvage the machinery and any of the supplies."

"That's great news."

"Yeah. I'm going to put everything in storage until I can find another place to rent, but I'd like to relocate to the area, although it might not be in Stoneham. I don't want to have to deal with Bob Kelly."

"I can't blame you for that. I'm glad you decided to stay. Stoneham needs an in-town sign shop."

Will handed her a slip of paper with his number. "In the meantime, can I kiss you good-bye?" he asked.

Tricia's smile was tentative. "Oh, why not," she said, expecting a buss on the cheek, but instead Will lunged forward, planted his lips against hers, and tried to force his tongue into her mouth. The desperate move took her by surprise and she pulled away and almost stumbled. "Will!"

The young man seemed to realize he'd made a serious faux pas. "Sorry. I kind of hoped you'd . . . that maybe after

last night we might have some fun together. Nothing permanent, but—"

"Friends with benefits?" she asked.

"Sure. Why not? After all, you and the cop are on the
outs—you're free as a bird."

That might be, but Tricia hardly felt desperate for male
company, especially knowing Will had probably spent the
night with Michele Fowler, if not some other woman he'd
picked up at the pub.

"I don't think so."

Will shrugged. "Could you still look for my aunt?"

"Yes. I'll . . . I'll let you know in a day or so what I come
up with."

"Thanks. I guess I'd better go." He said the words, but
he didn't seem in any hurry to leave the dining room.

"Good-bye, Will," Tricia said, put her hands on his shoulders, turned him in the right direction, and gave him enough
of a push to get him started. He took the hint and left.

Tricia turned to look at the front of the room, where
Angelica and Bob still seemed to be involved in a heated,
but very quiet argument. Their mouths moved, but she
couldn't hear a word they were saying. She looked down at
the photograph in her hand. Shielded by layers of fat, the
Eleanor of years past looked much older than the one Tricia
was familiar with. Had Stan Berry recognized her on the
morning he'd been killed? Could he have said or done something so outrageous that it spurred her to kill him?

Tricia wasn't sure what to do. She should just call Baker
and give him the photo and let him interrogate Eleanor. For
all she knew, Eleanor had already fled the inn, and if so, then
it might be imperative that Baker put out an APB to find her.

Tricia took a step into the lobby, looked past the cheerful, glowing Christmas tree, and saw Eleanor striding down the corridor, heading back to the reception desk. Her hands were clenched at her side, and her face was creased with worry.

Much as she didn't want to believe it, Tricia was afraid she'd found Stan Berry's killer. She forced herself to move forward. She would ask Eleanor a few innocent questions, anything to help her assuage her guilt at the knowledge that she'd have to turn in someone she truly had liked. And she prayed she'd believe whatever answers she received.

TWENTY-TWO

Tricia approached the inn's reception desk with trepidation. She could almost hear Grant Baker's plaintive voice inside her head pleading, "Why didn't you call me?"

Because he might not be available.

Because he might blow her off.

Because she had blown *him* off and he was hurt, because he'd blown her off one too many times and s*he* was hurt.

Because in the long run, she might just be wrong.

Tricia stopped before the reception desk, resting her hands on the oak top and forcing a smile. "Eleanor, I have good news."

"Oh? Did Angelica win?" Eleanor asked.

"Yes, she did."

"That's wonderful," Eleanor said without enthusiasm. "But how will that affect me?"

"It probably won't, but I think I might have some happy news for you."

"Oh?" Eleanor certainly didn't sound cheered.

"I met a young man on Saturday who said he might have a long-lost relative here in Stoneham."

Eleanor said nothing.

"He was looking for someone he called Auntie Yum-Yum."

Eleanor's eyes went wide with what looked like fear. She said nothing but turned. On her desk sat a small plastic container of what looked like chocolate powder. Beside it stood the glass of milk Tricia had seen earlier. Eleanor pried the lid from the container. "I'm not sure I understand what you're suggesting."

"Will Berry gave me a photo of his mother's aunt. I think it might be you."

Tricia wondered if she was making a mistake by handing Eleanor the photo. Would she rip it to shreds?

Eleanor stared at the picture in absolute horror, her face going deadly pale.

"Stan Berry was married to your niece, wasn't he?"

Still Eleanor said nothing. Instead, she set the picture down and reached for her purse. With trembling hands she withdrew a folded piece of paper and set it on her desk.

"He was an abusive man with unusual tastes—especially when it came to the women he was attracted to," Tricia said. Part of her wondered why she was torturing the poor woman before her, and another part felt compelled to find out the truth behind the violent act that had robbed Stan Berry of his life.

Eleanor swallowed, picked up a plastic spoon that sat on

a napkin next to the glass, and measured out a heaping teaspoon of the chocolate powder and dumped it into the glass. "That man stole my niece's life," she said, her expression hard and unforgiving. "He deserved to die."

"How did he steal her life?" Tricia asked.

"She was in her first year at Smith College, with a full scholarship—the first member of our family to ever go to college, but *he* talked her into dropping out. She wanted to be an industrial engineer, and instead she ended up behind a register at Shaw's grocery store in Nashua. She got pregnant. They had no money, and when the going got really tough, when that sweet child Will was little more than a toddler, Stan just up and left. Louise depended on welfare and the kindness of her relatives to stay afloat. That bastard left the state. He never paid her a nickel in child support. Is it any surprise she drank herself to death?" Eleanor shook her head in disgust, picked up the spoon, and added another portion of chocolate from the container to her glass of milk.

"Oh, Eleanor, Stan Berry's death has now ruined *your* life as well?"

Eleanor shook her head and stirred the contents of the glass. "What life? I work at the Brookview for not much more than minimum wage. I wait on people with better lives than me. People who have the cash to stay in a fancy-schmancy inn. Beautiful people who have careers. People who have retired and don't have to worry about paying the utility bills or wonder if they should buy their meds instead of food." She took a small sip of her drink.

Tricia didn't quite believe Eleanor's bitter words, or at least didn't believe she'd admitted the *real* reason she'd killed Stan Berry. Should she spout her harebrained theory? All Eleanor could do was deny it.

"I think there's a much more personal reason why you killed Stan," Tricia said, trying to keep her voice neutral.

Eleanor's eyes flashed, and her lips pursed, but she said nothing as she carefully set her glass on the desktop.

"I think years ago you weighed a lot more," Tricia ventured. "Stan was fascinated with extra-large women. I think he might have made unwanted comments. Comments that were insulting, or—"

"Insulting?" Eleanor accused. "You don't know the half of it, Tricia." Eleanor lowered her head, and for a moment Tricia thought of a bull getting ready to charge. "That man . . ." She closed her eyes for a moment, and when she spoke again, her voice was low and full of vitriol. "That man spied on me—took pictures of me. He sold them to a magazine. Worst of all, Stan Berry sexually assaulted me."

"Oh, Eleanor," Tricia said with a horrified gasp. Had Will thrown away the very issue that had contained those terrible photos?

"The first time it happened . . ." Eleanor stopped, took a breath, and swallowed several times before she could continue. She'd gone terribly white. Had she ever confided this awful secret to anyone else before now?

"Oh, Eleanor—it happened more than once?"

She nodded, and a tear slid down her cheek. "That man robbed me of . . ." Eleanor let out an anguished sob. "He robbed me of my self-esteem. He took all the joy out of my world. He . . ."

Tricia rested what she hoped was a comforting hand on Eleanor's arm, but she pulled away from the touch as though scalded.

Eleanor wouldn't look at Tricia. "I felt . . . dirty. Sullied. Forever. What he did ended whatever chance I had at having a loving relationship with any man." Her hand moved to clasp the glass on her desk. "I lost weight. I lost more than a hundred and fifty pounds, but I could never shed the image of that horrible man . . . how rough he was with me . . . For years and years, somewhere in the back of my mind I heard his mocking voice calling me the magic mountain mama."

Had Stan said those things in cruel jest or had he actually been aroused by his wife's aunt?

"How much older were you than him?"

Eleanor swiped a hand across her cheek, catching another tear, and practically fell into the office chair behind the counter. "Ten years. He said the age difference didn't matter when . . . when . . ." She choked on the words. "When the flesh was willing . . . and that I had more than enough flesh for both of us. And then . . . then he made a point of grabbing me in a very private place. And he . . . he . . ." Eleanor broke down completely, unable to go on.

Tricia felt like a heel for making the poor woman relive the worst moments of her life, and yet she couldn't forget that Eleanor had killed a man—viciously stabbing him through the heart with her own letter opener.

Eleanor's sobs began to slow and she took another sip from her glass, which seemed to calm her even more. "You were right, Tricia," she said at last, and set the glass down. "Life as I knew it is over. I guess I knew that the minute you found Stan dead. For a day or two I thought maybe no one would learn of my shame, but I should have known you would ferret out the truth. You always do," she said with an ironic laugh.

"What are you going to do now that I know?" Tricia asked.

Eleanor sighed and picked up the glass once again, but this time she drained it. "Funny you should ask. I figured if the truth came out, I'd have to spend the rest of my life living in shame. It wasn't a very pleasing prospect. And I couldn't bring that kind of shame to the only man who has ever treated me with kindness."

"Chauncey?" Tricia asked.

Eleanor didn't answer, but instead grasped the arms of her chair and continued. "So, I made a decision right after it happened. I'd decided that if there was even a remote chance that the world would ever find out about my shameful secret . . . that I'd kill myself."

The breath caught in Tricia's throat. "Oh, Eleanor. Please tell me you're joking."

Eleanor reached out to clasp the edge of the reception desk, and slowly swung her head to the left and right. "You were right, Tricia. My life *is* over." She shook herself and grimaced, as though she'd just tasted something terribly sour.

Tricia's gaze drifted to the glass Eleanor had so recently set down on her workspace. Could it have contained poison?

"Eleanor?" she said sharply.

Eleanor closed her eyes and hung her head.

Tricia rummaged in her purse for her cell phone, stabbed in 911. Within seconds the dispatcher answered. "Please send an ambulance to the Brookview Inn in Stoneham. There's been a poisoning. And send the police as well." Before she could say more, Eleanor's hands slipped away from the reception desk and she slid from her chair. Tricia dropped her phone, scooted around the desk, but couldn't catch Eleanor before her head crashed into the side of her workstation. The wound gushed blood, and Tricia grabbed the sweater from the back of Eleanor's chair to staunch the flow. She'd already lost consciousness.

Antonio suddenly appeared behind her. "I heard a crash. What happened?"

"Eleanor drank a glass of poison."

"Poison?" Antonio echoed, sounding stunned. "What for?"

"She killed Stan Berry."

"No, she didn't," came a frantic voice, and suddenly Henry Dawson was beside Tricia, pushing her away from Eleanor's prone body.

Eleanor's breaths started to sound like gasps.

"Where is that ambulance?" Tricia wailed.

"Henry, what are you saying?" Antonio demanded.

"I have a feeling I'll be repeating the story over and over again in the next few hours. Please, go outside and direct the EMTs to come here when they arrive," Henry pleaded.

Antonio nodded, and ran for the exit.

"Oh, Eleanor—you didn't have to do this," Henry said, his voice filled with anguish.

"Henry, please don't tell me it was you," Tricia pleaded, confused.

Henry smoothed Eleanor's hair back with great tenderness. "I told you, the staff here at the Brookview is like family. I have no one else. All my brothers and sisters are gone. Most of my friends are dead or moved south. I have no one but the people I care about here at this lovely old inn."

"But why?" Tricia practically begged. "What reason did *you* have to kill Stan Berry?"

"Eleanor, of course. She's like a sister to me. I saw that man taunt her with a disgusting photo. He violated her. Not just in the past, but I saw him touch her on Friday morning. He had no right to do that to her. Eleanor ran into Mr. Barbero's office, crying. That's when . . ."

"You picked up the letter opener and followed him down the hall," Tricia stated.

Henry nodded. "I waited until he opened the washroom door and I—I killed him."

Tricia's heart sank. "Oh, Henry."

Eleanor's breaths were coming in choking gasps. What kind of poison could have reacted so quickly?

The sound of a siren cut through the soft sounds of Christmas carols coming from a speaker in the ceiling.

Henry continued to stroke Eleanor's hair as silent tears wet his wrinkled cheeks. "Hold on, Eleanor. The ambulance is on its way," he crooned.

Tricia looked down at a deathly pale Eleanor and wondered if she would last even that long. She bit her lip and cursed herself for her impatience. If she had only called Baker would the outcome have been different, or would Eleanor have spooned the poison into her milk and drunk it in front of him—anything to avoid facing further humiliation?

It was something Tricia would never know . . . but would always have to live with.

TWENTY-THREE

If there was one thing Tricia was grateful for, it was that most of the Chamber members had already left the building by the time the ambulance and police arrived at the Brookview Inn. But she knew the gossip mill would already be churning out the news of Eleanor's attempted suicide, Henry's confession, and that she was nothing but a jinx after all.

She bit her lip and considered the possibility that she might just have earned the title.

Antonio had provided a straight-backed chair for her to sit in, since every other seat in the lobby had been occupied and no one seemed eager to provide her with any comfort, and so Tricia sat near Antonio's office door, where Chief Baker had been interrogating Henry for more than an hour. Despite the tragedy, cheerful holiday tunes still played throughout the inn's common areas, while the stately Christmas tree stood tall and beautiful and silent.

Darlene stood at the reception desk, glaring daggers at Tricia for her part in this terrible mess. Tricia had never felt so alone in her life.

And then a hand touched her shoulder. "Are you okay, Trish?"

Tricia looked up into Angelica's sympathetic face.

"No. Why couldn't I mind my own business? Why do I always have to play detective? Why—?"

"Hush!" Angelica ordered, the same command she gave her dog. It had the same effect and stopped what could have been a long tirade of self-pity and regret. "Are you still waiting to speak to Chief Baker?"

Tricia nodded miserably. "You don't have to hang around here, Ange."

"Don't worry. Frannie has already taken Sarge out. Bev and Tommy can get along without me at Booked for Lunch. I'll stay here as long as you need me."

Tricia reached up to clasp Angelica's hand and found herself smiling. It felt oddly comforting to realize she wanted— and needed—Angelica's company. She was also glad Christopher hadn't shown his face during the time she'd had to hang out in the inn's lobby. He was the last man on the planet she wanted to see.

Of course, she soon felt otherwise when she saw Chauncey Porter charging across the lobby and heading her way. "Oh, no," she muttered under her breath.

Angelica turned just as Chauncey practically skidded to a halt in front of them.

"What is wrong with you?" he hollered. "Why couldn't you just mind your own damned business?"

"Chauncey, there's no way Tricia could have known that Eleanor would try to kill herself when the truth became known about Stan." Angelica tried to reason with him. "The man may have been a scumbag, but it wasn't up to Henry to decide to make himself judge and executioner."

But Chauncey wasn't listening to her, his gaze was focused on Tricia. "I was going to ask her to marry me tomorrow. We could have had a beautiful life together."

"Chauncey, I—" Tricia tried, but Chauncey wasn't interested in apologies.

"I am so angry with you right now, Tricia, that I could murder you!"

"Now just a minute, pal," Baker said. Tricia hadn't heard the door to Antonio's office open. She turned, but before the chief could intervene, Chauncey's hand lashed out and struck Tricia's cheek, knocking her sideways.

Baker lunged forward, tackling Chauncey, wrestling him to the ground and manacling his wrists before Chauncey had a chance to react. A couple of officers charged across the lobby to give assistance, but Baker had everything under control.

Stunned, Tricia righted herself, her left hand moving to touch her face, which burned. She was sure she'd sport a bruise before morning.

Baker yanked Chauncey to his feet. "Come on, pal, we're heading for the station. You're under arrest."

"No, Grant," Tricia cried. "Let him go."

"The hell I will. He'll be charged with assault."

"Not if I don't press charges."

"Don't be foolish."

"Not foolish, Grant, compassionate."

"I don't need that from you, either. Just leave me the hell alone." Chauncey glared at Tricia. "I never want to speak to you again."

"Then don't," Baker said, unlocking the cuffs. "Go home, Mr. Porter, before I find something else to charge you with." He nodded toward one of the officers. "See to it that he gets to his car and leaves the premises." The officer nodded and ushered Chauncey toward the exit.

Angelica stood over Tricia, rubbing her back. "Are you okay, Trish?"

Tricia nodded and looked to Baker. "I suppose you want to talk to me now."

"Not here. This place is a fishbowl." Hadn't Eleanor said the same thing? The thought of her brought tears to Tricia's eyes once more. "Have you . . . heard?"

Baker shook his head. "Not in the past half hour. All I know is she was still alive when they arrived at St. Joseph Hospital in Milford." His voice was hard, cold. Did he blame her, too?

He turned back for Antonio's office and seconds later emerged with a handcuffed Henry, who looked like he'd been crying. He paused beside Tricia. "I'm so sorry you had to get involved in all this, Ms. Miles. I thought I was helping Eleanor, but I only made it worse. I don't want you to blame yourself for what happened. I guess she had to know her shame would become public at one point, and she was prepared for that eventuality. I don't want you to hold yourself accountable. If I hadn't taken matters into my own hands . . ."

"Come along," Baker said and grabbed Henry's left elbow, while the other officer took his right, and they practically propelled him through the lobby and out the door to a waiting patrol car.

"I guess I'd better wait for Grant to return," Tricia said.

"Uh-oh," she heard Angelica mutter. Tricia followed her sister's gaze to see Christopher heading down the inn's main staircase. He was dressed for outdoors, with a jacket, scarf, gloves, and hat, but he paused at the bottom step, looked around, saw Tricia, and headed her way.

"I've seen the cops coming and going for more than an hour now. Don't tell me you found another dead body," he said and laughed.

"Not now, Christopher," Angelica warned.

His grin disappeared as he studied Tricia's face. "Oh, Trish. I'm sorry. I never really thought . . ."

"You better run away as fast as you can," Tricia said coldly. "I'm the village jinx and people around me have a habit of dying."

Angelica jerked her thumb toward the exit. "Take a hike."

Christopher nodded. "I'm sorry." He reached down, patted Tricia's arm, and then pivoted. Without looking back, he strode across the lobby to the exit and disappeared behind the wood and glass door.

Typical. He always did leave just when she needed him most.

Seconds later, Baker reentered the lobby. He carried a cop's arrogant attitude with him, something Tricia had never seen on him before. This little talk wasn't going to be pleasant, and she had a feeling it would start with a stern lecture. He stopped uncomfortably close to her, his heavy boots nearly touching her shoes. "Inside." He nodded toward Antonio's office.

"I thought you said . . ."

"I changed my mind. I think it would be better for you if we talked here rather than down at the station."

Was he showing her at least a little mercy?

Tricia rose from the chair. Angelica began to follow her, but Baker stepped between them. "Not you."

"But I'm her sister."

"And your presence is neither wanted nor justified."

Angelica was about to protest when Tricia waved a hand. "It's okay, Ange. But wait for me, will you?"

"I'll be right here," Angelica promised and promptly took the chair Tricia had just vacated.

Once inside Antonio's office, Tricia sat on a chair in front of his desk, while Baker closed the door. Seconds later he loomed over her.

"Where do you want me to begin," Tricia asked, but then noted that they were alone in the room, with no one to take her official statement.

"I'm sorry to have to be the one to tell you, Tricia, but Ms. McCorvey has died," Baker said gently.

"Oh, no," Tricia wailed and buried her face in her hands.

Baker stepped close, crouched, and put his arms around her. Tricia hung on for dear life, sobbing. "I'm sorry. I'm so sorry," Baker repeated.

"I didn't know this would happen. I swear," Tricia said.

"It's pretty apparent she'd made the decision to try suicide before she even spoke to you," Baker said, patting her back.

"But if I *hadn't* spoken to her . . . I practically accused her—"

"Of killing Stan Berry?" Baker pulled back and shook his head. "I think she had a good idea who killed him. She left a note," Baker said.

"A note?" Tricia repeated, wiping her eyes.

"I can't show it to you, but I can tell you what it said. She took full responsibility for Berry's murder."

"But Henry said—"

"Yes, he killed Berry. But Eleanor didn't want him to get in trouble for it. I guess she thought she could save him from jail time, but that isn't going to happen."

"Could he be lying about it?" Tricia asked, and sank back into the chair.

Baker shook his head. "He knew pertinent information about the murder that we hadn't released to the public—and especially to you."

"Poor Eleanor. And poor Henry."

"He plans to plead guilty, to save the cost of a trial. Thoughtful man," Baker commented.

"I'm sure he likes to think of himself as a good citizen."

"Good citizens don't kill," Baker reminded her.

Tricia shook her head. "I still can't help thinking that it's all my fault—"

"Don't," Baker warned. "Now. If you're up to it, I'd like to get your statement now so that you can start putting all this behind you."

"I don't see how I can do that."

"I do. You've got a lot on your plate, what with Thanksgiving tomorrow, Black Friday, and the wedding on Saturday."

It all seemed terribly frivolous in light of Eleanor's death.

"Life goes on, Tricia. You can't help those that are beyond your reach."

"Sweep it under the rug and go on like Eleanor never existed?" she asked.

"No. But remember her as the smiling woman behind the desk. The one who helped the guests here at the inn. The woman you knew—not the one who lived in secret shame. I'm sure that's not how she'd want to be remembered."

No. Of that Tricia was certain.

"Are you ready to begin?" Baker asked kindly.

Tricia nodded.

Baker opened the door, signaled to another of his officers, and Tricia prepared herself for the unpleasant task ahead.

TWENTY-FOUR

Half the businesses in Stoneham closed early that Saturday afternoon, all so the owners could attend Ginny and Antonio's wedding at the Brookview Inn. It was a quarter the size of Tricia's overly elaborate wedding, but the setting was lovely, the company was great, and both the bride and groom looked stunning as they held hands and promised to love and cherish one another 'til death do them part.

At the sound of those words, Tricia's thoughts flashed back to her own wedding some thirteen years before. At the time, she'd believed she and Christopher were destined to stay together the rest of their lives. So much for happily ever after. She fervently hoped that Ginny and Antonio would weather the ups and downs of marriage and grow old together.

The inn's dining room was packed, even though the guest list was shorter by two: Chauncey and Eleanor.

Will Berry had returned to Stoneham earlier than he'd planned so he could attend Eleanor's memorial service that had been held at the Baker Funeral Home that morning. Tricia wanted to attend, but Will had called and asked her not to. He made it clear that he didn't blame her for what happened, but he didn't think Chauncey would ever forgive or forget. That hadn't helped assuage the guilt she felt, and always would. Would losing Eleanor cause Chauncey to give up his store and leave Stoneham? Only time would tell.

The music started again, shaking Tricia from her reverie. She smiled at Ginny, handing back the bridal bouquet. As she did, she caught sight of Angelica, sitting in the front row on the groom's side, which was totally devoid of family, decidedly short on friends, and entirely free from enemies. Frannie sat beside her, while Baker sat in the row behind Angelica, giving Tricia a comforting smile. These last few days had almost seemed like old times for them. Baker had come to Angelica's for Thanksgiving dinner after all and had picked Tricia up at Haven't Got a Clue in time for the wedding. And though he'd done everything right these past few days, she knew that they could not go back to the way things had been. They'd gone through too many periods where they'd been estranged—for one reason or another—for Tricia to face going through it all again. But at least they were friends, and Tricia was sure that no matter what, she'd always be able to count on Grant Baker.

Ginny and Antonio walked back up the aisle between the rows of chairs, heading for the lobby where pictures were to be taken and the receiving line formed.

Tricia filed along behind, without an escort. With Henry

in jail, they'd been short a groomsman. Mr. Everett was happy to stand in, but Joelle decided he should escort Grace back up the aisle. As she neared the doorway, Tricia caught sight of Christopher standing at the back of the room and her anger flared. How dare he crash Ginny's wedding! To make matters worse, he winked as she passed him.

The wedding party was soon joined by all the guests, who were shooed out the door by the inn's staff, who were charged with setting up the tables for the wedding dinner.

While the photographer set up shots with the bride and groom, Tricia snagged Christopher's arm and dragged him off to one side.

"What are you doing here?" she demanded.

"I came to say good-bye."

"Don't tell me you're going to drive back north tonight."

"No, but I intend to leave first thing tomorrow morning and since I knew I could find you here tonight, I figured it was probably best to say my good-byes here and now."

"Okay. Good-bye." She turned to go, and this time he grabbed her arm.

"It won't be for long."

Tricia's stomach tightened. "What do you mean?"

"It turns out my new employer doesn't want a long-distance financial advisor. She wants me closer to monitor all her investments."

My employer? Hadn't Antonio always called Nigela Ricita that . . . at least before he'd revealed their true relationship? "Don't tell me you've been hired by Nigela Ricita Associates?"

"Yes. How'd you know?"

"Lucky guess. Where are you going to be based? In Portsmouth?"

He gave a nervous laugh. "As it turns out, my office will be right here in Stoneham. In the same building that houses the Dog-Eared Page."

Kitty-corner to Haven't Got a Clue!

Tricia sighed. Was she going to be subjected to seeing the man who'd unceremoniously dumped her four years before on a daily basis?

"Where will you live?"

"That's something I need to work out. It won't bother you that I'm nearby, will it?"

"Of course not," Tricia lied with a smile. She became aware of a looming presence behind her.

"Is everything okay?" Baker asked.

Tricia's smile was rigid. "Just peachy." She turned back to Christopher. "Well, don't let me keep you."

"Aren't you going to kiss me good-bye?" Christopher asked, straight-faced.

"It's hardly good-bye if you'll be returning to Stoneham within weeks," Tricia said dryly.

"What's this?" Baker asked, not sounding at all pleased.

"I've got a job with Nigela Ricita Associates. I'll be based right here in Stoneham. Isn't that great?" Christopher asked, grinning.

"No!" Tricia and Baker said in unison.

"Tricia, hurry!" Ginny called. "The photographer is waiting."

Tricia turned so that she could take in both men. "If you'll excuse me." She pivoted and hurriedly left them.

Several Brookview Inn staffers threaded their way through the guests, holding trays of hors d'oeuvres and wine, deliberately avoiding Tricia while the photographer assembled the bridal party and put them through their paces around the lobby, on the staircase, and near the elegant Christmas tree. Except for Antonio, she doubted she'd be welcomed by any of the inn's staff for the foreseeable future.

Tricia smiled on cue and hoped it looked genuine, but out of the corner of her eye she could see Christopher and Baker having a quiet, but intense, conversation. What could they possibly have to say to each other? Perhaps they both regretted that they'd treated their relationships with her so cavalierly. None of that mattered now.

When at long last the photographer released the bridal party from their torture, Angelica appeared at Tricia's side with a wineglass in each hand. She gave one to Tricia. "You look lovely." She reached out to touch Tricia's bruised face. "Looks like you walked into a door, but it's almost completely camouflaged by makeup."

"Thank you. You look nice, too."

"What? In this old rag?" Angelica said with a laugh.

Tricia knew a designer dress when she saw one, only she wasn't sure what designer had created the lovely navy linen suit Angelica wore. Like a lot of other things, it didn't matter.

"So, I guess Nigela Ricita was a no-show," Tricia said to make conversation and sipped her wine.

"Oh, but she *was* here," Angelica said.

Tricia nearly choked on her wine and actually did a double take. "Did you meet her?"

Angelica shook her head sadly. "No. Antonio said she snuck in long enough to see the ceremony and then snuck out again."

"He saw her?"

Angelica nodded.

Tricia frowned. Ginny wasn't going to like that—not at all. She'd been more desperate than most to meet the elusive Ms. Ricita. "When did Antonio tell you? We've been stuck having our photos taken ever since the ceremony ended."

"No, you haven't. You were talking to Christopher for a while. Speaking of which, what's he doing here?"

"It's too long a story to get into now. Suffice it to say we haven't seen the last of him."

"Oh?" Angelica asked, her eyes widening with interest.

"Time to throw the bouquet," Ginny called out.

"No—no!" Joelle insisted. "That comes later—after dinner. After cutting the cake!"

Ginny seemed undeterred and stepped in front of the grand Christmas tree. All the single women in attendance gathered like a knot of fleas in front of her.

"Come on Tricia—and you, too, Angelica," Frannie called excitedly.

"Oh, no!" Angelica declared, stepping back. "Four times at the altar was enough for me."

Frannie grabbed Tricia's arm and practically hauled her over to the rest of the group. Angelica circled around, took Tricia's glass and her bridesmaid's bouquet, and moved back to the sidelines. She had no desire to be standing among the desperate gathering of women.

"Heads up," Ginny called, turned her back to the crowd, and tossed her bouquet into the air. It sailed in a direct arc straight toward Tricia, who, without conscious thought, reached out and caught it.

The gaggle of guests broke into laughter and applause. Tricia looked around her. The other single women were tight-lipped—even Frannie—but it was the sight of Christopher and Baker that held her attention as the flash from the guests' cameras made her feel like the object of desire from the paparazzi. Christopher's smile was euphoric, while Baker looked pensive.

Tricia looked down at the bouquet of white roses and baby's breath and sighed, wondering if this was an omen of things to come.

ANGELICA'S RECIPES

CRÈME BRÛLÉE

1 quart heavy cream
1 vanilla bean, split, the seeds scraped
6 egg yolks
¼ cup superfine sugar
boiling water
½ cup brown sugar

Preheat the oven to 325°F. Pour the cream into a saucepan. Add the vanilla seeds and pod. Place over medium heat and bring to a boil, then remove from the heat. Set aside to rest for 5 minutes. Meanwhile, combine the egg yolks and superfine sugar in a bowl and beat with electric beaters for 2–3 minutes or until light in color.

Remove the vanilla pod from the saucepan and discard or save for another use, then pour the hot cream over the yolk mixture and whisk to combine. Remove foam with a large spoon and discard. Strain the mixture into a large pitcher, then carefully pour it into six 7- or 8-ounce ovenproof ramekins. Put the ramekins in a deep roasting pan. Pour boiling water into the pan until it's halfway up the sides of the ramekins. Loosely cover the pan with foil, allowing some air to enter through the sides.

Bake in the oven for 40–45 minutes. The crème brûlée should still wiggle a little when done. Carefully remove the ramekins from the oven and the water bath, and set aside to cool. Place the brown sugar on a baking tray, turn off the oven, and place the tray inside for 15 minutes or until the sugar is completely dried out. Allow it to cool completely, then place it in a food processor and process to a powder. Store in an airtight container. Once the custards have cooled, cover with plastic wrap and chill overnight in the refrigerator.

When ready to serve, preheat the broiler on high. Sprinkle 2 teaspoons of the brown sugar on top of each custard, using the back of a teaspoon to spread it evenly. Place the custards under the broiler until the sugar melts and caramelizes. (You can also use a mini blowtorch to caramelize the sugar.) Allow the custard to cool for 5 minutes before serving.

Yield: 6 servings

Barbecue Bacon-Wrapped Shrimp

18 large uncooked shrimp
9 bacon strips (cut in half for each shrimp)
1½ cups of your favorite barbecue sauce

Preheat the oven to 300°F. Peel and devein the shrimp. Wrap a half strip of bacon on each shrimp and pierce with a toothpick.

Bake the shrimp on an ungreased baking sheet for 30 minutes. Remove to a slow cooker. Warm the barbecue sauce and pour it over the shrimp. Stir until covered. Simmer for 2 hours, stirring occasionally. Remove from the sauce to a serving dish and serve.

Yield: 18 pieces

Grandma Miles's Peach Upside-Down Cake

⅓ cup butter, melted
½ cup packed brown sugar
2 cups sliced fresh or frozen peaches (if using canned, rinse and drain)
⅓ cup shortening

1 cup granulated sugar
1 egg
½ teaspoon lemon juice
½ teaspoon vanilla extract
1⅓ cups all-purpose flour
2 teaspoons baking powder
¼ teaspoon salt
⅔ cup milk
whipped cream (optional)

Preheat the oven to 350°F. Pour the melted butter into an ungreased 9-inch square baking pan; sprinkle with the brown sugar. Arrange the peach slices in a single layer over the brown sugar.

In a small mixing bowl, cream the shortening and granulated sugar. Beat in the egg, lemon juice, and vanilla. Combine the flour, baking powder, and salt. Add to the creamed mixture and alternate with the milk. Spoon the batter over the peaches.

Bake for 45–50 minutes or until a toothpick inserted near the center comes out clean. Cool for 10 minutes before turning out on a plate. If desired, serve with whipped cream.

Yield: 6 servings

Baked Brie
with Raspberry Preserves

½ (17-ounce) package frozen puff pastry, thawed
1 (8-ounce) round of Brie cheese
¼ cup raspberry preserves (or ¼ cup of your
    favorite preserves)
⅛ cup toasted almond slices (optional)

Preheat the oven to 425°F. Lightly grease a baking sheet. Roll the puff pastry out slightly. Place the cheese round on top of the pastry (do not remove the rind). Place the preserves on top of the Brie. Sprinkle the preserves with the almonds. Wrap the puff pastry up and around the Brie. Bake for 20–25 minutes, until the pastry is golden brown. Remove from the oven and let cool for 5 minutes. Serve with crackers.

Yield: 4–6 servings